He was so close...

He was so close Penny had to lean against the desk in order to tilt her head back far enough to look at his face.

"Your inability to stay here? What about my inability to allow you to stay here? I don't want to be married-to you or to anyone else. I don't need your help, Mr. Owens. Nor do I want you to remain at my ranch. I could never allow a man who carries such low regard for women to remain in my presence."

"Low regard for women? I'll have you know, Miss Jordan, I have a very high regard for women, especially those who know what their role is! But that has nothing to do with the reason I can't remain here. I have a business to run in Pennsylvania. I have family there. I have commitments there. I have my life there!"

"Please, Mr. Owens, we both know you haven't paid attention to your business, family, or life in Pennsylvania for almost a year now. You haven't cared about anyone or anything. You've been too busy wallowing in self-pity. Let me tell you something, Mr. Owens, death is part of life, get over it."

"Get over it?" Jace had never wanted to strike a woman before, but right now, he had a great desire to do so. No, on second thought, right now he wished Penny Jordan was a man so he could punch that little, freckle-covered, nose.

"Yes, get over it! Quit being a burden to everyone around you! I for one, Mr. Owens, do not need another problem and that's just what you are, another problem."

Mail Order Husband

By

Lauri Robinson

Linda
Thank you
for attending the
event!
Lauri
Robinson

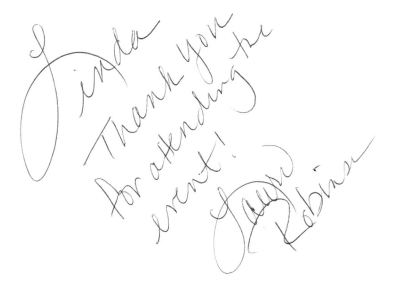

This is a work of fiction. Names, characters, places, and incidents are either the product of the author's imagination or are used fictitiously, and any resemblance to actual persons living or dead, business establishments, events, or locales, is entirely coincidental.

Mail Order Husband

Contact Information: info@thewildrosepress.com

Cover Art by *R.J.Morris*

The Wild Rose Press
PO Box 706
Adams Basin, NY 14410-0706
Visit us at www.thewildrosepress.com

Publishing History
Cactus Rose Edition, April 2007
Print ISBN 1-60154-062-0

Published in the United States of America

Dedication

To my husband, Jess, for all the hours I've spent with my laptop. Thanks for understanding.

Chapter One

Dakota Territory 1872

Regret, or was it fear that made her heart race and the fine hair on the back of her neck stand at attention? Penny Jordan didn't know, nor did she care. She was too tired. Sick and tired of the hell her life had become. Even more exhausting were the solutions others kept providing.

"I don't need a husband!" she shouted. The words echoed across barren grassland.

As they faded, sporadic visions of the past months fluttered into her mind. The memories, full of pain and corruption made her eyes sting. Chilly fingers of real fear crept up her spine. She bit down on her lips as a select few emerged. Her body shuddered. It took all the strength she could muster to keep the images at bay and prevent her body from sinking to the earth. She tightened every muscle, refusing to be ruled by her past and struggled to concentrate on the future. Her future.

"Use the past, don't let it use you." The unspoken words filtered through the images and split them into pieces. The strength she searched for surfaced. Stinging lids lifted from her eyes and blinked at the wetness of her lashes.

Fresh air filled her lungs, and she focused on the disfigured creature at her feet. Crouching next to the body, she felt for any sign of life. One fleeting thought passed through her lips. "Maybe it's more like I wish I didn't need a husband."

The never-ending wind that ripped across the flat land, tugged at her long braid. Several strands of golden-red hair let loose and the fine tendrils whipped around to snap at her face. With a hand she blocked the offensive hair, and scanned the surrounding area for hints of evidence the culprit may have left. Her ears tuned into any sound outside of the whistling wind.

For miles in all directions, short, native, buffalo grass provided a solid, durable carpet across the sandy soil. The thick, sturdy blades of brown concealed any footprints that may have been made. Sun-parched earth had absorbed the blood, but the animal's overall condition made it apparent the misdeed had been recent.

"Less than a day, probably no more than a few hours," she said aloud.

A low, haunting moan carried eerily by the breeze mingled with her words. Penny jerked and scanned the prairie's low, ever-rolling plains. She cupped her hand to defuse the glare of the sun and focused in on a silhouette several yards away.

The image grew into recognition. Hidden in the shade of a resilient elm stood the calf's mother. The large, white-faced head of the burnt orange cow slowly swayed to and fro. Her wet nose lifted now and again, sniffing at the scent of death floating on the breeze.

The air in Penny's lungs escaped with a whoosh. She tore her eyes from the mournful mother and back to the carcass at her feet. Another dead calf. This one was meant as a message- for her. Its throat had been slit.

The cold feeling of death crept up her arm. She pulled her hand from the soft hide of the dead animal and ran her fingers down her thigh. Her gaze went back to the mother cow. Behind it, the prairie grew and formed into the Black Hills of the Dakota Territory. Her blurred vision roamed the hidden valleys and steep inclines for a moment. Something snapped within her. Full-blown anger replaced fear.

Her lips puckered in a frown and her eyes squinted with resentment. "No-no, I don't want a husband," she said. "But, I think its time I admit, I need one!"

With newfound determination, Penny grabbed the wide-brimmed hat from the ground beside her, slapped it on her head, rose, and turned to her horse.

The heels of her boots stirred a faint trail of dust across the thick carpet of grass. One hand gathered the loose leather rein while the other gripped the saddle horn. With intent, she kicked her rear leg high and straddled her coal black steed. A fleeting glance flit between the mourning cow and small corpse. "I will put a stop to this killing," Penny vowed and brought the back of her boot down to touch a strong flank before it slid into the stirrup.

She settled into the saddle as Midnight took off in a swift, even gait. His solid hoofs barely hit the ground before lifting again as the animal obeyed her urgency. Their speed increased and almost soundless, they soared over the flatland.

Several miles later, their pace slowed as they drew near town. The fine dust covering the well-traveled road could easily become swirling billows, and Penny didn't want to draw attention to their arrival. Ignoring several familiar faces, she steered Midnight down the street to the telegraph office.

Small beads of sweat trickled down her back as she dismounted. Flipping a rein around the wooden hitching post before tucking the white cotton shirt deeper into the waistband of her dungarees, she made her way onto the boardwalk and through the wooden door.

Without a word of greeting, Penny wrote one line on a scrap of yellow paper and handed it to the smiling Mr. Smith. He read the message and looked at her expectantly.

She fought embarrassment, and ignored him by pretending to pick an imaginary cocklebur from the sleeve of her shirt. With downcast eyes she saw the way the telegraph agent peered down at the paper in front of him again. He scratched his whiskered chin before looking up. She refused to meet his questioning gaze and dug her hand deep into a hip pocket. She tossed two bits onto the counter. "Send it exactly as written and have the reply sent to the ranch as soon as it comes in." The tinkling sounds of the coins settling, mingled with the echoing clicks of her boots on the wide boards of the floor.

Penny felt Mr. Smith's gaze follow her through the window beside his desk. With a straight posture, she marched down the steps, hoping he didn't notice how shaky the fingers were that tightened the chinstrap of her Stetson. She mounted Midnight and left town as quick as they had arrived. Giving no heed to several onlookers who gawked at the lingering trail of dust she left in the heavy afternoon air.

Half of the town would wonder about her trip to Elm Creek in the middle of the day, and the other half would know of it before she made her way back to the ranch. Right now, she prayed Mr. Smith would remain silent about the contents of her message to Candice Berlin-Owens in Philadelphia, Pennsylvania.

After trotting past the last building, she urged Midnight into a full gallop. Her stomach flipped, and the tips of her ears burned as she thought of the words she had written.

IN DESPERATE NEED STOP PLEASE SEND HUSBAND STOP.

Shaking her head, she bent down against the thick leather horn and aligned her upper body with her horse's long neck. Her legs tightened to hold her in the saddle. She had to create distance between herself and the telegraph office, lest she change her mind and cancel the wire.

Midnight's smooth flowing gait did little damage to the dried ground as he swiftly carried her homeward. Without thought she leaned into each twist or turn as they sped across the grassland. Communication between she and her horse was silent and genuine, formed from a mutual relationship of love and respect.

Sweat dripped from her brow. The afternoon sun bore down on her as it glistened in the bright blue sky, giving dishonor to the forbidden gloom she felt. Penny blinked at the sunshine and salty tears formed in her eyes. She squeezed wet lashes together as their speed ate at the miles they had to cover.

Before long, a small grove of trees that followed a winding creek as it made its way southeast to the Missouri River came into view. Her lids felt heavy, and she wiped at the moisture with the back of her hand. Pulling her spine upright, she let her legs relax. Midnight felt the message and slowed his pace.

Both were breathing hard as they turned to saunter toward the stream parallel to the trail. When the horse stopped and lowered his head to slurp at the cool water, Penny slid from his back. Her legs wobbled beneath her. She grasped the saddle and waited for the trembles to lessen.

Needing a few minutes of reprieve, she lifted her face as a large cloud floated between the earth and the unrelenting sun. Her exhale was long and forced her lungs to empty. The last bits of air burned as she pushed it out.

With caution, not yet trusting her unsteady legs, she took a step away from the animal. They didn't stumble nor collapse beneath her. Little by little, her willpower returned. When complete control was restored, she arched her back, and then stretched the tension from her arms and legs.

The bandana around her neck held a tight knot. Her fingers finally forced the folds to let loose, she bent and soaked the material in the crystal clear water. The wet fabric felt refreshing against hot skin as Penny used it to wipe the sweat and tears from her face. She pressed the cloth against the back of her neck and crouched on the sandy bank of Elm Creek.

An image of a young girl with dancing green eyes and long braids swirled atop the water in front of her. She could hear her father's voice calling for his Copper Penny. As the imaginary voice faded, so did the image. It was replaced by an older version- a woman with sad, green eyes wearing a hat too large for her head and a man's, white work shirt. Penny tossed a pebble at the reflection, forcing it to dissolve.

A soft bump on the shoulder interrupted her thoughts. She ran a hand along the horse's chin. "It's the only thing left to do, Midnight. I am so tired of it all. No, I'm exhausted. I've seen nothing but destruction and devastation since the sun rose this morning. It feels like that's all I've seen for the past six months." The horse pulled his head up and large, brown eyes gazed down at her.

"This is our last option, Boy. You know, I can't give in to them-I won't give in to them. If having a husband is what it will take, then that is what I must do." Her words tugged at her heart. "Damn society! When are women going to get our due?" The horse raised his front hoof and pawed at the soft sand, twice, in answer to her mournful sounding voice.

She swished the bandana in the stream again,

disrupting the image that had returned. Wringing the water from the cloth, she turned away from the creek before her likeness could appear again. "Six months, that's all it will take. If this husband Candice has in mind will just stay for six months," folding the cloth into a triangle, she continued to talk aloud, "then he can leave, and I'll be able to run the ranch. Widowed, even divorced woman are allowed to take over where their husbands left off, but single women can't take over when their papa's die. It is so unfair and makes no sense, whatsoever."

The animal nuzzled his forehead against her shoulder as she replaced the tie around her neck. "Yes, I know, I have you. You will never let me down will you, Boy?" She laid her head against his. "Why couldn't you be a man? You'd put Luke James in his place for me." She stroked the silky hair under his thick, flowing mane. His foot stomped the ground again, and he released a soft whinny. A genuine smile formed. It lifted her heart. "You're right. Let's go home. The deed is done."

Her fingers moved along his neck until they grasped the horn. She pulled herself into the saddle with ease. "There is one other thing that really bothers me about that calf. The Copper Cow isn't running any cattle on the north ridge right now." Midnight shook his head and snorted as if he fully understood the conversation. Her boots, slipping into the stirrups gave the horse permission to continue on their journey.

The break had shed some of the urgency she'd felt, and the slower pace they settled on, gave her mind the opportunity to consider her actions and next steps. Maybe Candice won't be able to find someone willing to become her husband. Then what would she do? She wouldn't give up, that was for sure. Her parents had worked too hard to build the ranch for her to loose it to the no good scoundrels who were trying to take it from her. That much she knew with all her heart and soul. If only she had been born a boy. There wasn't anything wonderful about being born a girl. As a man, she would have the respect and reverence she deserved at being a cattle baron. She relished the thought.

The heart in her chest quickened when Midnight traveled through the tall, familiar gateposts, but the happiness Penny felt at being home, quickly slipped away. Tension rose and her stomach began to churn as she recognized two riders approaching. Her hold on the leather reins tightened and with determination she squared her shoulders and rode straight toward the men with a mumbled, "Welcome home."

"Miss Penny," the first greeted and touched the wide brim of a floppy hat. His quizzical look went clear to her bones, leaving no doubt he noticed her bedraggled appearance.

"Hello, Sam," she acknowledged the older of the two men.

"How were things over at O'Brien's?" he asked.

She felt disapproval in his stare. He was mad at her, again, for riding out alone, again. "Not good. They lost everything except the house. Thank goodness they are all alive. Mr. O'Brien has some nasty burns from trying to get the animals out of the barn. He was able to save one milk cow and the plow horses. A few chickens managed to escape the hen house, but …" Looking away from her hired man, she took a deep breath and shook her head.

"What do you want us to do?" His look softened.

"I don't know right now, Sam. I'll have some supplies sent over later today. I suppose we'll just have to wait and see what they decide to do."

"Hate to be the bearer of more bad news Miss," the other man started only to be interrupted by Sam's gruff voice.

"I'll ride with Henry, to take things over. I'll see if there's anything else I can do." Removing a tattered hat, Sam wiped the band of sweat that glistened across his winkled forehead with his forearm. He replaced the felt over his thick, gray hair and his weather-beaten face glared with anger at the younger man for a moment. "Miss Penny, what Jim here, was 'bout to say, is, he found a dead calf."

An eerie feeling crept up her spine. Penny looked at the younger man. Jim Calhoun met her gaze with defiance before he checked himself and turned his stare into one of compliance. The top button of his shirt was undone, and she watched as blood flowed into the area, turning his neck a deep red.

She felt tingles crawl across her skin, as they did every time she encountered the new ranch hand. Her gaze flowed from his head to his boots. He was young, a few years older than her twenty-one years. And fine looking. Too fine looking for a ranch hand. His curly blond hair and pale skin didn't belong on the range.

He also portrayed too much self-confidence for his role at the ranch. There was something about the newcomer, she couldn't put her finger on it, but something about him rubbed her the wrong way. As the owner of the Copper Cow, Penny understood the importance of hiring capable, knowledgeable help. Jim's presence at the ranch highlighted her failures of late.

She looked back at the older man, "You mean *another* dead calf, don't you, Sam?" The words caught in her throat. Regret was instant. Sam was only trying to protect her. Penny took a deep breath and let her apology come through her eyes before asking, "Where did you find it?"

Sam acknowledged her apology with a slight smile before he nodded in answer to her first question and replied to the second. "On the north ridge."

Relief fluttered. Thankfully it was the same one she had found. "Did you take care of it?" Her glance went toward the younger man as she wondered if Jim had found it before or after she had.

"Yeah," Sam nodded when her gaze met his again.

Penny rubbed her temple, "Is there anything else I need to know about?"

"No," Sam answered. Penny caught the way his eyes commanded Jim to remain silent.

The younger man puckered his lips and his cheeks puffed as he let out a long breath. The silence lingered.

Midnight shuffled his feet and drew Penny's attention back to Sam. "Where are you heading now?"

"We're going out to the south draw. Jim thought he saw some strays down by the creek."

"Really? I must say, Jim, you certainly seem to get around the ranch well. The north ridge and the south draw all in one morning. That almost seems impossible, considering the size of the Copper Cow." Penny couldn't hold the bitterness from her voice. She pulled her lips between her teeth and bit down. Managing the Copper

Cow was all she ever wanted, but carrying the tremendous weight that came with it was beginning to get the best of her. She had to be careful. Even if she didn't trust him, she couldn't afford to loose another cowhand.

"I saw the strays the day before yesterday, Miss Jordan." Jim paused, emphasizing her name with a spiteful glare. "This is the first chance Sam's had to ride out and check them." He draped an arm across his saddle horn and leaned forward. "Besides, that's what you pay me for isn't it?" His attitude said more than his words.

"I suppose it is," she responded, willing herself not to react to his underlying tone. It was never what he said that bothered her. It was how he said it. She should be use to it- his attitude was like most of the other men in the Dakota Territory. Disgust for a woman who thought she could accomplish anything without a man.

Keeping her eyes locked onto his, she forced him to look away first. When he did, she nodded toward Sam and nudged Midnight with her knees. The horse separated her from the men before she instructed, "Let me know how it goes, Sam."

"Why didn't you tell her its throat had been slit?" Jim asked the older man, knowing Penny was still within hearing distance. "You can't keep sugar coating everything. It's time she learns a woman can't run a ranch, it takes a man!"

Penny didn't hear the grumbled answer Sam supplied and pretended she didn't care what it was either. She clicked her tongue and lifted her seat in the saddle. Midnight picked up his pace, until the uneven trot smoothed into a placid run.

Making their way into the protective area of the homestead, she brought the horse back to a walk and addressed another old man with a wave as he stepped out of the double doorway of the large, red barn. Henry's brilliant smile always warmed her heart.

"I was startin' to fret 'bout youz, Miz Penny. You wuz gone a long time!" One of his dark hands took a hold of Midnight's bridle.

With a smile, she slid out of the saddle. "You don't need to worry about me, Henry. You know I can take care of myself. " She gave the stout man a quick hug. Even though he was as sturdy as ever, she could feel how age had started to wither his frame- another reminder of her deteriorating circumstances. Her smile was forced to remain bright. "But, please give Midnight some extra grain. We had a long ride today."

"Youz shouldn't have ta be takin care of youzself." Henry finished his hug with a slight pat on her cheek before he turned to escort the horse into the barn. "Come on, boy, Henry iz gonna brush youz down real good, too."

"I already have enough men trying to tell me how to take care of myself and my ranch, I really don't need another one underfoot," Penny whispered beneath her breath as she turned to take in one of her favorite sites, the big, white house in the center of the ranch setting. Its two-story, side pillars made it look somewhat out of place on the desolate prairie. The bright white paint glistened in the sunlight and seemed to invite the lush leaves of the tall oaks to shade it. Penny loved everything about the big house. Just as her mother had when she modeled it after her childhood southern plantation residence.

Penny climbed the deep stairs leading her onto a spacious porch that surrounded the large structure on all four sides. A curious glance scanned the windows lining the exterior walls as she inched to the door. The large knob clicked and opened one of the double front doors. She paused to listen for any sounds of movement. Silence met her. With relief, she slipped into the house and crept into the large room on her right.

Pushing the door shut, she leaned against the solid frame. The room had once been her father's office. She could still feel his presence here and relished in the notion of the strength it gave her. An after thought made her turn the skeleton key that brushed against her fingers beneath the knob. The snap of the lock echoed in the room.

The large, hide-covered chair was pushed back from the desk and inviting her to sit down. She slipped onto the seat and pulled herself forward, careful not to scrape the floor with the chair's solid legs. She looked around the room before leaning down to open the bottom drawer of the desk.

A beaded leather bag lay on top of several ledger

books. Penny retrieved the pouch and laid it on the desktop. A slight tug released the drawstring. Tipping the bag, she watched the contents cascade out. Her hands examined each piece. Memories flowed. One by one she placed them in a circle atop the black writing pad. A hard shake forced the last item, a well-worn book, to tumble out. Her hands clutched it close to her chest before positioning it in the center of the other items. She caressed the writing on the top of the book. Letter by letter, fingertips traced the words Holy Bible. She bowed her head and wondered aloud about the telegraph she'd sent. "Do I ask for your blessings, or for your forgiveness?"

Chapter Two

Two Weeks Later

"It takes a good driver to hit every hole in the road!" The voice beside her was filled with sarcasm as the woman clutched onto the side of the buckboard seat.

"Mary Alice, you're making me question my sanity in asking you to accompany me today." Penny's gloved hands flipped the long reins, encouraging the matching team of buckskins to pick up their pace. "It's not my fault the rains have turned the road into a washboard. Now please, your constant complaints are frazzling my nerves." She pointed at the ever-stretching plains and said, "Just sit back and enjoy the view."

"What view?" Mary Alice mumbled as she attempted to straighten the bonnet that covered her graying hair and protected her sun-browned face from the morning sun.

Penny bit back a retort. Her aunt was right; there was no view, just miles and miles of prairie grass. The few trees that spouted up here and there looked lonesome and weary as they strived to survive in the sometimes-harsh Dakota weather.

Mary Alice arched her brows and asked, "I'm frazzling your nerves? I think going to pick up your mail order husband is what has your nerves all frazzled. Why, I never heard of such outlandish behavior in all my born years. Your Papa is rolling in his grave. I can feel it in my bones, I tell you. He's even been talking to me in my dreams you know, saying, "Mary Alice, what is happening to my Copper Penny? You must stop this outrageous idea of hers." I try to tell him, I've done all I can, but you just won't listen to reason. Why I…Oh!" Stifling her chatter mid-sentence, Mary Alice caught herself from being tussled out of the bouncing wagon. "I saw that," she advised, when she was once again settled on her seat.

Pinching her lips together, in an attempt to control the smile she had caused for herself by steering the wagon into a deep rut, Penny forced her gaze to stay on the identical light brown rumps in front of her. She was well aware of the fact her actions could cause a broken axle. But at the moment even that seemed less irritating than her father's sister's un-relinquishing prattle. "I'll make you a deal, if you stop ranting and raving, I'll stop driving in the ruts," she suggested, yet knew nothing on earth was going to suppress the woman's opinion of the task they embarked.

"Humph!" Mary Alice folded her arms across her chest.

Penny tossed a glance at her aunt. She hoped the disgust her long time companion demonstrated was more for show than true feelings. She longed to see a teasing twinkle in Mary Alice's eyes. They had traveled this road more times than either cared to count over the years. Their journeys had always been fun, even when rain, snow, or sand filled winds, had joined them. The trips had been their time alone together, and Penny always looked forward to them.

Holding a solemn stare straight ahead, Mary Alice said nothing. Penny steered the vehicle beyond a long rut and their gait continued on a smoother course.

"Would you care to drive?" Penny asked a short distance later.

"No, you are perfectly capable of driving. You've been doing so since you were no more than three or four." Mary Alice let out a deep sigh, unfolded her arms and rearranged her twisted skirt.

Penny forced her sigh to remain silent. She knew Mary Alice was worried about the mayhem that had overtaken their lives. It was taking its toll on all of them, which was a large part of why she had sent the telegram.

Everyone at the ranch had worked hard to save her inheritance, the Copper Cow. Penny scowled at how her slight build, long, copper-colored hair and soft voice made people think she was immature and in need of protection. It infuriated her. No one believed she was a competent, grown woman, capable of running a ranch. A husband would help with that. Once a woman was married, she became valued and someone people listened to. She glanced toward the older woman.

Mary Alice had her eyes locked on the never-ending horizon. Would everyone react as Mary Alice was to the news of her pending marriage?

Penny felt the deep silence from her aunt- it hurt. She let out a sigh in regret of her behavior. Couldn't they see how it would benefit all of them? Didn't they see it was her only hope? She was tired, so very tired.

Penny had accepted how everyone noticed the dark bags that had settled below her eyes. Her mind couldn't remember when she had had a full night's rest. Hours in the sun had also allowed the band of light freckles stretched across her cheeks and nose to become more noticeable. Weeks ago, she quit attempting to hide her fatigue. No talc powder on earth could lesson her speckled skin's appearance, or hide her weariness.

But it had been just this morning she realized how thin she'd become. After a restless night, she had crawled from the cotton sheets with the hope a soak in the large brass tub might boost her energy and courage. Stepping out of the water, the early morning sun had haloed her reflection in the adjacent mirror. Her mouth had gapped open in shock. The woman whose ribs and hipbones stuck out like those of a neglected calf was almost unrecognizable. The mirror image also caught the way her collarbones jutted across her upper body highlighting the fact that the small, but firm orbs of her breasts had depleted into miniscule, two-toned lumps.

The cloth of her cotton wrapper hid the view from her eyes before she escaped the room. Her frustration grew while attempting to choose one of the many outfits, which hung unused in her closet. They all emphasized her thinness. She finally settled on a pale blue contraption. One that she now wished she'd hung back in the cabinet with the others. The confining collar irritated her neck, and the tight sleeves made driving the wagon more difficult than necessary.

After donning the irksome dress, she had gone downstairs to eat twice the normal amount for breakfast, hoping the act might add a little meat to her bones and allow it to become a bit more appealing. Now, she recognized her over indulgence, along with the long, rough ride was making her nauseous.

As if she had the ability to read minds, Mary Alice began again, "At least this fiasco of yours has made you put on a dress. I'm so tired of seeing you in men's clothing. Why your poor Mother, she would die all over again if she knew you were running around in men's britches. She was a real lady you know. A real southern belle, I still remember the first time I met her...."

Penny took in a deep breath and attempted to close her ears as Mary Alice began sharing old reminiscences. Letting her aunt rattle on without comment, she focused her own thoughts on what the day would bring- her first encounter with her husband.

A mail order husband is what Mary Alice called him, which in part, was the truth. But to Penny, it was her last hope of reclaiming her life and ranch. The outlandish activities that had been happening had become too difficult for her to control, and the Cattleman's Association would not listen to her concerns.

"Women are not allowed at our meetings Penny, you know that. If you want anyone in this room, or town for that matter, to listen to what you have to say, you have to find yourself a husband. Your Papa was one of my best friends, and I want to help you, but I can't go against all of these men. I know Luke has asked you to marry him. Why don't you? It would settle a lot of matters." Silas Osborne had said last month while escorting her out of the hotel. She had, once again, attempted to attend a gathering of the association.

"Because I don't want to get married, and I would never marry that snake, Silas. He's no good and you know it." Standing outside of the hotel's front doors, she had felt eyes boring into her back. "He's watching us right now isn't he?" When Silas didn't answer, she'd asked again, "Isn't he?"

"Yes, Penny, he is." Small beads of sweat had popped out on his forehead when he answered.

"Oh, Silas, he has you too, doesn't he?"

He'd ignored her question. "You have Sam take you home now, Penny. You be a good girl, and go straight home. I have to get back to the meeting." Silas had tossed a quick glance at the window behind her before he'd leaned forward, gave her a soft kiss on the cheek, and whispered in her ear. "And have that black man, Henry, move from the barn into the house."

Those parting words had instilled a chill in her bones that still remained. She had gone straight home. And she had asked Henry to start sleeping in the house. Not because she felt he would be able to protect her if needed, but because he would be safer there. He had been her mother's slave since childhood and still remained faithful to Miss Charlotte's family. Henry was part of the original group that made the move to the Dakota Territory before the War Between the States. When Harold and Charlotte Jordan left the south to claim thousands of acres in the vast northern hills.

The next day she re-read Candice's latest letter:

Dearest Penny,

I worry about you so! All of those terrible incidents you keep writing about are so frightening! I can't bear to think of you trying to manage that ranch all by yourself. I so wish you would come to live with us.

I know I have asked you many times over the past months, and I know you keep saying you can't. But Penny, I do not think you are safe there.

You are like a sister to me. The only sister I will ever have. And I so want to know you are happy and safe.

If you won't move here, to Philadelphia, please let me find you a husband. Married life is so wonderful. It is all I ever dreamed it would be! Daniel is magnificent. I can't wait for you to meet him.

We have someone in mind for you, Penny. All you need to do is say the word and he will be on the next train west. I know we have written of this before, please reconsider!

Daniel and I both want to help you!

With all my love,

Candice

Penny had re-folded the letter and put it in the bureau drawer with several others. She'd been unable to answer it. For six months, every letter she had written Candice had been full of bad news. She refused to write again. Not until she had something fun and exciting to share. Not until she could tell her friend she was happy, and safe.

Two weeks later, instead of a letter, she had sent the telegraph.

She and Candice had been writing to each other since her return home three years ago, on her eighteenth birthday. Two days after her trip to town, a breathless rider had delivered an envelope containing Candice's response to the Copper Cow.

COMING STOP MEET STAGE IN ELM CREEK AUGUST 10 STOP.

Penny had destroyed the note. The following day, Mary Alice kneaded a batch of bread dough and questioned, "When are you going to tell me what was in that telegram?"

"What telegram?" Penny had made a bad attempt at ignorance and left the kitchen, knowing Mary Alice couldn't leave the task she was up to her elbows in. For almost a week it had worked. But apprehension of meeting her future husband, or perhaps traveling three hours across the prairie with a stranger, made Penny concede to Mary Alice's merciless questions.

"It was an answer to a telegram I sent to Candice," she'd begun, as her aunt settled herself upon the bed.

"Go on."

"It's my only hope. I've tried everything I can think of and nothing is helping. Farmers are being burned out of their homes; every week I have cattle dying or disappearing. The Cattleman's Association won't let me attend their meetings nor heed my warnings. And I don't believe that the Lakota are the ones responsible for it all. I have to do something before anyone else dies."

"And what does Candice have to do with it?"

"I asked her to send me a husband."

"You what?" Mary Alice's hazel eyes had all but popped out of her head as her mouth hung open in astonishment.

"I asked her to send me a husband. I have to go meet him in Elm Creek in a few days. Perhaps, you would like to ride with me? I would appreciate the company," Penny had answered while she climbed out of bed and strolled to the door, knowing her aunt would follow. It was customary for them to share a cup of tea when one or the other couldn't sleep. Once they were both standing in the hall, Penny turned and re-entered her bedchamber. "Now I really am tired. We can talk more tomorrow. Goodnight, Auntie. Oh, and could we please keep this just between the two of us for the time being?" She had shut the door on the stunned woman, turned the key in the lock, and crawled back into bed.

For several days, her aunt acted as if she had a bee in her bonnet, and it was continuously stinging her. But to Mary Alice's defense, she kept the news a secret, and no one else knew the real reason they traveled to Elm Creek this morning.

Penny brought her mind back to the present and allowed the wagon to come to a halt. They stopped at the crest of one of the hills encircling the valley in which the small town was established. She dropped the reins onto her lap and shook her hands in an attempt to ease the numbness created by too tight of a grip on the leather.

"Well, we are almost there." Mary Alice looked down at the buildings below. The long trail they followed led through the middle of town and intersected with another roadway from the north that continued south out of town. The roads created a pattern that made the town's structures look like they were built on four interlocking squares of a quilt. Smaller, newer establishments were littered along the outskirts of the squares and butted up to the winding creek the village was named after. Both women took in the view for a few, silent moments.

Mary Alice reached over and clutched one of Penny's trembling hands. "I'm sorry, honey. I know I haven't been very good company this morning. This whole thing came as quite a shock to me. But, now that it is about to happen, I'm beginning to think it is a good thing. Maybe it's the answer to our prayers. I want you to know, I am proud of you. You have done a very good job of keeping the Copper Cow running. I know it hasn't been easy." She patted Penny hand. "A husband might be exactly what you need."

A response wouldn't form. The backs of her eyes burned and Penny swallowed against the lump in her throat.

Mary Alice snatched the reins and flipped them across the backs of the stilled horses, "Getty-up now boys, we got some mail to pick up!"

Caught off guard, Penny grabbed the side of her seat to keep from being tousled over the edge. She couldn't help but allow a nervous chuckle to join the older woman's giggles at almost unseating her.

****

"Candice! Candice, what are you doing here?" Penny exclaimed, recognizing the female who stepped down from the dust-covered stagecoach.

"I just had to see how you are doing for myself!" The young woman engulfed Penny in outstretched arms. "Where's your wagon?" she asked as soon as their heads met.

"It's over at the general store. We had supplies to pick up." Stepping back, Penny took in Candice's beauty. Lush, blond hair was piled expertly upon her graceful head and covered with a lace-fringed cap that matched her traveling dress of bright pink. The traveler's well maintained appearance showed no signs of the long ride she had just endured. "It is so good to see you!" Penny exclaimed.

"Yes, yes, it's good to see you too, but, quick, go get your wagon!" Her friend demanded with a slight shove as she turned to address the other woman. "Mary Alice, how are you? You look fabulous! I love that color on you. You have the ideal complexion to wear yellow. And those glasses, they fit your face so well, they really frame your eyes."

Penny heard no more, because the whole time Candice flattered Mary Alice, she waved for Penny to obtain the wagon. It took only moments to retrieve and pull the buckboard beside the stage, to the spot Candice directed.

"Here is our wagon now, Mr. Adams. Please place our bags in the back. NO! No, I will get Mr. Owens, thank you so much. Miss Jordan, will help me, please?"

Confused and somewhat shocked by Candice's impatient actions, Penny tried to shake off her stunned demeanor and tossed a nervous smile at the driver. She moved to the coach door as instructed and waited to follow Candice up the steps. Leaning into the darkened area, the first thing that struck her was the stench. "Good Lord, Candice."

"Shhh, don't say a word, just get in here and help me!" Candice demanded.

The shades on the windows were drawn, making the tiny space appear dank and gloomy. Penny pushed the door open further. The sun blazed in through the open space and settled onto the back wall of the stage. That was when she saw him.

Slouched in the corner, was something that almost resembled a human shape. Long arms and legs sprawled in all directions. Candice moved the limp legs toward the door before she jammed a brown, derby hat upon greasy, dark hair. Positioning one lank arm around her shoulders, Candice pushed the other arm at Penny as she heaved the long body upwards.

"Here grab his arm!" Looking down, she used a sweet voice to address the man, "Jace? It's Candice. Come on, we have to get out of the stage. This is Penny. She's here to help us. That's it try to stand up. Good. Now put that arm around Penny." Candice cajoled the being to comply with her instructions.

The long arm snaked its way around Penny's neck and shoulders. Shivers ran up her spine. She braced herself to take on the extra weight and helped to lift the heavy mass from the bench seat. His head fell her way. She got a full whiff of his breath and almost passed out from the smell. Turning her face away, she coughed and swallowed against the rumbles of her already nauseous stomach. Holding her breath, she half carried—half dragged the body as she led the way to the stage door and fresh air.

"Good job, now here's the step. Good. One more. Good job, Jace. It's not too far to the wagon. You can do it. There, now hold your head up, you can do it." Candice continued to encourage as they guided him off the stage.

"What is this, Candice?" Penny seethed through clutched teeth when she felt it was safe to take in a breath of air.

"Why Penny, dear, you know Jace, my brother-in-law. I wrote about him in several letters." Candice said, in a voice louder than necessary, before she whispered, "Jace, you have to pick up your feet a little."

Penny alternated with Candice in using their legs to make his move, but as they rounded the stage, his long boots were toe down in the dirt. They drug his lengthy body to the wagon.

"He became ill on the train, and Mr. Adams has been very concerned. But I told him, we would get Jace to the doctor as soon as you picked us up," Candice said as she smiled at the other two people standing next to the wagon. "Mary Alice would you be a dear and climb in the back of the wagon, so Jace can lay his head on your lap? Thank you, darling."

Penny felt the flaccid weight slipping from her grasp as they waited for her aunt to climb in. Thankfully, Mr. Adams noticed it as well and moved around to grasp the limp form before it slithered all the way to the ground. With haste, the driver settled the lifeless looking creature into the back of the wagon, before he turned to cover his mouth and cough.

Candice picked up the derby hat from where it had tumbled to the dirt and continued leading the group's movements with a voice that was sweeter than honey. The watery-eyed driver and Mary Alice scrambled to do all she asked of them. "There we go, all settled! Mr. Adams, thank you so very much. I hope I get to ride in your stage again when I return home. You have been so wonderful and most helpful during our trip."

Complying with the hand instructions Candice continued to give, Penny climbed onto the driver's seat as soon as Jace and Mary Alice were settled in the back.

Her friend placed a gentle kiss upon the driver's cheek then turned and leaped onto the wooden seat.

"Let's go, Penny!" Candice demanded before her bottom hit the seat.

The horses moved forward. Penny glanced back to see how the rear seat travelers were doing, "The doctor's office is just around the next corner," she assured.

Candice smiled and fluttered four fingers at Mr. Adams. "That's good." As soon as they were out of earshot she asked, "Which way is it to the Copper Cow, and how far is it?"

"The doctor's office is on the west road, we just follow it for about three hours and we will be at the ranch." A shudder ran up her neck when her eyes caught a glimpse of how the man's greasy hair lobbed across the folds of her Aunt's traveling dress.

"Good, I can't wait to see it." Candice removed her traveling gloves and shook them into the breeze.

"Good luck at getting the smell out of those," Penny muttered as she steered into the curve if the road.

"Oh, no!" Mary Alice exclaimed when they turned the corner.

"What?" both young women asked in unison.

"Look, the doctor's not home. There is a note on his door. I'll go see what it says. Maybe he's eating lunch or something." Mary Alice clearly wanted a different task than the one she had been coerced into.

The doctor's house looked like most of the other buildings in town. Two stories tall, painted white, and adorned with a large, wooden sign hanging from the porch roof. This one simply said 'Doctor'.

Candice shook her head, "No, Dear, that's okay, we aren't stopping. We are going straight to the ranch."

"What?" Penny began to pull the wagon over. "That uh-that man is very ill, we must find the doctor!"

Grabbing the reins, Candice gave them a quick shake. "He is not sick. He's drugged. I've been giving him something called opium, since before we left Philadelphia." She threw Penny a quick smile before the long reins slapped across the backs of the buckskins again. The wagon jolted forward as the horses reached a matching gallop. Their churning feet filled the air with dust. "I think he's getting use to it. I've had to almost double the dose to keep him quiet. I truly hope I didn't give him too much. I'm sure Singing Dove can help him. You did say she still lives on the ranch right?"

Penny snatched the reins from her friend's hands and guided the horses into a more sensible trot. "You did what? You have been doing what, since when? Candice! I can't believe this!"

"Singing Dove does still live on the ranch doesn't she? You always said she could heal people. That she was better than any doctor. Oh, Penny, she is at the ranch isn't she? I couldn't live if I killed Jace! Accident or no accident, it would be terrible if he died!" Tears began to fall from Candice's frightened eyes.

"Now, now, dear, it's okay." Mary Alice reached a hand forward to comfort the young woman by patting her back. "Singing Dove still lives at the ranch, and Mr. Owens is not going to die. He has a strong heartbeat and is breathing deep and even. His only true chances of dying right now are Penny's reckless driving, or if I decide I can't stand the stench any longer and throw him overboard."

"Oh, thank you, Mary Alice! Thank heavens! I guess I am just becoming a little anxious. He didn't wake up all morning! Most days, he's came around enough for me to give him a little water or broth, but since we started traveling by stage, I started to give him a double dose in the middle of the night. I had to have a boy at the hotel, help me get him into the stage this morning. We had a private car on the train ride, all the way from Philadelphia, so that part of the trip was easy. But, I was frightened that we would have several others on the stage with us. I couldn't take the chance that he would wake up. As it turned out, we were the only two on the stage, except for one day and that man slept all day as well. And Mr. Adams was so very accommodating; he's a wonderful driver. Oh, Penny, I wish you had been with us, it was quite a fascinating adventure!"

Penny stared at her friend in disbelieve and tried to make sense of her garbled tale. "A fascinating adventure? Candice, I can't believe this. You have been drugging this man for days, weeks, and you call it a fascinating adventure? You could have killed him!"

"Well, I didn't kill him. Mary Alice said he is going to be just fine. What are you getting so grumpy about? I did all this for you. And it was fascinating. It has been a true adventure." Candice turned her face away from her friend and clasped her hands upon her lap.

Penny leaned forward, and noted the way Candice's lower lip quivered. "I'm sorry, Candice, I don't mean to sound—uh-grumpy, but I am a little concerned about Mr. Owens." Penny shook her head, hoping to clear her thoughts. "Wait a minute, Jace Owens, that's Daniel's brother! This man really is your brother-in-law. What is he doing here?"

"He's your husband!"

Chapter Three

"My what?"

"Your husband. You asked me to send you one." Candice turned and flashed a look of righteousness at Penny.

"I know! So why are you and *he* here?"

"I told you, he's your husband."

"What?" Penny's body quivered as she glanced to the man in the back. "I thought Daniel's brother was already married."

"Jace is who I was talking about for your husband. And yes, he is Daniel's brother. That's why it would have been so terrible if I had killed him. Well, it would be terrible if I killed anyone, but especially Daniel's brother. And, he is not married any more. Well he is, but not to his first wife. Karin died in childbirth almost a year ago. I told you about it in one of my letters."

Candice let out an exaggerated sigh. "It was so sad. Daniel and I have been very worried about him. When we decided that I needed to find a husband for you, I thought of Jace. Daniel thought it was a wonderful idea as well. When your telegraph arrived, Daniel and I asked Jace about it. I must say he wasn't the least bit excited about the news. In fact, he refused to do it. So, Daniel and I decided I would drug him and bring him out to you."

Pointing at a small grove of trees, Candice added. "Oh, do pull over Penny. I have had to relieve myself since I got off the stage."

Penny steered the horses off the road and drove toward the creek where she and Midnight had found rest a few weeks earlier. Her mind reeled haphazardly as the wooden wheels of the wagon groaned, bounced, and jostled off the dirt trail and over the uneven ground covered with prairie dog mounds.

Trying to avoid the larger hills, Penny focused on

driving and seethed between clutched teeth, "Your husband helped you drug his brother and send him west? He really is the perfect mate for you." Her mind recalled a few of the many harebrained escapades Candice had talked her into when they were younger. *Oh, what have I done?*

The wagon came to an abrupt halt. Penny turned to her friend, "And what do you mean, he is married but not to his first wife? How many wives has he had?"

Candice was already scrambling off the wagon. "Oh, only two. Karin and now you."

"Me? We aren't married yet."

"Yes, you are. You married Jace by proxy, or Jace married you by proxy, I can't remember which way it went, but it happened before we left Philadelphia," Candice said before she ran toward privacy.

"How can you marry someone without knowing it or being present?" Mary Alice asked Penny as they watched Candice slip into the grove of trees.

"I have no idea." Penny threw her hands into the air and used them to cover her face as they floated down. "Oh, Mary Alice, what have I gotten myself into now? I had forgotten how crazy some of Candice's ideas could be. Why did I believe this one would work? This-this mail order husband scheme?"

"Well, Dear, if it makes you feel any better. He's not really a mail order husband. A mail order husband would have come to you on his own accord. What you have is a kidnapped husband, or as the Lakota call them, a stolen husband. However, I believe they steal wives. I don't think I have ever heard of a stolen husband. But then, I had never heard of a mail order husband either..."

"Mary Alice, please, not right now." Penny lifted the reins from her lap. After securing them around the wooden brake handle, she climbed down and said, "I might as well relieve myself as well."

"What about me, I might have to go too, you know?" With caution, Mary Alice re-positioned Jace's sleeping form and scrambled over the bags and boxes of supplies covering the back of the wagon. She climbed over the rope tailgate and landed on the ground with a "Humph." Brushing the dust from her long skirt, she joined Penny to proceed toward the trees.

****

He could see them, lying together in the cold, pine box. His small son swaddled in blankets and nestled beside his tender, adoring wife. Then he heard the hammers; one by one they drove long, stiff nails into the coffin. The loud bangs echoed through his head. Pain ripped across his chest, his heart began to constrict.

"No, no, no!" Jace protested against the throbbing ache, against the loss and prayed for the dark fog to over take his existence again.

"Oh, dear! He's waking up!" Candice exclaimed as Penny emerged from the grove. Her friend hitched her pink skirt high above her ankles and ran through the knee-high grass. Penny followed suit. Her eyes grew wide when Candice pulled a small flask out of a hidden waist pocket before scrambling into the back of the wagon. "Jace? Jace? It's Candice and it is time for more medicine."

"Stop!" Penny arrived at the wagon and reached for the bottle Candice was opening. "Don't give him any more of that stuff."

Candice slapped her hand out of the way. "I have too. We can't let him wake up here!"

His arms began to flay about without control. His feet quivered and jerked, smashing into the supply cartons.

"Candice? Candice, let me die!" he moaned. One out of control armed flapped against her friend's bodice before long fingers snatched a hold of the pink material. "They're gone, gone. Just let me go to them."

Penny pulled her hand out of the way. Any other words of prevention stilled in her throat as his eyes flew open. They were black as night. His head jerked from side to side. The opaque orbs sent a chill up her spine. They reminded her of an abandoned cabin. It was like the door was open, but no one was home. She shivered, took a step back, and looked toward her aunt, who stood beside the wagon, wringing her hands together.

"No, Jace, I can't let you die. But I will give you some more medicine. It will help you sleep." Candice stilled his head with one hand. "Here now, open your mouth. That's good." She poured thick liquid onto his tongue and lifted his chin. "There, now swallow and lie still. It will only take a minute to start working."

In silence, Penny watched his Adam's apple move up and down.

"Good job, Jace. Now just go back to sleep. It will all be better soon, I promise." Candice laid a hand on his chest and waited until his thrashing body grew still. She pushed a strand of hair from her face and scampered out of the wagon.

"Will you sit with him again, Mary Alice?" Candice asked as she returned the flask to her pocket.

"Well, Dear, I really don't think…" Mary Alice began.

Candice placed her hands on the older woman's shoulders and pleaded, "Please, he will sleep now. It really has been an exhausting trip for me."

Penny shrugged her shoulders as her aunt looked her way. She had also forgotten how good Candice was at getting what she wanted. Not knowing what else to do, Penny climbed back onto the driver's seat. "Can we go home now? Before…before Mr. Owens wakes up again," flashing an angry glare at her friend, she finished, "or dies."

"Very well," Mary Alice let out a long sigh as she began to climb in the wagon and take her former seat.

Penny refused to watch either woman as they resettled the man and themselves into traveling positions. Once they were seated, she slapped the reins against the buckskins. Her mind would have sent up a prayer, if it had known what to pray for.

The midday sun was strong. Her thin bonnet did little to prevent the heat, and the burning rays encouraged the pain in her temples to increase. Penny wiped the moisture from her forehead as Candice broke the silence that had engulfed them for several miles.

"Daniel assured me it's all legal," she said.

"What, poisoning your brother-in-law?" Penny snapped. The closer they got to the ranch, the more nervous she became. Sweat rolled from her armpits. How on earth would she explain the emaciated, stinking sack of bones in the back of the wagon to the rest of the ranch's occupants? A husband would have been hard, but this…

"I didn't poison him, I drugged him. Drugging someone is not the same as poisoning them. And, no, I don't know if that is legal or not, I never asked Daniel. But since he gave me the medicine, I assume it is." She stiffened her spine. "I was talking about the marriage. Daniel is a lawyer you know. So he wrote up the papers, and I signed on your behalf. Daniel signed on Jace's behalf, since he was already being medicated, and Daniel's friend, who is a judge, married the two of you. All you two have to do is sign the marriage certificate. It's in my carpetbag. I will give it to you when we get to the ranch."

She let out a deep sigh, "Oh, Penny, I do wish you weren't so angry about the whole ordeal. Daniel worked very hard to see that every thing was taken care of."

A twinge drew across her chest. "I am sorry, Candice, I'm not angry at you or Daniel. I'm angry at myself for getting into this entire mess," Penny admitted.

"I know. It did sound much better and easier in writing didn't it? I must admit I've been second-guessing myself for over a week now. Ever since that train left Philadelphia." With confidence only Candice could portray in extreme situations, she assured, "But it will all turn out, I know it will. Just wait. It will be the answer to all of our prayers."

"Not the answer to my prayers!" Penny closed her eyes for a moment, trying to calm her escalating frustration. But it didn't help. She was overwhelmed.

"Candice, I asked for a husband. Not some man who is so ill he can't walk. Nor one who is so distraught over the death of his wife and baby he can't even function. How is your brother-in-law going to help me?"

She held her hand up when Candice began to interrupt. "No, no, let me finish. I don't need another problem. I need a man who can help me solve the problems I already have. I need a man who can stand up to Luke James and make him leave me alone. I need a man who can stand up to the Cattleman's Association and say "listen to my wife, she knows what she is talking about". He doesn't have to love me. He doesn't have to want to live with me forever or have babies with me. He just needs to help me save my ranch!" Her voice crackled and croaked as the words gushed from her chest. She couldn't stop the tears from flowing. Penny's final words were barely audible, "That man would be the answer to my prayers."

Candice leaned over, the bouncing of the wagon made it difficult, but her friend persisted until their heads rested together, and Penny was wrapped in a loving hug. "Jace can be that man, Penny, just give him a chance. Please, I beg you. Just give him a chance to be the answer to your prayers."

From the back of the wagon, Mary Alice instructed, "Well girls, prayers aren't answered without hard work, and I do believe that we have our work cut out for us. So, dry your eyes, and roll up your sleeves…were home."

Penny shivered as her blurry vision saw the tall posts that held a wide board, displaying the brand of the Copper Cow, high above their heads.

****

"Now, that wasn't so bad was it?" Candice said, entering the office.

Penny looked up from recording her recent purchases into the ranch's ledger books. "Thank the good, sweet Lord Singing Dove and Henry were the only two around when we arrived. I just don't know how I'm going to explain your brother-in-law to Sam. I don't even want to think about trying to explain him to some of the other folks around." Penny rubbed her forehead. An uncontrollable shiver ran up her spine every time she thought of the man, who now was her husband. "Is h-he settled in?"

"He's comfortable. Singing Dove is tending to him. She says he needs to get the poisons, I mean drugs, out of his body. She'll start the cleansing process first thing in the morning. It has something to do with the sun rising." Closing the door behind her, Candice continued, "Penny, I have to leave tomorrow. I don't think I should be here when Jace wakes up."

Penny watched her friend walk to the desk, lay an envelope on top of the ledger, and then sit down on the long adjacent couch. Candice's fingers caressed the material of the plush cushion. The covering was the same as the chair Penny sat on. The red-brown cattle hides were from two of the original Herefords that aided her father in creating the Copper Cow Ranch. She gave her head a slight shake as Candice's words registered.

"You're leaving tomorrow? You just arrived. Can't you stay for a few days?"

"No, Jace has been drugged for too many days. And, I really don't want to be here when he wakes up. I have to warn you, Penny. He's going to be angry. Jace is one of the most wonderful men I know. He's a lot like Daniel. But losing Karin and the baby was hard on him. We have been so worried about him. He's been drinking—a lot, and just didn't seem to care about anyone or anything. I was afraid he was going to die if someone didn't do something."

Pointing to the envelope, she continued, "There's your marriage license and certificate, as well as the permission papers. You'll have to have Jace sign it too. The judge I mentioned earlier, the one who married the two of you. He is, was Karin's father. He too was very concerned about Jace.

"Penny, you must make this work. You can't let Jace return to Philadelphia, nor can you let him start drinking again." She paused for a moment and placed a hand over her chest. A small sob escaped before she whispered, "He needs a new life Penny, and you are his only chance."

Penny didn't have a response. What could she say? She watched as her friend pulled a neat, pressed handkerchief from beneath her sleeve and used it to dab at the tears rolling down her face. A few moments later Candice folded the cloth and replaced it under the cuff of her outrageous, yellow, chiffon dress. The garment was covered with long, frilly lace and wide, stiff ruffles. Penny wondered how anyone could maneuver in so much material.

Candice straightened her posture and looked at Penny with glistening eyes. "Now, finish up what you're doing so you can show me around this beautiful ranch of yours. We only have a few hours before it gets dark. Henry agreed to give me a ride back to the stage in Elm Creek first thing in the morning. I will catch the train in Yankton again and meet up with Daniel in Omaha. He has a cousin there I'm going to stay with for a few days, until he arrives. Then we are going to travel to the Pacific Ocean before we return to Philadelphia. Doesn't that sound exciting?" Candice flashed a mischievous smile. "We figured it would be best if Jace couldn't get a hold of us for a few weeks."

Penny sat for a moment, her mouth gaping in astonishment. With both hands, she pushed her chair away from the desk and shook her head. "You are amazing, Candice Berlin-Owens. One minute you're asking me to save a man's life, and the next you're talking about seeing the Pacific Ocean. Yet, somehow, coming from you, it all makes sense, and somehow fits together. How do you do it? You amaze me."

"Oh, please, Penny!" Candice rose from the couch and walked around to embrace her in a hug. "Come on, you're the amazing one. Running this ranch all by yourself, living with Indians and black people. I really wish I could stay for a few days." Stepping back to separate the two of them, she tugged on the shoulder of Penny's white, cotton shirt. "To teach you how to dress again if nothing else…those pants and that shirt! Where did you ever find men's clothing to fit you? This reminds me, Jace doesn't have any other clothes with him. You'll have to find some for him, Sis. You do realize we are now sisters don't you?"

Penny opened her mouth to speak, and then closed it. Shaking her head, she resolved to worry about her new problem later. Instead, she took hold of Candice's hand and pulled her to the door.

"Come on, I'll show you around and introduce you to Midnight, you're going to love him!"

****

Jace felt the pain rip across his stomach again. With a moan, he rolled his head toward the bucket that had been strategically placed beside him for several days. There was nothing in his stomach to erupt, but his body still went through the motions. The bile burned his dry throat. Cold sweat broke out across his naked body. When the dry heaves came to an end, a cup of sweet smelling liquid was pressed to his lips. "No, just let me die," groaning in protest, he turned his face away.

"Hiya." A strange voice came from above him. "You not die." The owner of the voice poured the contents from the cup into his mouth. Firm fingers lifted his chin, forcing him to swallow. "Drink *phejuta*, good medicine for *Maka Wichasha*."

Jace felt the liquid settle into the empty basin in his abdomen. He braced himself, waiting for the convulsions to come again. When none came, he forced his raw vocal cords to emit croaked whisper, "Where am I?"

"Shh, you sleep now. Tomorrow you will wake and be healed," answered the voice he recognized as Native American and of the woman he knew had been nursing him for several days. Her words seemed to carry wisdom and knowledge, providing his body with peacefulness he couldn't explain. He accepted the black void that came to take over his mind and fell into a deep, comforting sleep.

A number of hours later, the rumblings of his stomach woke him again. This time it was not in illness, but in hunger. A sense he hadn't recognized in sometime. He tugged heavy eyelids open.

Nothing was familiar. Sprawled across a large bed, covered with a single white sheet, he let his eyes roam. Cream-colored wallpaper with tiny brown flowers decorated the room. A large dresser and clothes cabinet stood along one wall. A chair and dressing stand were on the opposite one, which also hosted the open window where a cool breeze flowed into the room. He ignored the gurgling of his stomach and forced his mind to recall how he came to be in this room. Hazy, confusing visions floated through his mind. Closing his eyes, he attempted to focus in on the revelations.

One picture became clear. "Candice!" He threw the sheet from his naked body and flipped his legs over the side of the bed. The quick movements made his stomach jolt, and his head swirl. The room spun. He stilled his actions and waited for his weakened body to catch up to his fast moving mind.

With caution, he stood and looked for his clothing. Slow even steps moved him across the room where he pulled open several dresser drawers. Nothing. His steps grew stronger as he made his way to the cabinet. But it was bare as well. He searched for options. Ripping the sheet from the bed, he wrapped it around his waist and made his way to the solid, wooden door.

The hallway was long and vacant. Tall windows at both ends filled the area with sunlight. Several doors lined the corridor. He moved forward and tapped on the door across from his. "Candice?"

No one answered. He pushed it open and took in the scene of an unoccupied room very similar to his. Frustrated, he strode to the next door. This one was a bathing chamber. He stared at the large brass tub. A vision of his body lying in it flashed before his eyes. Warm water and a scented steam had swirled around him. He could almost feel the comfort it had provided. Shaking his head, he removed the image from his mind, and pulled the door shut.

"Candice!" he shouted. The word floated across the emptiness of the hallway. "What is this some kind of a hotel?" Zigzagging left and right, he continued to shout her name as he thrust each door open. His mind recalled a few hazy visions of a train and stagecoach.

"No, it's not a hotel, it's an insane asylum. That little twit put me in an insane asylum!" Angry disbelief filled him.

He came to the top of a deep staircase. "Candice! Where the hell are you? When I get my hands on your scrawny neck, I am going to squeeze it until your eyes pop out!"

Flipping the long tail of the sheet over his right arm, his bare feet marched down the varnished stairs. "Candice! I know you're here! Get your sweet, little carcass out here right now!"

He stopped at the bottom of the stairs. Straight ahead, tiny dust motes danced in the sunlight shining through the large windows of a set of double doors. He glanced down at his attire and turned away from the front entrance. Several other doors dotted the long walls that led away from the foyer. To his right French doors were open wide and showcased a large, formal dining room. On his left, he could see a large desk settled in the middle of either an office or library. A sixth sense pulled his attention to a door further down on the right. A door he knew held people on the other side.

****

The women, busy in the kitchen, stilled their actions

as sounds wafted down from the upper floor. One particularly loud phrase caused Penny's spine to tingle. She dashed a look at the other two.

"Maka Wichasha awake. This is good. He is healed." Singing Dove resumed stirring the slices of potatoes that sizzled in the frying pan on the iron cook stove.

Penny looked at her stepmother, the Lakota woman her father had married a few years after the death of Charlotte Jordan, fifteen years ago. "Skunk Man? You named him, Skunk Man?"

"Han," Singing Dove nodded her head in affirmation. Her golden brown skin matched coffee colored eyes. A slight smile raised her high cheekbones.

Penny's mouth fell open, but no words emitted, her mind swirled.

"Seems pretty fitting, if you ask me." Mary Alice started to set the plates she held onto the table.

"Nobody is asking you." Penny dashed a look of disbelief at her aunt.

"Well, maybe if people would start asking me what I thought, they wouldn't keep finding themselves in peculiar situations," Mary Alice supplied with a sweet smile. "And right now, I think you better go greet your husband, before he tears the house apart looking for your friend."

Penny slammed the lid on the coffee pot and marched to the swinging door of the kitchen. With both hands she gave it a hard shove, using more force than necessary.

The door hit something solid with a thud. Her hands caught the edge as it swung back at her. She looked around the perimeter.

"Oh!"

A man well over six-foot tall stood on the other side. His midnight blue eyes glared at her. She let go of the door, but grabbed it before it went all the way shut. She squeezed her eyes shut. One at a time she opened them and peer through the small opening, almost hoping he was a vision of her imagination.

Blood began to gush from his nose. He brought both hands up in an attempt to quell the flow. Penny's gaze followed the white sheet that slipped from his waist to form a pile on the floor, covering nothing but long, bare feet.

Her face burned with embarrassment, "Mr. Owens, oh, here, let me help you." She slipped through the narrow opening. As the door slapped shut behind her, she reached for the sheet and concentrated on keeping her gaze away from of his male parts.

Two large hands grabbed the sheet from her grasp. Startled, she glanced up and shivered as blood continued to flow over stiff whiskers. The man gathered the sheet and wrapped it around his waist before using a corner of the long material to apply pressure to his nose. Once he had blocked the stream a deep nasal voice demanded, "Where is Candice Owens?"

She stood, but before she could respond the swinging door smacked her backside as someone pushed it open. Penny jolted forward. Her steps faltered, and the man took a quick step back to avoid another collision with her.

"Oh, my! Here, Mr. Owens, let me help you," Mary Alice said. She threw Penny a glare that was laced with dismay before she sidestepped around her. With open friendliness, Mary Alice placed one hand on the man's shoulder and the other on his folded elbow. "Come into the kitchen and sit down."

Thankful she didn't have to touch him; Penny tugged on the door handle and held it open for their passage. The man held his stance. Weary eyes glanced between her and Mary Alice. A noise seemed to draw his attention through the open doorway to where Singing Dove stood. Her stepmother bowed her head in greeting, and her hand rose to point to the kitchen table. Recognition seemed to enter the man's deep blue eyes. He tossed a look of loathing at Penny before he allowed Mary Alice to lead him into the room.

Her two relatives fussed about until they had him settled onto one of the tall-backed, kitchen chairs. Mary Alice instructed him to tilt his head back to stop the flow. When it appeared to slow, she wiped the blood from his face, hands, and chest. "I don't believe it is broken, Mr. Owens. It should stop bleeding in a minute or two. Just sit still," her aunt assured him.

"Where is Candice Owens?" Jace inquired.

The other two women gave Penny expectant stares.

The room grew eerie with silence. She let go of the swinging door and took a step forward. Her mouth opened and then closed again. She brought her hands up and shrugged her shoulders.

Singing Dove nodded at her and then toward the man. Her deep brown eyes insisted Penny say something. Anxious feelings filled every pour of her system.

She hadn't seen him since they carried him into the house, almost a week ago. Penny brought both hands up and rubbed her temples, trying to stimulate some sense of stability. Though he appeared to be much thinner than a man of his height should be, his aura was one of authority. He made the atmosphere in the kitchen feel foreign, and his scant attire made his masculinity very visible. She felt the blood flow to her face and had to clear her throat with a slight cough before she could speak.

"I'm afraid she's not here at the moment, Mr. Owens."

One long arm stretched out and his hand waved, clearly indicating that Penny was to step closer to where he could see her. She glanced at the other women. Neither acknowledged her silent plea for help. Her lips puckered with distaste, and she forced her feet to shuffle across the floor.

"Where is she and when is she returning?"

Startled, her body jumped as the deep voice shook the walls.

His head was still tilted back. Thick, dark lashes surrounded the deep blue eyes that glared at her. High cheekbones jutted out below those unapproachable eyes, and his nose appeared to be too large for his face. Was it swelling? Had she broken his nose with the door?

"Where is she!" he repeated.

"I don't believe she will be returning," squeaked out of her mouth.

"Oh, and why is that?"

Penny watched the unkempt mustache and beard move up and down as he spoke. The hands hanging at her sides trembled; she clenched them into tight fists. "Because, I believe, she is on her way to the Pacific Ocean."

His index finger touched his wide nostrils and patted

the scraggly hair of his mustache. When he appeared to be satisfied the flow had stopped, he brought his face forward and resettled himself on the chair. “Who are you?” he asked. His tone was softer, but still laced with aversion.

Her nails dug into the palms of her hands. “My name is Penny Jordan.”

Thick eyebrows almost met as his forehead creased into a frown, “Jordan? Penny Jordan.” Sparks flew from his eyes. “You’re the friend she and Daniel wanted me to marry!”

Chapter Four

Penny didn't answer. The lump in her throat was too large for words to maneuver around. She bit her bottom lip and tried to pull her gaze from his.

Anger seemed to ooze from his being. "I will tell you just what I told them. I am already married!"

Her body jolted away from the table as his voice boomed like thunder rolling across the prairie. She caught her balance by placing a hand on the kitchen cupboard.

He pulled his eyes from her and turned to stare at the window on the far side of the room. No one moved. Soon his head bowed and a voice, which seemed to be filled with remorse, whispered, "Even though she is no longer with me in person, I will remain faithful to my wife until the day I die."

Except for the pop and crackle of food sizzling on the stove, silence filled the room. The moments ticked by. Penny looked at Mary Alice, who looked at Singing Dove, who looked back at Penny. Simultaneously, their gazes went back to the man who sat at the table, eyes closed, face lowered.

Several minutes later, one of his hands came up to massage his forehead. A deep sigh left his chest, he looked at Penny and asked, "Where am I?" His eyes were filled with loneliness or loss.

Her voice cracked, "Y-you're at the Copper Cow Ranch."

"And where is the Copper Cow Ranch?" he growled, letting his frustration be heard.

"About three hours, by wagon, less by horseback, west of Elm Creek," Penny answered. Even his anger couldn't diminish the regret forming in her chest.

"Can you tell me, Miss Jordan, in what state are the Copper Cow Ranch and Elm Creek located?" Jace practically bellowed at her.

Beset with tension, her shoulders drooped. With a deep sigh, Penny pushed away from the counter and walked over to pull out the chair across from his. She sat down, braced an elbow on the table, and laid her forehead in her palm. From below her hand, she peered at him.

"Technically, Mr. Owens, we are not a state. We are still a territory. You are in the Dakota Territory." An overwhelming sense of guilt, of her—and Candice's—actions, tugged at her conscience. "Your sister-in-law has no intention of returning. As a matter of fact, she and Daniel decided it would be best if you wouldn't be able to locate them for a while."

Penny took responsibility seriously. Knowing she was responsible, at least in part, for the position this man now found himself in, she couldn't blame him for his anger. Feeling some of her inner strength returning, she straightened her spine and looked squarely at her guest. She had to deal with this current problem, quickly-but how? "Believe me, Mr. Owens, I am no more impressed by this situation than you are. I don't want a husband anymore than you want a wife."

Accepting the sharp daggers his eyes threw at her, she continued, "However, right now, I suggest you have the breakfast Singing Dove has prepared for you. Mary Alice will locate your clothes, and once you are more appropriately dressed, you and I will meet in my office to discuss the predicament we seem to be in. If you will excuse me, I have some work to attend to."

Jace was somewhat stunned. The quivering, young girl had transformed herself into a very self-assured, determined woman right before his eyes. His bewildered mind seemed to be unable to communicate any response.

Bemused, he watched as her small hand snatched a fresh biscuit from the plate on the table. She broke it apart, popped a small piece into her mouth and rose from her chair. Without another word, she slipped from his view. He heard the door swing shut as she made her exit.

****

Jace pulled the drawstring of his brown, wool pants as tight as he could and twisted it into a tight knot. He knew he had lost a significant amount of weight the last few months, but this was ridiculous. The pants threatened to fall below his hips.

However, he felt better than he had in weeks. He wondered about Singing Dove and her healing ways. He felt cleansed, reborn even. At the table this morning, when he spoke of his wife, pain hadn't overtaken his body. The heart-wrenching ache that had been his lifeline had disappeared. He searched, but couldn't find it, and the melancholy feeling that had been engulfing him was gone as well. Remembrances of Karin and the baby were still with him, but thoughts of them didn't fill him with remorse. Instead, he felt a sense of joy at what they had shared. Shaking his head in disbelief, he finished dressing and left the bathing chamber.

He took in the condition of the home while strolling down the long hall. Most of the upstairs looked as if it had never been lived in. The long carpet runner showed only a small amount of wear. Faint trails led into the first three bedrooms and to the bathing chamber. The whitewashed walls were bare except for the lanterns that could illuminate the walkway during the dark hours of evening. Yet, the lamp wicks where white, demonstrating the majority of them had never been lit. The house was neat and clean, but there was something deeper. Almost an empty feeling, like no one lived here.

One hand slid along the solid oak banister running parallel to the wide stairs. He sauntered down the even steps. The design of the staircase reminded him of the one in his parent's house, the one that he and Daniel had slid down too many times to count. The thought of Daniel should have renewed his anger, but a tantalizing smell registered in his mind first.

His nose led him to the kitchen. Both arms came up in protection as he approached the hinged door. It remained still. His reflexes relaxed, and he gave the solid wood a push while taking a deep breath, inhaling the sweet scent.

Basking in the mouth-watering aroma, he pushed the door wide and entered the room. "Ah, hello again, ladies."

Mary Alice looked up as she lifted a baking dish from the oven. With a clatter, the tin pan hit the floor, and its contents rolled across the wooden boards. Her mouth hung open. Her stooped form appeared to be frozen as she stared at the doorway.

Jace let the door swing shut behind him, scooped up the hot loaf, and tossed it from palm to palm before he placed it on the table next to several others.

"Mr. Owens?" Mary Alice questioned.

He pulled his lips into a bright smile and nodded. "At your service, Ma'am." He gave a slight bow at the waist. "I—ah-guess I look a little different cleaned, shaved, and dressed."

Mary Alice straightened her stance and closed the oven door. Her face displayed merriment as she retrieved the pan off the floor. "Yes, I guess you could say, you clean up right nice, Mr. Owens."

"I hope I'm not disturbing you ladies, but my appetite has returned with a vengeance. Would it be possible to have a slice or two of this fresh bread?" He pointed to the line of golden brown loaves.

"Well of course. You sit down. I will get you some berry preserves to go with it. Singing Dove, will you please get Mr. Owens a fresh cup of coffee? Or, would you prefer tea, Mr. Owens?" Mary Alice handed him a knife and plate.

"Coffee would be wonderful. Thank you both, very much." Jace settled himself at the table and ate two slices of bread before the preserves and coffee arrived. It was warm and all but melted in his mouth. Without a doubt, the best bread he had ever tasted. "Please forgive me, I just couldn't help myself."

"That's quite alright. You look like you need the nourishment," Mary Alice assured. She placed a large glass of milk next to his coffee cup.

"Would you ladies, have a moment to join me?" He needed answers and figured this was the best place to start. Using a spoon, he spread deep red preserves across another slice of bread.

The two women looked at each other, nodded in unison, and pulled out adjacent chairs. Jace stood and waited for them to be seated. Once settled, Mary Alice poured two additional cups of coffee from the pot on the table.

Jace offered them each a slice of bread, but they shook their heads in decline. "So, tell me, how did I come to be in the Dakota Territory?" he questioned between bites of what he believed to be the best raspberry jam he'd ever tasted.

"*Wakhan Thanka*," Singing Dove's soft voice stated.

Jace looked from Singing Dove to Mary Alice.

"She said, the Great Spirit brought you here," Mary Alice supplied.

"Really? Does my sister-in-law know this Great Spirit?"

The women smiled at his comment. He took in their images. They appeared to be about the same age, ten or maybe fifteen years beyond his age of thirty.

Mary Alice was a little taller than Singing Dove, maybe five-three or four, her torso was thicker, but she still held a slender, feminine shape. Her brown hair was streaked with several gray strands. They glistened in the sunrays that streamed in through the glass paned window. A pale sprinkling of freckles banded across her nose provided a striking similarity to her niece.

"No, Mr. Owens, I do not believe Candice is acquainted with the Great Spirit. At least, not the one Singing Dove is referring too." Mary Alice commented as the three shared a chuckle.

"So then, how else did I come to be here at the Copper Cow?" Having ate his fill, Jace pushed his plate out of the way and sat back to enjoy his coffee and company.

"I believe Penny should be the one to tell you," Mary Alice looked to the other woman before responding. Singing Dove gave no sign of her thoughts.

"I see," Jace replied. "Has she returned yet?"

"No, I don't believe she has. Is she here, Singing Dove?"

The Lakota woman gave a negative shake of her head.

"Well, then, perhaps, you could just explain the physical way that brought me to the ranch? We will let Miss Jordan explain the reasons behind my travels."

Mary Alice looked once again at the other woman. When she received a slight nod, the aunt's eyes lit with merriment at the approval.

"By train," Mary Alice answered.

"Do you think you could provide a few more details?"

With eyes sparkling, Mary Alice leaned across her coffee cup and began her tale. "Well, you see, my brother, Harold, Singing Dove's husband and Penny's father, died of a heart attack about six months ago."

"Hiya."

Jace looked at the Indian woman, then back to Mary Alice.

"Singing Dove said no, she doesn't believe that Harold died of a heart attack. But that is what the Doctor said it was. It happened one morning out in the barn. Henry found him lying dead in one of the stalls. Anyway, ever since then Penny has had to run the ranch, and the men folks around here aren't taking to it real nice. There's been, well, a lot of trouble." Mary Alice paused to take a swig of coffee.

"Penny and Candice have been writing to each other for years," she began again. "After Penny told her about all of the trouble, your sister-in-law decided that Penny needed a husband. She said she would find one and send him to the Copper Cow. Candice also said she asked you to do it, but you said no. That was when she gave you some medicine and brought you out here herself. I think, she said you traveled by train as far as Yankton, then by stage to Elm Creek, where we picked you up and brought you to the ranch. Of course, we didn't know it was going to be you. We thought it was going to a real mail order husband. We didn't know Candice was coming either. Penny was furious! It took Singing Dove a week to get all of the poison out of your system."

Jace held up his hand to halt her speech, trying to take in all she was saying as her tale jumped from topic to topic. He zeroed in on her last statement, "The poison out of my system?"

Mary Alice nodded, "The opium that Candice was giving you."

Jace stopped his cup mid way to his mouth, "She was feeding me opium?"

"Yes, and by the time you arrived, she was worried that she might have been giving you too much. She said she had to double the dose once you got on the stage, so you wouldn't wake up in front of the other passengers.

"You were in a sorry state by the time we picked you up. That is why Singing Dove named you *Maka Wichasha*. Ouch!" Mary Alice shot a furrowed look across the table at Singing Dove.

Jace looked from woman to woman. He had witnessed the kick delivered beneath the table, but let the action go and asked Singing Dove, "How did you clean the opium out of my system so fast? It usually takes months, if not years, to cure a person from an opium addiction. Some are never cured."

"*Phejuta*, good medicine," Singing Dove explained, "and I put you in a boiling pot."

"A boiling pot? Oh, the big bathtub upstairs."

Singing Dove nodded her head, "Han."

"I do remember bits and pieces about it all. I owe you my gratitude, Singing Dove. I believe you saved my life with your good medicine and boiling pot." Jace took a drink of coffee as Singing Dove bowed her head in acceptance of his thanks.

"Should I tell you the part about you and Penny being married, or should Penny tell you that?" Mary Alice changed the subject.

Hot coffee spewed out of Jace's sputtering lips. He grabbed the towel lying next to the loaves of bread and tried to wipe up his mess while still coughing and attempting to catch his breath.

Mary Alice glanced from Singing Dove to Jace. "I probably should let Penny tell that part."

"No, Mary Alice, now that you mentioned it, I believe it would be best if you told me. At least, as much as you know about it," Jace answered once he was able to speak. He wiped the wetness out of the corners of his eyes and put on a charming smile for the women.

"Well, I only mentioned it because I don't understand how it can happen. Maybe you can tell me. You being from Pennsylvania and all, they must do things differently there." Mary Alice paused to refill each of their cups with fresh coffee.

Jace took a deep breath, waiting to exhale until he felt his nerves begin to calm. "I'll try Mary Alice. Go on. Tell me what you know." He thought of his brother and sister-in-law. This had Daniel's name written all over it.

Of all the hair-brained ideas those two came up with-this had to top them all.

"Well, Candice said it is called, uh- a proxy. Yes, that's it—a marriage by proxy. She said it is legal. Daniel is a lawyer, you know. He wrote out some papers and a judge, who is their friend, married the two of you. Penny didn't know anything about it. Oh, she was upset! I thought she was going to make the wagon crash right there and then. She was driving over prairie dogs hills and everything. I can't believe you slept through it all."

Jace held up his hand again in silent command for her to stop talking for a moment. He closed his eyes — again. A judge friend had married them. It had to have been his father-in-law. A man he greatly admired. How could Charles have done this to him? Why would Charles have done this? Another vision entered his mind, one of a man wallowing in a drunken haze. So lost in his own sorrow, he wasn't paying attention to anyone else around him. He braced himself and waited for pain to rip across his chest.

"Mr. Owens? Mr. Owens, I'm sorry, I didn't mean to upset you!"

The pain didn't come. His heart didn't constrict. It just continued to beat at a steady pace. Jace took another cleansing breath before opening his eyes. "No, Mary Alice, you didn't upset me. I was just trying to absorb all you have told me."

"Can two people really get married without neither of them knowing about it?"

"Well, that is a difficult question to answer. Yes, marriages by proxy are legal. They are done quite often. But, usually, it is because the couples that want to get married are unable to be in the same place at the same time. Like, in the situation of a mail order bride for instance. The woman can sign a piece of paper giving her permission to be married to the man who has invited her to travel to where he lives and to marry him. This is allowed, because often the woman is relocating out into unknown territories where the opportunities for the couple to get married are few and far between. I do not believe I have ever heard of a time where both parties were unavailable. But I assure you, if Daniel completed the paper work, and if my f-I mean his friend, married us, then by all means Miss Jordan and I are legally married." Jace let out a deep sigh as he completed his explanation.

"Really? That is quite interesting isn't it, Singing Dove?" Mary Alice said as she leaned back in her chair and folded her arms across her bosoms, appearing to be a woman deep in thought.

The group sat in silence for several minutes before Jace questioned, "Tell me, if Miss Jordan wanted a husband, why didn't she just marry someone from around here? There must be a few eligible bachelors in the Dakota Territory."

"It's not that my niece wants a husband. She needs a husband."

"What do you mean needs a husband? Is she with child?"

"With child, good heavens no! Mr. Owens, why would you say such a thing?"

Jace held his hand up in front of him almost afraid that the now disgusted aunt might throw the coffee pot at him. "Mary Alice, I'm sorry, I didn't mean to imply anything. I was just wondering why a woman would feel that she needs a husband."

"Our Penny is a good girl. A good, upstanding citizen!" Mary Alice stood and walked over to the stove where she retrieved a long, wooden spoon.

Jace felt relief when she used it to stir the stew that simmered over the fire's low heat. "Mary Alice, please accept my apologies. I assure you I did not mean to insult Miss Jordan. I am sorry if my words offended you."

"I accept your apology, Mr. Owens. I'm sorry I became so angry. Our Penny has just worked so hard, and she is doing a good job too. I guess I just wish there was more that we could do to help her."

"It is because of *Zuzeca*," Singing Dove said as Mary Alice laid the spoon down and returned to the table.

Jace rose and waited until Mary Alice was once again seated before he sat down. "Why, Singing Dove?"

"*Zuzeca*, he is why Penny needs a husband. He is no good." Singing Dove's words were laced with loathing.

"The James Ranch is our closet neighbor to the North," Mary Alice began to fill in the details. "Bob James became ill last year, and his son took over their ranch. His name is Luke, but Singing Dove calls him *Zuzeca*, it means the snake. Luke has asked Penny to marry him several times. He has also told all of the other men, for miles around, to stay away from her. He keeps implying that someday she will marry him."

"And how does Penny feel about this Mr. James?"

"She doesn't like him at all. She says that he has too many cattle on the small amount of grassland he owns. I don't like him either, he's short and ugly and mean."

"Short, ugly, and mean," Jace repeated. His eyebrows rose, "Ah, I see." He couldn't help but smile at the way the woman was steadfast in defending her niece. "Well, Penny might be right. It takes several acres for one cow to get the right amount of nutrition from grassland. If he is over crowding them, disease or malnutrition could overcome his heard as well as the neighboring ones."

Mary Alice had a look of surprise on her face. "That is what Penny says too. Were you a rancher back in Pennsylvania, Mr. Owens?"

"No, Mary Alice, I'm not a rancher. I'm a veterinarian."

"A what?"

"A veterinarian."

"Say that again- a vetern-what?"

"During the War Between the States, I was commissioned by the government, to attend the Ontario Veterinarian College in Canada. To study the diseases affecting the soldier's horses."

"Oh, so you're a farrier," Mary Alice concluded.

"No, I'm not a farrier. I am a doctor of medicine for animals." This was a conversation Jace was used to. The United States was just beginning to understand the need for separate training for doctors and veterinarians. Glanders disease in horses as well as Texas Fever in cattle and cholera in swine during the war encouraged the government to look at Europe and Canada, and their advanced studies of these diseases as well as their schools of veterinarian studies. As a pioneer in the field, he rarely came across someone outside of his circle of associates, family or friends, who had heard of a veterinarian.

"So you're a doctor?" Mary Alice asked.

"Yes and no. I am doctor, but only for animals."

"I've never heard of such a thing. You sure you aren't making this up?"

"I assure you, I am not making this up. I am an animal doctor, a veterinarian."

Singing Dove stood and began to gather the empty coffee cups. "Time to eat."

Mary Alice rose to follow suit by removing the other debris from the table. "Almost, Penny's not home yet."

Singing Dove nodded her head, "She just rode in. Fast."

****

The long ride had been just what Penny needed to clear her mind. But the discovery she made was now causing her heart to race. She allowed Midnight to slow his pace as they drew closer to the homestead. After a few minutes the horse blew two deep snorts and tossed his head, communicating a warning to his rider.

"What is it, Boy?" Penny scanned one full circle, surveying the outlying area. A second glance picked up two riders heading for the ranch parallel to her route. They were too far away for her to recognize, but she could guess their identity. The emptiness of her stomach churned with fear. How long had they been following her?

She pulled her knees tight against her mount and leaned over the saddle horn. The horse needed no further urging. Chunks of dirt flew several feet in the air as his hoofs hit the hard ground with force. Penny knew the moment the other riders picked up speed. Midnight threw a load squeal into the air, claiming the territory as his own and challenging the other horses to try and overtake him.

The black steed was in the barn and Penny was just about to walk up the front steps of her home, when two horses came to a sliding halt beside the white fence that protected the house lawns.

"Miss Jordan, may I have a word with you?" Luke James blew the words out of his lungs as he slid from the back of his still panting horse.

Penny took a deep breath before she turned to face the intruders. "Mr. James, you, nor your men, are welcome on my property. Please take your leave."

Sharp spurs, strapped onto his boots, jingled as he strolled through the fence opening and up the gravel walkway toward the steps. The sound as well as his proud strut stirred her anger. His condescending smile was more fuel than she needed. Her hands balled into fists.

"Penny, it will only take a moment." His dark brown eyes challenged her to defy him as he attempted to halt her with his stare.

Penny turned and flew up the remaining steps. Stopping short of opening the door, she recalled what Luke might see if he followed her into her home. With a frustrated stomp of one booted foot, she turned to glare at the approaching man. He was no taller than she, a little over five feet, but acted as if he were ten feet tall. "If you have something to tell me, Mr. James, send a telegram."

"And miss the pleasure of your company? Never, my dear." He continued to approach.

She could tell the hard ride was more of a task than he had been prepared for. The slow way he climbed the steps demonstrated his breathlessness. She placed her hands on her hips. "What do you want?"

He arrived on the top step and reached out to touch her. "We need to talk."

Penny took a step back before his hand made contact. "I have nothing to say to you."

Luke lunged and grabbed the upper part of her right arm with thick fingers. "What were you doing up on the north ridge, Penny?" he seethed through tobacco-stained teeth.

The black colored clothing he always wore was covered with dust from his rough ride. The smell of dirt mingled with the foul scent of his body odor.

"It is none of your business what I do on my property. Now, let go of me." She attempted to pull her arm out of his grasp by twisting sideways.

Luke surged forward and took a hold of her other arm, forcing her to stand in front of him. He squeezed down on the flesh. One bushy brow lifted in surprise at the feel of solid muscles beneath her cotton sleeves. His thumbs drove into the softer flesh of her inner arms.

"I've decided to make it my business. I've decided to make everything about you, my business!"

Small drops of spittle from his mouth splashed onto her face. Penny turned away from the offensiveness of it.

"Let go of me, or I'll..." The words stopped forming. Over her shoulder she noticed a tall, handsome stranger, stroll out her front door.

"Or you'll do what, Miss High and Mighty?" Luke seemed to take her silence as a result of his power. His glaring face was within inches of hers, brooding eyes revealed his mind's sweet acceptance of victory. He smiled, and his mouth moved closer.

"She'll tell her husband, and he'll make damn sure you never touch her again!" A deep voice snarled.

Chapter Five

In one swift moment, Luke found himself lying on his back upon the wooden, porch floor. The air gushed from his lungs as he stared up at a man, whom appeared to be Satan reincarnated. With eyes black as coal and nostrils flaring, the tall beast glared down at him, almost daring him to move. Luke's body began to quiver from head to toe.

When those black eyes left him to glance toward Penny, Luke scrambled to his feet. Sweat oozed from every pore of his body. He took a few steps backwards, stopping when his back pressed against one of the solid, two-story columns. He gulped for air, trying to find his voice.

"Wh-who the hell are you?"

"I just told you. I'm her husband." The man turned, and rested a hand on Penny's shoulder. "Are you okay?" he asked.

Penny willed herself not to faint. She managed to nod her head twice. Words refused to form. All she could do was gawk at one of the most remarkable faces she had ever seen. Pictures flashed in her mind before full recognition hit her. "You shaved," she whispered.

"I don't know what you two think you're doing, but I do know you are not her husband. Penny Jordan is not married. I would have been informed of any such occurrence well before it happened," Luke stated vehemently.

Luke's finger trembled as he pointed it at her and the handsome man. The pressure from a hand slipped away from her shoulder. Instantly she missed the warmth it had provided her chilled body. Jace took a menacing step forward. Ominous eyes starred down at the shorter man. Beads of sweat rolled down Luke's face. His entire body seemed to quiver.

"Oh, I assure you, Mr. James, I am her husband. And

if you ever lay a hand on her person again, I will make you wish you hadn't. Now get your sorry carcass off the Copper Cow," her rescuer ordered.

The shorter man was dismissed as Jace Owens turned and placed an arm around her shoulder.

"Come on, Penny, our lunch is getting cold." He escorted her into the house. Penny couldn't help but glance over her shoulder at Luke James and the way he still held onto the porch pillar.

"Oh, that was magnificent!" Mary Alice exclaimed as she closed the door behind the couple.

"Mary Alice, not right now," he said. "Take Penny into the kitchen. I need to watch and make sure our visitors take their leave." Jace Owens drew his arm from Penny's shoulder and walked into the office.

"Okay, Mr. Owens. Come along Penny, lunch is ready." Mary Alice placed a hand on Penny's elbow.

Penny stood still. Her gaze followed her rescuer through the office door. She shook her head, "No, Mary Alice." The tall, trim form strolled past her desk to take a stance at the window. His shape reeked of masculinity. Broad shoulders tapered to a narrow waist and into hips that supported long, lean legs.

This couldn't possibly be the same man she hauled out of the stage a week ago- could it? She unfolded Mary Alice's fingers from her arm and gave them a slight squeeze. "I think it is time Mr. Owens and I had our talk. Would you please bring our lunch into the office?"

"Of course, dear, but do you think now is a good time? Are you up to it?" Mary Alice wrapped both of her hands around Penny's.

Penny tore her eyes from his shape. "I'm fine," she assured while thinking of the quivering form they had left on the porch. "And now, is the only time. Within a few hours everyone for miles around is going to know I have a husband." She pulled her hand away, nodded at her aunt, and made her way into the room.

Penny walked through the office and over to the double windows. Taking a stance beside him, they watched the pair of riders exit the yard. She tried to remain still. But it was hard, her hands were sweating, her heart raced, and her stomach seemed to be flip-flopping. Could it be true? Could this man somehow have been transformed into the answer to her prayers while she had been away? Or had she been dreaming about someone saving her from Luke for so long that her mind conjured up the scene on the porch?

"Who are the other two riders approaching?" The sound of his words broke into her pondering thoughts.

Penny forced her eyes to focus on the horizon and willed the answer to emit without stutters. "Sam Watson, the ranch foreman, and Jim Calhoun, a ranch hand. They have been out in the south draw, looking for strays."

They both watched as the two groups of riders met up. "Do you trust your men?" he asked.

"Yes, and no," Penny answered, "I trust Sam with every ounce of my being. But Jim is new, and there is just something about him that makes me leery."

Jace turned and waited until Penny lifted her face and returned his gaze. He questioned the reality of the porch scene. Puzzled as to what made him fly to her defense. What made him react so irrationally? He had no intention of staying. Why on earth would he have proclaimed her as his wife?

The array of questions left as she filled his vision. Long, golden-red hair folded into a braid that cascaded down her back. Sparkling, green eyes highlighted a heart-shaped face and sooty lashes fluttered as she held his gaze. A band of light freckles dusted the bridge of her nose. The sun-kissed skin surrounding pink lips, quivered. Jace wondered what she was thinking and offered a smile. "Thank you, Miss Jordan."

Thin brows rose in question. "For what, Mr. Owens?"

"For an honest answer. I appreciate it." He turned back to gaze out the window. She copied his action. The pairs of riders separated and the ranch hands rode into the yard.

The older man threw a perplexed look toward the house. Penny covered her face with both hands and emitted a deep sigh.

"Are you ready to have our talk, Miss Jordan?"

"Yes, Mr. Owens, as ready as I'll ever be." With a sweep of her hand she pointed to a small table and two side chairs. "Please have a seat."

Jace pulled out the chair closest to him, and with a nod of his head, offered the seat to Penny. He waited while she removed her Stetson and riding gloves and tossed them onto the desk before accepting the chair. Jace remained were he stood until she was settled, then walked around the table and took his seat. The rambling of wheels signaled Mary Alice's entrance to the room. He let out a silent sigh of relief, recognizing his need of a few moments to gather his thoughts before conversing with the female ranch owner.

Mary Alice pushed the teacart next to the table, and without looking at either occupant, began to transfer the appetizing scented dishes on to the table.

Sensing her nervousness, Jace commented, "You were right, Mary Alice."

"Pardon me, Mr. Owens?" Mary Alice questioned.

"Mr. James. He is short, ugly, and mean."

Mary Alice opened her pert mouth, but the drawn brow look she received from her niece stifled her reply.

"I'll leave you two to your lunch," she said and concluded her tasks by placing a small container of raspberry jam next to his plate.

"Thank you, Mary Alice. It looks delightful." Jace gave her a broad smile.

"Please close the door on your way out," Penny instructed.

"Of course, Dear," Mary Alice agreed, but only after receiving an acknowledging nod from him.

"Shall we?" Jace took the lid off the kettle of stew.

"By all means." Penny unfolded the cloth covering the bread and both settled into the tasks of serving themselves.

After watching her for several minutes, Jace commented, "I wish you would start to eat the food in front of you, instead of playing with it, Miss Jordan."

"I'm really not very hungry, Mr. Owens."

"Well, I find myself very hungry, and I don't like to eat alone. Our talk can commence once we've eaten. Here." He handed her the, now half empty container of preserves. Watching as she spread the jam across her bread, he continued, "Your attire leaves no doubt that you need the sustenance."

Penny glared across the table.

He could see the fight she was having with herself to remain in check and teasingly flashed her a flirting smile.

Stabbing a potato with the tongs of her fork, she lifted her eyebrows as she raised the food to her mouth. "Mr. Owens, my attire ..."

Jace interrupted, "Is very enticing to say the least. So tell me, Miss Jordan, how large is the Copper Cow?"

Her brows pulled together and her mouth puckered. She gave him a stony glare and dabbed at her lips with a napkin before she answered, "About twenty square miles, give or take."

Jace continued to throw questions at her until she was fully drawn into the conversation. He asked about the lay of the land, available water, grazing plants, and winterfeed. She gave quick, competent answers for each one.

"How many head are you running?"

"Currently, only about two thousand. Two years ago we were upwards of five thousand, but we've had a lot of set backs this last year."

"What sort of set backs?"

"Well, Mr. Owens, you name it, and I've probably experienced it."

"Hoof and mouth? Texas Fever?"

"No, I don't mean diseased cattle. We've been lucky on that count. I mean loss of breeders, loss of wholesalers, loss of cowboys, renegades, rustlers, and run-a-ways. My spring round up netted me a thousand less than we had last fall. I sent two of my best cowboys out to search for them, but they never came back either." Penny laid her fork down beside her plate.

"Deserters?"

"No. Both Tom and Jake had been with the Copper Cow for years. They just disappeared. Sam and a few members of Singing Doves' family found some tracks, but a spring rain made it impossible to trail them any farther. Their horses never came home either. It was not long after Papa died. I still don't know what to think."

Jace watched as her gaze traveled around the room. The melancholy expression on her face told him she thought of happier times.

He scanned the room. It was characteristic of the rest of the house, spacious, yet homey and comfortable. Shelves holding various books and magazines lined two walls. A large, oak desk in the center of the room faced the door and provided the occupant with the full service of the large fireplace that consumed the back wall. A couch, two large cabinets, and the table, they sat at, completed the furnishings. A large set of horns hung above the mantle, and a map of the Dakota Territory, as well as several framed documents adorned the walls.

"Your father died this spring?" He broke the heavy silence befalling the room. Their earlier conversation had been stimulating. Her knowledge of ranching was very apparent. She fascinated him. Jace shook the thought from his head. He was too old to be awestruck by a female.

"Yes, well, actually it was in February."

"What happened?" he asked.

"Heart attack."

"Singing Dove doesn't think it was a heart attack."

Green eyes flashed at him. He saw the anger. Pushing herself away from the table, Penny laid her napkin next to her plate before she rose to walk over to her desk. She pulled out the massive chair and settled upon it.

"And that, Mr. Owens, brings us to the real reason we are here." Looking at him she continued, "Why don't we start with how much Mary Alice has already told you? I say Mary Alice, because I know Singing Dove would never have told you about Papa's death."

Jace wasn't intimidated by the regal stance she attempted to portray. "Alright, Miss Jordan. Let's see, I know I was drugged, put on a train, and then the stagecoach that delivered me to Elm Creek. Where you picked me up and brought me to the Copper Cow Ranch. I was of course, accompanied the entire way by my sweet, little sister-in-law, who is now on her way to California. I could have died or become addicted to opium for the rest of my life, but a wonderful Lakota Medicine Woman saved my life and gave me a Lakota name, which is quite an honor I might add."

Penny agreed with a false looking smile as she

smugly agreed, "Quite an honor, *Maka Wichasha*."

"Yes, that's it, *Maka Wichasha*," Jace repeated with pride. "I also know that I am married to you. But I can't give Candice all of the credit for that. That goes to my brother and father-in-law. I became this ah, mail order husband, I believe is the term Mary Alice used, in order to help you save your ranch. That's about it, give or take." Jace left the table to sit on the couch in front of her desk. He leaned back against the soft cowhide and extended his long legs onto the rug covering the floor.

"She did a pretty good job. Really hit all the high points I guess," Penny answered as she leaned back into the chair.

"You know, Miss Jordan, technically I was kidnapped. I should contact the sheriff and press charges."

Penny rolled her eyes. "I didn't kidnap you."

"But you are an accessory to the crime."

"I knew nothing about it!"

Jace lifted one eyebrow.

"Well, okay, I knew about it, but I didn't know it was going to be you. I thought it was going to be someone who wanted to marry me, or I mean at least wanted to become my husband, or a husband to someone. I uh..." She leaned forward and laid her forehead onto the palm of her hand. "I can't believe I ever thought one of Candice's hair-brained ideas would work. I just can't believe this."

"What do you know? We agree on something. Candice is full of hair-brained ideas. And they usually are just as outlandish as she is. Do you know that she believes she is starting a trend by keeping her maiden name and adding her married name as a hyphenated word? It will soon be a rage, just ask her. Or, tell me, Miss Jordan, do you have any idea why she and Daniel are going to California?"

"To see the Pacific Ocean?" Penny asked with doubt.

Jace shook his head. "No, to campaign for Victoria California Claflin-Woodhull. The Equal Rights Party has nominated her for the United States Presidency. Candice is completely obsessed with this woman, who by the way also hyphenates her name. And Daniel, my dear brother, has bought into the ridiculousness of the entire fiasco."

"Excuse me, Mr. Owens, I know all about the name

thing, and I have heard of Victoria Woodhull. I support her efforts to run for the presidency. She is a remarkable woman, one of whom I greatly admire. It's time for women to be heard, not just seen." Her trim body straightened in defense of her answers.

"But you said the fundamental words, she is a woman," Jace stated. He let his relaxed stature demonstrate his enjoyment of their quarrel.

"What is wrong with her being a woman?"

"Nothing is wrong with her being a woman. It's the fact that a woman will never rule the greatest nation in the world. Beside, it's a moot point. No man is going to vote for her, and we both know, women can't vote," Jace casually explained.

"Women will soon have the right to vote Mr. Owens, mark my words. And a woman will rule the United States-someday," Penny said as she stood to walk around the desk. "But, let me clarify your beliefs, if I may. You believe a woman can't rule a government, which I might add, greatly needs to be reformed. Do you also believe a woman can't run a ranch?"

Jace looked up at the woman standing in front of him. Her hands were braced upon trim hips, highlighted by the thin leather strap that gathered the denim around her slim waist. Her tiny chest heaved with anger as she glared down. The thin cotton of the white shirt tucked into the enticing jeans, allowed him to see the faint outline of the under garments she wore. Shaking his head to remove the direction his thoughts had preceded, he pulled his feet beneath him and rose to tower over her.

"I believe our conversation has detoured off our subject, Miss Jordan. But just for future reference, I didn't say a woman couldn't run the nation. I said a woman never will run the nation. Nor did I say a woman couldn't run a ranch. I have seen many women manage farms, plantations, even businesses. Your Mrs. Woodhull, runs her own newspaper and stock brokerage business, and does a remarkable job of it. I have even encountered very successful women ranch owners."

"Tell me, Mr. Owens, are any of these successful women single?"

"What does that have to do with it?"

"Everything!" Penny braced her stance and continued, "None of them are single, are they? Oh, they may be widowed, or their husbands may have deserted them, but I'll bet my life that none of them have never been married!"

"Which is our subject isn't it? Our so-called marriage, your ranch, and my inability to stay here and help you." Jace glared down at her.

He was so close Penny had to lean against the desk in order to tilt her head back far enough to look at his face.

"Your inability to stay here? What about my inability to allow you to stay here? I don't want to be married-to you or to anyone else. I don't need your help, Mr. Owens. Nor do I want you to remain at my ranch. I could never allow a man who carries such low regard for women to remain in my presence."

"Low regard for women? I'll have you know, Miss Jordan, I have a very high regard for women, especially those who know what their role is! But that has nothing to do with the reason I can't remain here. I have a business to run in Pennsylvania. I have family there. I have commitments there. I have my life there!"

"Please, Mr. Owens, we both know you haven't paid attention to your business, family, or life in Pennsylvania for almost a year now. You haven't cared about anyone or anything. You've been too busy wallowing in self-pity. Let me tell you something, Mr. Owens, death is part of life, get over it."

"Get over it?" Jace had never wanted to strike a woman before, but right now, he had a great desire to do so. No, on second thought, right now he wished Penny Jordan was a man so he could punch that little, freckle-covered, nose.

"Yes, get over it! Quit being a burden to everyone around you! I for one, Mr. Owens, do not need another problem and that's just what you are, another problem."

"*I'm* a problem for *you*? Who do you think you are, Miss Jordan, the answer to every man's prayers? Not hardly. Why, there's not enough meat on those bones to keep a snake warm at night. Let me tell you who you are, or better yet, what you are. A simple-minded twit! One, who has driven her father's ranch so far into the ground she can no longer see daylight. One who is so vain, she believes any man on earth would want to travel half way across the country to become her husband. One, who is incapable of..."

Penny gave his chest a mighty shove as she screamed, "Get out!"

Jace caught himself before toppling backwards. His eyes followed her movements as she flipped around and stomped behind her desk. His anger was boiling, making his torso heave with each intake of air. His hands clenched at his sides.

Penny needed to put distance between them. She had watched those blue eyes turn black during his rant, just as they had on the front porch while confronting Luke. Her heartbeat increased another degree. It raced in her chest, making it hard to breathe. He didn't frighten her, but she couldn't remember ever being angrier with someone. Who did he think he was? His comments were outrageous. She planted her hands on the top of her desk and yelled, "Get-get out of my sight. Get out of my house. Get off of my ranch!"

He glanced at the door, opened his mouth, but pulled it shut before anything emitted. Jace threw his arms into the air and walked across the room.

Placing a hand on the doorknob he turned back to her, "Believe me there is nothing I want more than to leave this God-forsaken land. I will be using one of your animals to transport myself into town and have it returned to the ranch. Maybe under different circumstances it would have been a pleasure to meet you, Miss Jordan."

Penny picked up the only thing within reach and threw it as the door slammed shut. A solid thud echoed throughout the room. She stared at the door and shuddered. The thin, metal letter opener was stuck deep into the wood, near the same spot Jace's head had been.

"Oh, dear Lord, please forgive me," she whispered as her body slithered onto the chair behind her. She laid her pounding head on the top of the desk and listened to heavy male feet stomp up the stairs. Moments later they came back down and out the front door.

****

Jace entered the front of the barn. The size of the building made the immense house seem small. His eyes caught dust motes floating in the streaming sunlight, and he slowed his pace to walk along stalls filled with fresh mounds of hay. A strange sense overcame him. A shiver run up his spine and soft words resonated in his ears. He twirled around, recognizing the voice and looking for its owner. *This place is driving me crazy,* he thought, *now I'm hearing voices.*

A black man watched him from near the rear of the long walkway. Jace felt the temper that had overcome him in the house weaken as he made his way toward the man. He continued to glance around, still searching for the now silent voice.

"Hello," he greeted. "I'm Jace Owens, I need to borrow one of Miss Jordan's mounts." He nodded at the back paddock filled with fine looking animals.

"Iz know who you iz," the man answered. "Iz Henry, it wuz me who helped Singing Dove heal you."

"Well, then it is my pleasure to meet you, Henry." He took the other man's hand in a firm shake. "Are you the caretaker of this barn?"

"Yes, um."

"You do a marvelous job. This is one of the cleanest barns I've ever seen, and believe me, I've seen plenty."

"Thank ya, sur," Henry responded with pride. "It keeps the horses happy. That it does. Iz just wish Miz Penny would let me clean out that stall." He pointed to the end booth.

Jace walked over to the stall. The hay was brown and stiff, he kicked at it with his foot and the smell of mold penetrated the air. "Why won't she let you clean it out?" he asked and stepped into the area. His footfalls churned up a thick fungus under the top layer of old straw.

"Wuz where Iz found the master. Dead. Right there he wuz." A look of sadness overtook the old man's features.

His boot kicked a large chunk of the spoiled grass. The movement revealed something. Bending down Jace picked up a square piece of cotton cloth. Recognizing the material as one that came with a new bottle of ether, he walked out of the stall and over to a bucket near the railing. He lifted the dipper. The contents were clean and clear. After taking a drink of the cool liquid, he drizzled a small amount of water onto the cloth. A scent wafted into the air.

"Henry, tell me about the day Mr. Jordan died," he encouraged while directing the black man to walk out into the fresh air of the back paddock.

"Ain't notin' to tell. Iz come out to sees if'n he wuz back from his ride and dere he wuz, dead. Never even gotz his horse saddled," Henry explained, shaking his head.

Jace looked around the paddock. A man sat on the top rung of the fence on the opposite side of the corral. Squinting to get a better view, he wondered if his eyes were also playing tricks on him. He turned back to the farmhand when the man waved. "Who is that, Henry?"

"At's Mr. Calhoun, a ranch hand."

"Henry, I'm going to need that horse now. Could you saddle one for me?"

"Yes, sur."

Jace tucked the cloth into his back pocket and started to walk toward the corral. After a couple of steps, he turned back to the barn and said, "Oh, and Henry, go ahead and clean out that stall." When he saw the old man was going to protest, he continued, "I'll tell Miss Penny I told you to do it. It's full of mold, that's not good for the horses."

"It sure ain't. Thank ya, sur! Iz get ya that horse right quick." The old man's step picked up a pace as he walked into the barn to retrieve a saddle.

Jace turned back around. The cowboy still sat on the fence. His stride slowed as he paused to open and close the latched gate and side step several horses. He patted a few of them as he made his way to the ranch hand.

Jim Calhoun stepped down from his seat. "Owens. It is you."

"Yes, it's me." Jace stopped a few feet from the man. "What are you doing on the Copper Cow, Calhoun?"

"Shouldn't I be asking you that? Or maybe I should ask why they made you marry her?" Jim responded with a snide chuckle.

Jace turned and saw Henry start to saddle a large

sorrel. "Get a horse, Calhoun, you're going to show me the way to town." Without waiting to see if the other man would follow his command, Jace walked over to greet his mount.

As the two men rode out of the barn, Jace looked up at the house. Movement caught his attention. He touched his hat and continued to watch the area until he saw the curtain fall across the glass panes of the office window.

Penny felt her face burn and let the material block her view. She ignored the knock that sounded off the office door for a second time. Her mind questioned what Jace and Jim Calhoun would have to say to one another. An eerie feeling wafted up her spine. She brought her arms up and folded them across her torso. As her body shivered, she turned toward the sound of a door opening.

"Not now, Mary Alice."

"Mary Alice is busy in the kitchen." Sam Watson pushed the door shut behind his thick frame. His gaze riveted on the letter opener sticking out of the door panel. Reaching up, he gave it a mighty tug. His fingers ran down the hard metal shaft before stony eyes rose up to meet hers. "When were you going to tell me, Penny?"

"Sam?" Her eyes stung. She blinked against the discomfort. "Sam, I'm sorry, I…. Oh, I don't even know where to start." Her hands rose, she couldn't face him. Peering through her fingers, she saw him place the instrument on the desktop and continue across the room.

"I've really messed up this time. What am I going to do?" A sob emitted from her throat.

Sam engulfed her into his arms as soon as she was within reach, "Hush now, Princess, it's going to be okay." He held her as the tears fell. When the flow started to ebb, he continued, "There now, let's sit down. It's time we had a talk."

"I just thought a husband would solve all my problems," Penny began once he had aided her to the couch and sat down beside her.

"Like a knight in shining armor." He chuckled and handed her his handkerchief.

Penny nodded and wiped the tears from her face, somewhat embarrassed. She hadn't cried in front of Sam for years. "They don't exist do they, Sam?"

"No, I don't think they do" A smile softened his wrinkled face. "But princesses do." He touched her nose with his forefinger. "And I know a princess who now has a pea the size of a boulder under her mattress."

"What am I going to do, Sam?" She laid her head on his shoulder, thankful for the comfort.

"You have to make this work, Penny." He wrapped is arm around her.

"I know I have to make this ranch work, Sam. That's what I've been trying to do. I also know this whole husband fiasco is going to make things worse."

"It certainly is. That's what you have to make work, Penny, your marriage."

She lifted her head. "What? There is no marriage, Sam. I sent a telegram asking Candice to send me a husband. So she did."

"I know. I've known about it all week. Do you honestly think you could keep a man hid, in your upstairs, for days and I wouldn't know about it?" Sam raised his eyebrows. "Now you have to make it work. It is the only choice you have, Princess."

"You've known?" Penny looked at the man who had been at the Copper Cow longer than she had. "Of course you would have known. How could I imagine you wouldn't know everything that went on around here? But what do you mean, my only choice?" Penny pointed at the window. "He's an evil, sick, man. Believe me, Mr. Owens was not a mail order husband. He was a mail order problem!"

Shrugging her shoulders, she continued, "Besides, he's left. He borrowed a horse to ride to town. From there he will find his way back to Pennsylvania."

"Then you have to go to town, ask him to come back, and ask him to stay married to you for at least a little while."

Penny shook her head. "Oh, no!"

"Look, Penny, we both know what a *zuzeca*, Luke James is, a snake of the lowest kind. He's wanted you since he first saw you, when you were knee high to a jackrabbit." Sam took a hold of her hand and continued, "Thing is, Penny, now that Mr. Owens put him in his place, so to speak, Luke could get real nasty. He has always gotten what he's wanted, except for you. And it's eating at him. Has been for the last year. With Mr. Owens here, you, Mary Alice, Singing Dove, Henry, and even myself, will be safer." He waited for her nod of agreement.

Penny turned to gaze at the wide set of horns hanging above the fireplace. Her mind filled with all of the people who depended on her.

Sam lifted a finger, placed it under her chin, and forced her to look back at him. "We both know Luke and his rough riders have the rest of the ranchers believing his Indian tales. And that's just what they are, tales. You know the rest of the ranchers are good men. Most of them have been ranching on this prairie for years. They believed in your Pa, and would have gone up against Luke, if he were still here. But, they don't have anyone to follow right now. I believe they may not go along with Luke's plans of retaliation as long as Mr. Owens is your husband. He's already proven he isn't afraid to take a stand against, the *zuzeca*. I think he is the type of man the rest of the ranchers would follow."

Penny looked down at their clutched hands. His looked so weather-beaten, and used. She patted the top of it with her other hand, opened her mouth, and then closed it again.

Sam laid his other hand on top of hers. "Real husband or not, without Mr. Owens here, you'll become, well, a soiled dove. And Luke will have one more thing to use in convincing the rest of the men to do what he wants. He will fill them with all kinds of tales of what happened between you and your husband. No matter how much they respected your father, they'll listen to his side of the story. You do understand what I'm saying, don't you, Princess?"

Penny's shoulders drooped. "Without Mr. Owens, Luke will win." Her thoughts were in turmoil. She pulled her hands from his, stood and walked to the window. Pulling back the curtain, the homestead and stretching prairie came into view. Land that was as much a part of her as she was of it. "Oh, Sam, I've really done it this time, haven't I?"

"Actually Penny, your friend's hair-brained idea wasn't so bad. It may be just be what we need to stop Luke James and all of his shenanigans."

"I am so sick of society and all the rules we must live by. When are women ever going to be given our due? It's so unfair. I didn't want a husband. I don't want to be married. I just want to run my ranch. I want-I want things to be how they use to be."

"I know, but that's not going to happen. Things can't go back to how they use to be. You've grown up. You're no longer a little girl. You're a grown woman with grown up responsibilities." Sam laid the truth out for her to accept. "Princess, you have to find a way to make Mr. Owens stay here."

The invisible weight on her shoulders seemed to intensify. An hour ago, on the front porch of the house, that weight had been whisked away by Jace Owens. She had felt triumph and pride as her husband had come to her rescue. Was it possible? Was Sam right? Could Jace Owens be the answer she had been looking for? Or did she simply not have any other options? She could no longer think only about what she wanted. She had to think about what everyone else needed.

Taking a deep breath, she turned back to the room. "So Sam, do you have any idea as to how a woman convinces a mail order husband to stay with her?"

"Well, I'm not for sure, but a dress might help."

Penny gave Sam the smile he searched for and felt her spine stiffen with determination. She stopped to give him a hug before she made her way to the door. Pulling it open she yelled, "Mary Alice, please put the pressing irons on the stove, and I need your help upstairs."

"I'll hitch up the buggy for you. A princess can't go riding around in a buckboard," Sam said as he followed her out of the room.

An hour later, shimmering pink ruffles bounced off each step as Penny made her way down the stairs. The dress was created to enhance curves she thought no longer existed. A square cut neckline exposed the fair skin of her throat and framed a glistening, gold pendant. Matching earrings dangled from lobes that peeped out beneath the trimmings of an enticing bonnet. She felt more feminine than she had in over a year and concluded the feeling also brought a certain level of power with it.

"Here's your wrapper, in case it gets chilly this

evening, but remember if it gets to be too late, just spend the night in town. It is too far for you to be traveling in the dark," Mary Alice said as she continued to fuss and pick at the flouncing fabric.

Penny stopped her aunt's movements by placing her hands on the older woman's shoulders. "Thank you, Auntie." She kissed a soft cheek and whispered, "I love you."

"I love you too, Sweetie." Mary Alice nodded and pointed at the door. "Now go bring your husband back home."

The sun was high in the sky, sending rays of heat onto the black awning of the buggy as Penny climbed onto the warm, leather seat. With a flick of the reins, she set the elegant vehicle into motion. Sam Watson nudged his mount to follow the buggy down the dusty lane.

Penny used the long drive to formulate her plan. A powerful speech grew as she rehearsed each sentence aloud. Changing lines, she practiced it again. Preparing exactly what she was going to say, how she was going to say it, and when- she took special care in the placement of specific lines. As buildings began to dot the horizon, she felt confident of her abilities and her bargaining measures.

However, when the structures began to grow, her confidence shrank. By the time the buggy rolled down the main street of town, she wasn't able to recall her lines and her trembles were almost uncontrollable. Tied to the hitching post in front of the general store, she spotted a large sorrel with the double C brand of the Copper Cow decorating its hip. A lump formed in her throat, she tried to swallow it, but couldn't. Her mouth felt as if it was stuffed with cotton.

The buggy came to a halt next to the boardwalk that connected the establishments of the small town. Penny twisted the long leather straps around the thin brake handle, and climbed out. Stepping onto the wooden boards in front of the carriage, she lowered her hand and splashed the tips of her fingers into the cool water of the horse trough. "Here Maize, that a girl, have a good long drink. It was a dusty, hot ride."

"I'm sure it was." A deep voice startled her.

Chapter Six

Jace watched the high heals of her boots become tangled amongst swirling, pink fabric. Flaying fingers searched for something to grasp. He lifted a hand and the tiny digits clasped on with vengeance as they grasped his arm to save her from an imminent fall. A deep sigh of relief floated out of pert, pink lips, and she opened her eyes to look up at her stabilizing aid.

"Oh!" A startled look flashed on her face.

He couldn't help the smile that crossed his face as she realized she clung to the arm of her husband. She pulled her hands away and her body tipped backwards.

"Ohhh." The swift movement caused her precarious balance to linger again.

Wrapping one capable arm around her shoulders, and placing the palm of his other hand on her torso, Jace stifled her staggering actions. "I apologize, Miss Jordan, I didn't mean to startle you."

Her feet stilled. She took a deep breath, stepped out of his embrace, and ran a hand down her dress. "You, um, you didn't startle me, Mr. Owens. I was just surprised to see you, that's all."

"Surprised to see me? And here I thought you came looking for me." Jace allowed his gaze to follow along the stylish lines of the pink fabric. His conclusion was quick. Candice must have patterned the creation. It would have been something his sister-in-law would wear to a tea party or a shopping excursion, in the city. Though the design made the redhead look very feminine by highlighting her curves, it was too restraining and frivolous for her free spirited personality.

"Looking for you? Why would I be looking for you, Mr. Owens?" Penny raised both hands to tug at the position of her bonnet.

"I assumed you traveled to town to fill me in on how I

should behave at the meeting tonight."

"Meeting? What meeting?" Her gaze snapped up to stare hard at him.

"The Cattlemen's Association meeting," he stated with a slight shrug of his shoulders.

"There's not a Cattlemen's meeting tonight."

"Yes, there is," he answered. Her reactions were sincere. She hadn't known about the meeting. He felt a sense of satisfaction. Not in her ignorance, but in his ability to be of assistance. "A special meeting has been called. The whole town is talking about it." Jace glanced around, the fine hairs on the back of his neck stood on end. He felt the questioning stares they received from bystanders.

"Let's take the buggy and my horse down to the livery stables." His fingers wrapped around her elbow.

Penny looked around. He knew the moment she too noticed several people standing outside of area businesses, watching them. The ears of the onlookers almost bulged from the sides of their heads.

"Marion."

"Excuse me?" Jace looked around to see whom she was referring to.

"Your horse. His name is Marion." She fell into step beside him.

"I'm riding a horse named Marion." Jace nodded with humored acceptance.

"His name was supposed to be Mary Anne, but when he came out a colt instead of a filly I had to rename him."

"I see." Jace placed his hands on her waist, guiding her climb into the buggy.

She accepted his help, but he saw the way her torso gave a quick shiver, resembling a horse shaking flies off its back, before she gathered the reins and waited for him to secure Marion to the rear of the buggy. She made room for him in the narrow seat and released the reins after he clutched them, as well as her hands, with a solid grasp of male authority.

"What's this about a meeting tonight?" she waited to ask until rambling wheels prevented anyone from hearing their conversation.

Jace took a moment to reflect before answering. From

the moment he had stepped into the colossal barn this afternoon, an overwhelming sense of purpose had descended on him. It was as if a supernatural force had interfered with his life and redirected all of his thoughts. His anger at Candice, Daniel, even Penny had quelled. Thoughts of righting the wrongs at the Copper Cow appealed to him.

In all honesty the woman sitting beside him had become the true center of his thoughts. He was astonished at how a simple argument with her had made him feel so alive again. The long ride into town, with the companionship of Jim Calhoun had been, insightful, to say the least. The arrival of his wife solved his pressing concern of being able to attend the Association meeting. Now, he just had to convince her to give him a second chance at being her mail order husband. The idea seemed strange to him, but also gave him the feeling of excitement. A feeling he hadn't felt in a very long time.

"First things first, Miss Jordan. If you didn't know about the meeting why did you come to town?" He made his lips form a grimace.

"Excuse me?" Penny questioned, her brows furrowed.

"Why did you get dressed up, in your Sunday best, and travel across the prairie in the heat of the day? If it wasn't to attend the meeting."

Penny lowered her lids and her fingers toiled with the lacy cuff at her wrist. Her reply was slow in coming, "I came to ask you to reconsider."

Stunned, Jace questioned his hearing and tried not to grin. He made his brow form a perfect arch above his right eye as he threw her a sideways glance. "Excuse me?"

"I came to ask you to please reconsider staying on at the Copper Cow, for just a little while," she repeated.

The woman amazed him. Jace glanced at the hands that now lay motionless on her lap. She could transform herself from a frighten child to a self-assured woman in mere seconds. The transformation intrigued him. "What makes you think I would reconsider?"

"Well, I was hoping that you might look at this as an opportunity for a second chance." They were almost to the stable, and he could sense she was waiting until he brought the buggy to a halt before continuing.

When they did, she twisted her body and placed a hand on his knee.

"Mr. Owens, I apologize for some of the things I said to you back at the house. I know your loss was a great burden for you to endure. I can't begin to imagine the pain you went through. I can however, compare it with my own loss, and know the pain does get lighter and easier to bear. It is my hope that by staying in the Dakota Territory, the change of environment might be of assistance to you, making your loss easier to accept.

"Maybe give you a second chance to find new hope in life, to set new goals for yourself and to explore new wonders. And to be honest, it is also my hope that our situation, or marriage, will give me the assistance and defense I need to restore my ranch, and now my social standing as well. I know..."

"I'll stay," Jace interrupted. Grasping her wrist, he lifted the hand that sent electric shock waves up his thigh. His fingers took a moment to caress the softness. Tiny bones were covered with skin that was smooth and supple to the touch, almost fragile feeling. Tiny flames licked at his fingers. He pulled his hand away, and let hers fall to her lap.

"Let me stable the horses." Afraid his voice would crack he didn't attempt to say more.

Her heartfelt confession had stirred feelings that had been forgotten. Suppressed so deep he no longer knew they existed. Hopes. Dreams. Goals. It took concentrated effort to jump down from the seat and proceed around the wagon to untie his horse. Using the back of his hand, he wiped the corners of his eyes, extinguishing the final tears of his past. Jace did need a second chance at life. He wasn't quite sure if he deserved it, but he wanted one. Jace Owens wanted to live again.

Leading Marion around the front of the buggy, he motioned for her to stay seated and walked to the stable. Nearing the doorway, he shouted into the muted darkness, "Hello? Need a couple of stalls for the night!"

Penny watched in astonishment as he entered the wide doorway. With a will of their own her eyes made an appraisal of his physique. Mary Alice had used her handiwork to restore the luster to his brown suit. The tailored jacket fit across broad shoulders with precision. Pinstriped contrasting black trim, outlined his lean form, and the shimmering white shirt made the ensemble appear very dapper. The squat, brown derby cap had been re-shaped and balanced on his head of thick, dark hair. She pondered her view as Jace Owens disappeared into the stable. He looked just like the men she used to encounter back east. She glanced down at the pink material surrounding her legs and concluded—he looked just as out of place on the prairie as she felt covered in lace and ruffles.

But, he said he'd stay. Penny couldn't believe it. She had only used a small portion of her well-prepared speech. Once she had been able to recall it. Piece by piece the words filtered into her swirling mind. Why had he agreed? She hadn't even gotten to the good parts. Nor the bargaining parts- the money she would offer in exchange for six months of marriage. Serious thought had been given as to what she could afford before a sizeable figure had been decided on. An amount she felt would allow him to start a new life.

Confused and pondering his quick decision, she shifted in her seat. The palm that had touched his knee still throbbed, and her wrist felt as if it was on fire. Anxious to dispel the sensations, she rubbed the hand against the material of her dress. It didn't help. She could still feel the brazing heat. Pulling a handkerchief from her small bag, she used it to wipe at the beads of sweat that formed while she'd searched for her speech. Since the moment his hands stilled her twirling motions and impending fall, her heart had begun to beat out of control, making rational thinking incapable. When those hands had spanned her waist to aid her into the buggy, she'd felt the beats hitting the inside wall of her chest.

Shaky fingers returned the hanky to its place. What was happening to her? Maybe she was coming down with something. Why else would her body be so out of sorts? This was ridiculous. She didn't have time to get sick.

A silhouette approaching the doorway caught her attention and dispelled her thoughts. With haste, Penny scrambled from the wagon seat, long before Jace was close enough to assist her.

****

"But I didn't pack a bag," Penny protested as they walked along the boardwalk headed for the only hotel Elm Creek hosted. Once the horses had been settled for the rest of the day, her husband suggested they get a room for themselves.

"The meeting will not conclude until late. It would not be safe for us to travel after dark. We will spend the night at the hotel and return to the ranch in the morning." Rolling his eyes, he concluded, "You will come to no harm by wearing the same dress two days in a row."

"Mr. Owens, why does my attire seem to concern you so? It is not my dress I am concerned about. Mary Alice will be worried if I do not return to the ranch tonight," she disputed.

"We will ask Sam to let her know our plans before he leaves town this evening, Mrs. Owens." He raised his voice in volume, making it easy for passerby's to hear his use of her married name as he steered her toward the hotel entrance.

Stopping in her tracks, Penny gave a civil smile to the startled couple brushing past them. She brought an angry gaze up to meet his and opened her mouth to speak, only to be interrupted as an older woman burst out of the door.

"Penny! Oh, Penny, darling! I was so surprised when Silas told me you had gotten married. I insisted on coming to town with him so I could meet the lucky man." The plump woman threw both arms around Penny for a long squeeze, before turning, "And this must be Mr. Owens. I'm Sue Ellen Osborne, and I am so happy to meet you, Mr. Owens." She took the liberty of wrapping her arms around his middle for a solid squeeze.

"My pleasure, I'm sure," Jace gave Penny a wide-eyed look as he patted the older woman's back with both hands.

"Come along now, I reserved the best room in the house for you. Of course Mr. Larsen tried to tell me he was booked up, but when I told him it was for Penny and her new husband, he found the space right quick." Sue Ellen explained as she pushed them into the spacious lobby of the hotel. "And Silas and I insist you join us for supper. We'll eat here at the hotel prior to the meeting. Oh, and Penny, while the men folks are meeting you can tell me how you snagged this wonderful buck here."

Penny would have spoken to Sue Ellen, if she could have thought of anything appropriate to say. Instead, she ignored her warm cheeks, nodded, and allowed her husband to guide her to the hotel desk with the hand he had placed in the small of her back.

She watched as Jace signed the registry ledger, Mr. and Mrs. Jace Owens, with a fluent hand while he addressed Sue Ellen. "Thank you for reserving the room for us, Mrs. Osborne, we appreciate your thoughtfulness." From behind the desk, Mr. Larsen handed him a single key.

Penny felt the color drain from her face. She tried to step around his large frame, but his hand slipped to her hip, halting her movements.

"We would be honored to join you and Mr. Osborne for dinner." A bright smile covered his face, and he flashed a quick wink at Sue Ellen. "But, right now, we need to freshen up a bit. We'll meet you in the dining room, at say, seven?"

"That will be perfect, my dear." Sue Ellen's blue eyes glistened with merriment. "Just perfect! See you then," she proclaimed before she placed a quick kiss on Penny's cheek.

Her face burned. She was led to a room on the second floor, where her voice returned as soon as they entered. "How could you?"

Jace closed the door. "How could I what?"

"How could you sign for the room as Mr. and Mrs. Jace Owens?" Penny tossed her pink drawstring bag on the table as she walked over to the poster bed, tugging at the ties of her pink bonnet. "You should have insisted on having two rooms. We can't spend the night in one room together!" Frustrated with the tight knot she now had created below her chin, she plopped onto the bed.

"Oh, the whole town will know by the time we go down for dinner. Sue Ellen is probably making her way over to the mercantile to talk with Ann Marie as we speak. Oh!" She couldn't stomp, her feet didn't quite reach the floor. So, she swung them in aggravation and slapped the patchwork quilt covering the spring bed instead.

Jace removed his coat and hat, hung them on the hook protruding out of the solid oak door and turned to make his way across the room.

"I signed our names as Mr. and Mrs. Jace Owens, because that is who we are. Or did you forget I'm the husband you commissioned?" He stopped in front of her. With one finger, he titled her head back to allow him to investigate the pink satin knot below her chin.

"Furthermore, the hotel is booked. I'm glad Mrs. Osborne was able to get us a room. And you should be too. The whole town is talking about your marriage." He portrayed a look of disbelief. "It appears some thought the occurrence would never happen."

The knot took his eyes from hers again. "If we don't share this room, they may begin to wonder if our marriage is real. Besides, I couldn't even consider allowing you to stay alone in a room tonight, not with Luke James and his gang in town."

His movements were as tender, swift, and competent as his words. The freed bonnet slipped from her head. He leaned forward and placed it on the bed beside her. "Did I answer all of your questions, or did I forget one?"

He was mesmerizing. She couldn't move or think. Her gaze refused to leave his features, which were stalwart and alluring. For the first time she noticed a faint scar ran down his right temple. It was somewhat hidden by dark wisps of hair that fell across his forehead in a disobedient style. The rich brown hair crowning his head was longer in the back, falling over the top of his collar. His shirt was a bright white, stiffly starched and stretched across his torso, molding the hills and valleys.

Once again she questioned if this was the same foul smelling mass she had hauled out of the stagecoach a few days ago. No repulsive odor protruded from his masculine form now, just the opposite. As if they had a will of their own, Penny's hands reached up and untied the thin band that formed a tie around his neck. He didn't move, just stared down at her. She gave the string a gentle tug. In slow motion it slipped out from under his collar.

She slid it threw her thumb and forefinger before handing it to him. "Thank you, Mr. Owens, and no, I think you answered all of my questions."

Shocked by her own actions, she twisted around to retrieve her bonnet. Her face felt hot and small beads of sweat began to roll down her torso. She waited for him to take a step backward. When he did, she slipped from the bed and made her way over to hang the cap on the wall pegs near the headboard. Her heart raced, and she could only hope the overwhelming sensations rushing through her body would soon dispel.

Out of the corner of her eye, she saw him walk to the window and pull the curtain aside.

"Jace," he muttered.

Startled by the sound of the high-pitched tone of his voice, she turned, "Excuse me?" Her fingers still tingled. She forced them to smooth the wrinkles from the ribbon of the bonnet positioned on the peg.

A slight cough emitted before he spoke. "Jace, my name is Jace." He gave a deeper cough and his voice returned to normal. "I suggest you stop calling me Mr. Owens, especially since it appears you were right." A finger tapped on the glass of the window. "Mrs. Osborne is on her way over to the mercantile."

The heart in her chest flipped. She scurried across the room. With an elbow, she nudged him aside and peered out the panes of glass. The back of Sue Ellen's blue linen dress flowed to and fro in her hurried steps to cross the street. One hand held the small linen cap upon her head; lessoning the chance the wind or her swift movements would uproot it.

"She appears to be on a mission." Jace glanced down at Penny.

"That she does, Mr., I mean Jace," Penny answered. Embarrassment made an unsure smile lift the corners of her lips as she peered up at her husband. Queasiness entered her stomach. White teeth peered out as his smile matched hers. Blood gushed through her body, followed by unexplainable warmth. It was a pleasurable sensation, too new of a feeling for her to examine or comprehend.

Jace turned and using both hands reached down and pulled open the sash of the window. A cool breeze flowed into the heated room. Fresh air and muted sounds from the street below soon encircled them.

"Shall we sit down and plan our attack?" He ran a hand through his hair and nodded at the table and chairs adjacent to where they stood.

The connection between them subsided. Penny sighed at the experience. What had it been? It was unexplainable, but she had felt a silent connection to him. Trying to clear her thoughts, she took a step back and slightly stumbled. He looked down at her expectantly. She glanced to the table, scurried toward it and agreed, "Yes, I think we should plan our attack."

"You really didn't know about the meeting?" Jace asked once they both were seated.

"No, after you left I uh, spoke with Sam and then drove into town." Nervous energy filled her. She clasped her hands together and laid them on the table. "Did you hear about it as soon as you got to Elm Creek?" She plucked at the lacey cuff covering her right wrist.

"You are going to pull that lace right off of there." Jace laid his hand on top of hers. The touch was swift. With sudden, jerky movements he broke the contact and used both hands to unhook the top button of his shirt. Once free of the confines, he twisted his neck and sucked in a deep breath of air.

Penny didn't know if she was glad or sad. The fleeting touch promised the warmth she had felt earlier, but it had also reminded her of a mosquito bite, a rapid sting that left a burning impression. Still pondering the feeling, she blinked when he spoke again.

"Actually it was before we got to town. We encountered a messenger not far from the Copper Cow. Calhoun recognized him as one of James' men. We stopped him to ask where he was going in such a hurry." Jace fluttered a light wink. "It appears Luke decided he needed to call an emergency meeting in light of our marriage. He sent messengers out to all of the Association members, except for the Copper Cow?" He paused, and waited for her to nod her head. "The meeting is here at the hotel at nine tonight. I think it would be helpful if you were to tell me as much as you can about the Association, what's been happening, and whatever you think is important, before we have to meet the Osborne's."

"I don't even know where to begin," Penny admitted.

She drew her hands down to rest in her lap.

"I'll ask a couple of questions to get you started. Tell me about the Cattlemen's Association. Who belongs to it, when was it started, and what do they do?"

Penny felt his sincere interest and without questioning it, she began, "It was organized several years ago by my father, Luke's father, Bob, Silas Osborne, and several other area ranchers. The aim of the organization was to set up the area branding system, to prevent rustling, to deal with contagious diseases, water rights, and to organize roundups. Through the years it became clear they also needed to be banded together to better regulate beef prices and legislation. At first anyone who raised cattle was able to join, but at some point, I believe while I was out east, it was determined a ranch had to run at least five hundred head to belong. My father was the president for several terms, and then Silas Osborne was while I was at school. It must have been two years ago he relinquished the job to Mr. James. When Bob became ill, Luke took over as president."

"Why five hundred head?" Jace asked.

"I don't really know." Penny pondered the thought for a moment. "I never asked, I only heard about the rule last winter."

"Was Luke voted in or just took over his dad's reign?"

She rubbed her temple. "Bob became ill last fall. Doc said he wouldn't make it through a bad winter. So his wife, Susan Leigh, insisted Bob and their daughter, Katie Jo, go on an extended trip to Europe to visit her family. I think she was hoping it would prove to be the cure he needed. I haven't heard if he is okay now or not." Penny wondered if Anne Marie had heard anything. She made a mental note to ask next time she was in the store before continuing, "As far as I know Luke just assumed the role. I think the officer's terms are for four years, so he has at least another full year left yet. It would be in the secretary's report. All of the meetings are recorded and kept on file at the bank."

Jace rose from the table, went to the window, and gazed at a building across the street. "What time does the bank close?" he asked.

Penny lifted her small traveling bag and pulled a

pocket watch from its confines. "Five, I think. Why?"

"I think I would like to see a copy of the original by-laws and the meeting minutes," Jace answered. "I'll be right back. Lock this door and don't open it for anyone, except me," he ordered before he slipped out.

Penny walked to the door, turned the key and then went to the window to watch as Jace sprinted across the street. He pounded on the bank door until Mr. Horn opened it for him to enter.

Feeling restless, Penny retrieved her bag from the table and hung it on the wall hook. The stiff leather of her dress shoes had a painful way of squishing her toes. Pulling a chair in front of the window, she sat down to remove the confining ankle-high boots.

Shadows were all she could see through the large window on the front of the bank, but her eyes continued to stare toward the building. Several minutes later the door opened and Jace exited. Her eyes followed his path back across the street, observing the manner in which he carried himself. His back was straight, holding his shoulders in line with his hips. His walk was proud and astute. One could sense an aura of good character surrounding his person. Though his dapper look seemed out of place on the dusty street, she couldn't help feel a sense of pride in knowing him.

A breath caught in her chest as she realized it was her husband she openly admired. The answer to her prayers, her knight in shinning armor. A warming sensation flowed in her veins again. Maybe this all would work out. A soft smile stayed on her lips as she returned the chair to its rightful position, and went to stand by the door, listening for his signal for her to open it.

"I got it." Jace slipped into the room and held up a thick, leather binder. He set it on the table and waited for Penny to be seated.

"When did a significant change happen and what was it?" he asked as he opened the book, glanced down at the neatly written notes and back up at her.

Feeling that ever present weight lessoning from her shoulders again, she began, "Well, I guess some of it started when Bob took over. Luke had just come back from the war. He talked about the railroad and how the

Cattlemen's Association needed to be ready when it came through Elm Creek. I was never interested in attending the meetings then, my father would tell me all about them when he came home. I remember him saying Bob was holding too much credibility in Luke and the connections he made out east."

"Do you mean the transcontinental railroad?" Jace questioned with disbelief.

"Yes, our sector is the Southern Dakota Railroad, right now it comes as far as Yankton." A blush covered her face, remembering it was the train that had brought him to her. "Luke claims to be corresponding with the owners and professes to have convinced them to bring the rail through Elm Creek. That's the main reason he can behave the way his does, everyone for miles around thinks he's a hero. The railroad will allow ranchers a quicker, easier way to get our beef to markets all across the nation."

"Elm Creek become a real cattle town?" Jace questioned. The sarcasm in his voice was unmistakable. "What about you Penny, do you think Luke is a hero?"

Penny shook her head. "No, I don't think Luke is a hero, I think he is a bully. He's not…well he's not a likable person. I have a hard time believing he made friends with all of the politicians he claims to be friends with."

Jace glanced down at the open book in front of him and flipped through a couple of pages before looking back up to catch green eyes gazing at him. The way they flashed with each emotion she felt captivated him. His heart skipped a beat. The thought of aiding her, of investigating the troubles she was experiencing, filled him with purpose. The whole situation intrigued him. His conversation with the banker had been interesting to say the least. There was so much more to the story. He flashed a smile, "And do you believe this little town could become…" he thought for a moment, then with flair added, "Jamestown, the Abilene of the Northern Plains?"

Penny's eyes snapped. Jace immediately noticed flashes of anger. He was amused and stretched his body to balance his chair on the two rear legs and folded his arms across his chest.

Her chair scraped the floor as she rose to her feet. Small, firm fists formed at the end of her arms. His eyes followed her movements around the table.

His amusement left as he watched her anger transform into fear. Concern rose in his chest. He brought the chair down on all four legs and rose to meet her. Reaching out to lay a hand on her forearm, "Penny," he started.

She twisted her arm out of his reach the moment contact was made. Her voice was laced with fear. "Don't touch me!"

Tremors rumbled over her body, her eyes were glassy, and seemed to be starring right through him. Perfectly formed lips quivered. She looked petrified.

"Penny, it's me, Jace," holding her gaze, he spoke soft and slow, not wanting to scare her any further. "I'm not going to hurt you. I'm sorry, Penny, it appears I frightened you."

The sound of his voice entered her mind; he could tell by the way she tilted her head. Her eyes blinked several times as if her vision was blurred. The haze must have cleared because he felt anger shoot out at him. "Penny?" he questioned with concern.

"You didn't frighten me, Mr. Owens, you infuriate me. It appears I have a traitor in the mist. I believe it would be best if you left now," she seethed between clinched teeth.

"What? What are you talking about? Leave now? You think I'm a traitor?" Jace was relieved to see her fear diminish, but wondered what brought it on. "I'm afraid I don't understand what you're talking about." The whole scene didn't make any sense to him.

Stomping to the window, Penny raged, "How did he get to you so quickly? Or were you in cohorts with him before you ever arrived. Going along with Candice's plan. Agreeing to stay. Oh, how could I have been so foolish? How could I have been taken in so quick?"

Following her across the room, Jace placed both hands on her shoulders and turned her, forcing her to look at him. "Penny, calm down. Who do you think I'm in cohorts with? What are you talking about?" He tightened his hold when she attempted to pull away. Stilling her in movements, he continued, "What did I say to give you that impression?"

"Jamestown!" she spat. "Only Luke uses that name, and," a deep shudder vibrated through her body, "and only in..." Her mind seemed to search her vocabulary to find the word she was looking for, "Private."

Jace saw fear enter her eyes again. "Penny, I'm sorry. It was just a play of words, something I merely thought James would come up with. No," he refused to let her go despite her struggles. "No, look at me, it is me, Jace." He framed her face with his hands. "You're safe with me."

He could feel her fear growing and without second-guessing his actions, he pulled her into an embrace. Her curves were a perfect fit to his. Both arms wrapped around her small form, and he leaned down to whisper comforting words into her ear. As the seconds turned into minutes, the vibrations rippling through her body began to quell.

Her cheek nestled onto his chest and a soft sigh left her body. He felt the blood rush to areas of his body that had been dormant too long. Pulling his head up, he looked at the ceiling, and tried to force his mind and body to ignore the fresh, flowery scent that surrounded her. He shouldn't take advantage of her fear. He couldn't take advantage of her fear. But it had been so long...

Chapter Seven

"Feeling better?" he questioned, several moments later, after he had control of his throbbing body and racing mind. He felt her head nod. "Here, let's sit down and then I'll get you a cool drink."

She didn't attempt to pull away from his embrace. Instead, she leaned onto him as he guided their bodies to the bed. He settled them both at the edge of the mattress and lessoned the embrace. His hands slid up to massage her shoulders and the upper parts of her arms.

"I apologize, Mr. Owens. I can't imagine what came over me," Penny attempted an explanation for her actions.

Jace felt her vulnerability returning to its hiding spot, becoming buried inside her, to once again become masked by self-proclaimed independence.

"There is no need for an apology. Let me get you that drink of water." He gave her hand a soft squeeze and held onto it as he rose to stand in front of her.

Almost as an afterthought, he placed a light kiss on her delicate knuckles before releasing them. Without a word, he crossed the room to the bureau. He poured water from the porcelain pitcher, which had been filled prior to their occupancy, into an adjoining glass. Before grasping the beaker, he flexed the muscles of his hand to lesson their shakiness.

It had been a long time since he'd been needed, or had comforted someone. He'd almost forgotten how enriching it could be. She was so young, so alone, so in need of protection. It felt rewarding to be here for her. What was happening to him? How had his life become so turned around?

One more question came to his mind as he turned and took in the scene before him. What had James done to scare her so intensely? Jace pasted on a smile and walked back to the bed. Determined to help her. He had to get to the bottom of it all, for her and for him. “Here you are.”

“Thank you.” Taking the proffered glass, but offering no additional words, Penny sipped at the cool liquid.

Jace strolled to the window, giving her the time she needed to gather her wits by pretending to take in a non-existent scene.

It was several minutes before she slid off the bed, placed the glass on the bureau, and took a moment to light the oil light in the middle of the table. After placing the spent match in a silver tray, she adjusted the wick to provide a soft glow across the room. Jace glanced back out the window. The sun was making its way behind the hills. Soon the valley would be basked in moonlight.

A soft cough broke the silence before she explained, “I can’t imagine what came over me, Mr. Owens, I assure you, I’m usually not such a ninny.”

He turned toward her voice and held out a hand, a silent invitation for her to come closer. The smile he formed was meant to be sincere and comforting. When she was within reach, he clasped her hand and used it to draw her in closer.

“I don’t think you’re a ninny, and I’m sorry I upset you so.” Bending his elbow, he obligated hers to fold and drew their entwined forearms to his torso. He pressed her hand onto his chest.

She didn’t resist his movements. The meager space between them felt electrifying. He tilted his face down lower to whisper in her ear, “However, you must start calling me by my given name.”

He studied the fine features of her face, the perfection of her skin. The flicker of the lamp made the small, brown freckles look as if they danced across her cheeks. Gold flecks encircled center black dots and highlighted the sea green of her eyes. Long, sooty lashes patted her cheekbones with each flutter.

Every atom of his body wanted her, needed her.

Jace knew her fear and anger had disappeared. He could feel her trust in him. The entire room seemed to become engulfed in some magical spell. They were connecting. Her soul seemed to flow from her eyes. He could see it, feel it. It was beautiful, pure, and more of an enticement than he could resist.

Their gazes entwined. “I shall have to think of a way to prevent you from calling me Mr. Owens.” Placing his other hand on the small of her back, he pulled her closer. He could feel the quickened pulse of her heart against the back of his confined hand and knew she could feel his matching one. His knees felt weak.

“It may take me some time to get use to it,” her voice shook, and her pink lips barely moved as she spoke.

They were parted just so, and too alluring for him to ignore. “Hmm, I wonder…”

Penny’s eyes never left his as his lips descended. Her lips were soft, like the petals of a flower and as sweet as honey. He took one more taste.

Her silent acceptance thrilled him. Blood surged through his body. He ran his tongue across her lips, pushing them apart. Intensity grew as he savored her sweet nectar. There was a soft ringing in his ears. He felt her body sway as she accepted the kiss and joined his actions. Her free hand crept up to his shoulder. Time stopped. Every sense filled with wonderful, tempting sensations. His mind held no thoughts. He was incapable of thinking as the movements drew them deeper together.

An undistinguished shout from below wafted through the window and filtered into his mind. It took all the conviction he could muster to lesson the kiss. His body was engulfed with sexual stimulation. Taking a deep breath, he opened his eyes to examine the angel in his arms. Her thick lashes had yet to lift open. His hand ran up her back and over her shoulder to allow his thumb to outline the fine features of her face. “Yes, I think that will do,” he acknowledged.

Her eyes fluttered open and encountered his amused expression. Tilting her head, she questioned, “What will do?”

“I have decided how I can help you remember to call me by my given name.”

“Oh and how is that?”

“I will have to punish you every time you call me Mr. Owens.”

“Punish me?”

“Yes, every time you call me Mr. Owens, I will punish you…with a kiss.”

"I do not believe that could be considered a punishment," Penny responded.

He watched her cheeks turn red and let out a deep chuckle, "I believe I am going to enjoy this marriage, Mrs. Owens."

Her face remained only inches from his. Thoughtful eyes searched his for a few moments before she asked, "Why did you agree to stay?"

He mulled her words around. How should he answer, did he even know how to answer? One knuckle ran over her eyebrow and down the length of her face. Encountering her chin, he tilted her head back. "Because you were right. I do need a second chance at life. I can't say if I deserve one for sure, or not, but I have to believe I do. I also believe you have been the victim of a grave injustice, and I want to help even the score. I want to see how it all plays out."

Penny believed him. Even with a body filled with sensations, which were new and enticing, and impossible for her to understand, she knew he did not lie. Her mind couldn't begin to analyze it all, but a sixth sense told her his answer was sincere. Somehow she also knew he was a man she could trust, with her own life if necessary.

"It's been quite a day," she sighed.

A loose wisp of hair dangled down the side of her face, Jace twirled it around one of his fingers. She could feel the touch all the way to her toes.

His head gave a quick bob, "Yes, it's been a long day already, but I'm afraid it's not over yet."

Her mind played a full circle of the day's event. "Oh, the meeting and supper with the Osborne's. What time is it getting to be?" She pulled away from their appealing setting and moved into the brighter light near the table to check the time on her father's watch.

Jace remained near the window. "We still have a little time. But before we get back to the association- you didn't happen to bring our marriage license, did you?"

"Yes, I did." She retrieved her small bag from its hook beside her bonnet and withdrew the papers. They were still sealed in an envelope. "I thought if you didn't agree to stay, you might need them when you got back to Philadelphia," Penny explained as she handed him the license.

His fingers broke the waxed seal and pulled out the parchment. Deep blue eyes scanned the sheets. "We have to sign them yet. We will stop and use the ink well at the desk on our way to supper. I have a feeling we might need these at tonight's meeting."

Penny nodded in agreement.

The papers were folded and slipped into his breast pocket. "I'm glad you thought of them, Penny." He reached over and caressed her arm. "I —uh-we better get back on subject."

"Oh, let's see, where was I?" Penny couldn't think when he touched her. Overwhelming sensations seem to overtake her. Taking a step aside, she broke their contact. "Oh, yes, the railroad. Luke has most everyone convinced the railroad is coming to Elm Creek next year. But that's not the real problem I see."

Encouraging her to sit with a wave of his hand, Jace settled himself on the opposite chair. "What is the main problem you see?"

"That Luke is hell-bent on creating an Indian uprising." The use of such words caused her cheeks to burn. "Excuse my outburst, but I am one-hundred percent convinced the raids on neighboring farms has been his handy-work, not that of the Lakota. Four farms have burnt, almost to the ground, this spring and summer. Each time the owners have not seen anyone, but arrows and other Indian belongings have been discovered in the ruins. Every time someone has been left injured. Twice people have died trying to put out the fires or save their families." Her serious manner never wavered. She had to make him believe her; assure him she wasn't making false accusations.

"Three of the families have moved on. If no one returns within a year, their homesteads will become available for someone else to claim. Three of the properties seem to be too far away from the James place to be of much good to Luke, but I still believe he is behind it all."

"Why would Luke want an uprising?" Jace's forefinger rubbed across his chin.

"My guess is to bring the army in, therefore creating

a larger market for beef. After the War Between the States, cowboys drove cattle from Texas clear into the Montana Territory, which is also where several Army bases have been established." She tried to stop her hands from emphasizing her words. It was a habit that overtook her, demonstrating her excitement or passion about the subject.

Lacing her finger together she held them close to her chest and continued. "We haven't had the Indian conflicts in this area like they have, but then again, we haven't been challenging the Lakota's property or way of life like they have over there." Her fingers pulled apart and she laid her palms on the table. "All of the ranchers in this area, through the Cattleman's Association, sold a lot of beef to the Army, but with the creation of all those new ranches in Montana, the Army started buying beef from them as well."

Hope of solving the pressing issues grew as she shared more. "My father claimed he wasn't too concerned about those ranches. He said it was too difficult to drive the cattle through the Black Hills to the Army forts. He preferred to drive our head to Yankton. From there the beef went to forts in Nebraska or into cities in Iowa and Minnesota." Shaking her head, she continued, "But even those contracts have lessoned lately. The only spread that seems to be surviving unscathed is the James Ranch. Every couple of months his hands drive a new herd through town, either on their way to market or bringing in fresh stock." She pointed at the book. "All cattle sales are supposed to be recorded." Excitement rose in her body, "I never thought to look in the books. What does it say? Is Luke really bringing in new stock or is he just rustling everyone else's? Which is something else he continues to blame on the Lakota."

While Jace flipped the pages, she pulled her chair around the table to sit beside him as they read.

****

Jace settled his hand on her back as they made their way around and between tables, zigzagging toward the lace trimmed, white handkerchief signaling the corner where their dinner companions were seated. Penny shared a smile with him as the material began waving with added madness. An older man attempted to snatch the cloth from Sue Ellen's hand, which forced her arm to flay to and fro faster- just out of the other's reach. By the time he and Penny arrived at the table, covered with a square of red and white checked oilcloth, the fabric was hidden in the sleeve of Sue Ellen's navy blue dress. The older couple displayed sincere smiles of greeting.

"Penny, my girl. You have made an aging man's heart gay again." The man stood to engulf Penny in a hug. Stepping back, he pulled his silk vest back down to cover his rounded middle, before offering his hand to Jace. "Silas Osborne," he stated as they grasped hands.

Introductions and pleasantries were put aside, and the smiling Mr. Larsen took their food order once they were seated. Silas began as soon as the waiter left the table; clearly displaying he had a role to fill and was intent on completing it.

"Penny is like a daughter to us, young man. I would be remiss if I didn't get to the point of asking your intentions. Harold was my best friend, closer than any brother I could have ever had. I will not allow his little girl to be swindled." His eyes grew deep with animosity as he stared across the table. "Tell me the truth, no bull shit, how did this marriage come about?"

Sue Ellen's gasp was loud enough to be heard across the room. Jace had no doubt every occupant at every table had their ears tuned into the foursome at the back of the room.

The goblet of water Penny had raised to her lips began to shake. Water sloshed over the rim and onto the table. Jace took the glass, placed it on the table, and took her hand in a tender embrace. He lifted the trembling fingers and brushed the knuckles with his lips before settling them below his on the tablecloth between them. He could sense his smile was not as reassuring to her as it was to him. Her fingers persisted to quiver beneath his calming ones. The tiny tears of fear that swelled and threatened to fall from her widen eyes encouraged his protective responsibility.

"I'm sure you are aware of the fact that Penny and my sister-in-law, Candice Berlin-Owens, went to school together out East. They were inseparable, and have kept in close contact ever since," Jace began. "Candice became convinced Penny and I were perfect for each other. And let me tell you, when my sister-in-law gets an idea in her head there is no stopping her."

Jace notice the quick glance Silas flashed at Sue Ellen. Encouraged, he squeezed Penny's hand in faith and continued, "Candice is one of the most persistent woman I have yet to meet, and though it took some-uh-doing, she did convince both of us she was right. A fact she will no doubt use to haunt us with for the rest of our lives. She made the journey out here with me, but could only stay a short time." He let a content look linger upon his wife until it brought a tinted glow to her cheeks.

A faint murmur of voices could be heard through the room as the tale traveled from table to table.

"You don't have to tell me how a woman acts once she gets her mind set. Nor how often they will remind you of how right they were." Silas rolled his eyes as he made an assumption. "So you knew each other when Penny was out East. I must say, that is a relief to my mind." Showing he wasn't quite satisfied, he persisted, "Mr. Owens, you seem to be a bit older than our Penny here. A little old to have never married."

"Yes, I am a few years older than Penny, a little more than half a dozen, and I was married before. My wife died in childbirth, along with our first child." Jace replied before adding, "And, please, call me Jace, my brother is the lawyer, he's the one who likes to be called Mr. Owens."

Recognizing the young man's previous loss, Silas bowed his head to Jace. "The missus and I never did have any children. I hope more for you and Penny," he stated with sincerity. Clearing his throat, he attempted to become stern again, "So, Jace, if your brother is a lawyer, what did you do back East?"

Jace caught the underlying message loud and clear. "I am well aware the Copper Cow is a prosperous ranch. Mr. Osborne, I would like to assure you, I am not a gold digger. I have a thriving veterinarian practice in Philadelphia, as well as several other successful investments. I have no need as far as finances are concerned. Our union is not about my financial gain. The marriage was truly Penny's choice."

Sue Ellen let out a soft cooing sound as she dabbed a tear slipping from the corner of her eyes. Turning to her husband, she patted his arm and concluded, "Silas, that is enough now, our meal is coming."

Penny thought she could have heard a pin drop. The dining room had never been so full before, it seemed every citizen of Elm Creek was eating out tonight. And she knew every occupant attempted to hear what was being said at her table. She held her breath, waiting for Silas to pick apart the holes in Jace's account of their courtship and marriage. He had told no lies, but left a lot to assumption.

Silas seemed to accept the story. The meal arrived and the food was consumed while Jace kept the conversation flowing by explaining to Sue Ellen, with great patience, what a veterinarian was, how it differed from a doctor, how it differed from a farrier, as well as how he had become one.

After the plates had been cleared, Silas suggested a short stroll along the boardwalk while they waited for the dining room to empty and be converted into the town's meeting space. Penny all but stumbled over her feet in her haste to leave the room. The cotton that covered her back had to have holes burnt in it from the stares of other customers in the room.

It didn't take long for the cool night air to penetrate the thin material of her dress. Penny folded her arms across her bosom to ward off the chill. Without missing a detail of the small talk between he and Silas nor a step in their leisurely walk, Jace removed his suit coat, draped it over her shoulders, and pulled her closer to his warmth.

The balmy sensation that engulfed her body every time he touched her was welcomed. Pride and honor grew to overtake her nervousness as they paused along the way to meet and greet many of the residents of Elm Creek. Their jaunt took them up and down the main street of town.

Upon their arrival back at the hotel Sue Ellen invited, "Penny, you come on up to my room, we will have a nice visit while the men folk are at the meeting."

Before she could answer, Jace interposed, "Thank

you, Sue Ellen, but Penny will be attending the meeting."

"Sorry, Son, but women aren't allowed at the meeting," Silas interjected.

"I'm afraid you have been misinformed Silas, I have read all of the by-laws and they say nothing about women not being able to attend. My wife will be joining me."

"Well of course it's not in the by-laws. It's just common sense. Cattlemen's meetings are no place for a woman, it's not proper," Silas said.

"And no woman wants to be there anyway, do we Penny?" Sue Ellen asked.

"Actually, I would prefer to attend the meeting, Sue Ellen. Jace is new in town, and I would like to be able to introduce him to everyone." The newfound determination and strength that Jace's presence instilled was miraculous. She was ready to tackle the world. It felt so good to have someone standing with her. Someone willing to share the load she carried. A load she hadn't realized was as heavy as the weight she felt slipping away.

"Really Dear, Silas can do that. You come along with me now." Sue Ellen took a hold of Penny's hand to lead her into the hotel.

Gentle actions removed Sue Ellen's hand from hers. Jace gave the older woman a slight bow of respect. "I apologize, I do not wish to offend you, Sue Ellen, but Penny is the rightful owner of the Copper Cow. A ranch that runs more than five hundred head and her yearly dues have been paid in full. Those are the only restrictions that prevent someone from attending the meetings. We have discussed this and she wants to attend, therefore I can not allow anyone to tell her she can't." He let go of the older woman's hand, and used the arm to encircle Penny's shoulders.

Silas looked from Jace to her and back to Jace. "You're gonna ruffle some feathers, Son. I think it would be best if she went on up with Sue Ellen."

"Half of the Dakota Territory believes just like you did, Silas, that I married Penny for the Copper Cow. And though I really don't care if they know the truth behind our union or not, I do want it to be clear- she is married-to me. I think the meeting tonight is the perfect place for me to establish my intent." His underlining message was completely clear to both Penny and Silas.

Penny looked up at her husband, hoping he could read the gratefulness she felt. No one spoke as they gazed at each other. Her heart slapped at the wall of her chest. Jace brought up a finger and ran it down the side of her face, brushing aside a corkscrew of hair. She felt the blood rush to her cheeks, but ignored it, and let a satisfied smile cover her face to match the one he displayed to her.

"Well, you're either gonna stir things up right good, or straighten everything out." Silas concluded, then with a chuckle added, "And I'm gonna sit back and enjoy the show!" He slapped Jace on the back before escorting his own wife into the hotel.

The room had been rearranged. Chairs now sat in short rows, facing a small platform that held a wooden podium. Several men were seated and others stood, conversing in small groups. The banker and acting secretary, Edward Horn, sat at a corner table, tablet open and pen in hand, recording the attendees as they strode in.

Side by side they entered the room. Penny felt her shoulders droop as she recognized several faces. Warm breath brushed her ear. "Don't worry, Mrs. Owens, I'm right beside you. Through it all, I will be right beside you." She leaned into the arm that came up to give a reassuring touch on her shoulder, took a deep breath, and with poise strode to the front row.

Jace settled his wife in a chair, took his rightful position on her left and encouraged Silas to sit on her right. Placing the large ledger in the empty aisle chair on his other side, he let his gaze wander around the room. Several of the men he had been introduced to earlier on the street nodded in greeting. He responded to each and with a supportive grin winked at Penny before he leaned back to wait for the showdown to begin. He was going to enjoy it. It felt good to be alive again.

Luke James entered the room, followed by the rough looking entourage Jace had heard accompanied his every move. With a pompous ring, his voice boomed above the others, "Alright gentlemen take your seats. Your President has arrived."

A few snickers and jeers rumbled off the walls as

everyone found a chair. Luke stomped onto the platform, the jingle of his spurs echoed off the hollow form as he made his way to the dais. Jace placed an arm along the back of Penny's chair and chuckled aloud in humor when he realized the short man had to stand on a wooden crate to see over the podium.

Luke glared into the first row while he pounded the wooden mallet on the desktop for attention and bellowed, "Order! I'm calling this meeting to order!" Focusing his beady eyes on Penny, he spat black juice out the side of his mouth and onto the floor. "Miss Jordan, I know you are aware of the rule that no women may attend our meetings." Without waiting for a reply or reaction, he barked instructions to one of the four cohorts who stood along the edges of the platform. "Butch, see Miss Jordan to the door!"

The burly looking man closest to them stepped forward and reached out to take hold of Penny's arm. The condition of his oily clothes demonstrated his objection to clean water and the smell of sour tobacco juice surrounded him.

"Touch her and I'll break your arm," Jace said. His voice came out as a low growl. Every muscle in his body tensed, ready for battle.

Butch peered down and sneered. Beady eyes strolled up and down Jace's brown suit as he emitted a short cockle. The way the desperado rolled his eyes was meant to display his belief Jace was a city man and that his threat was gutless. A loud snort came out of his mouth, and a grimy hand darted toward Penny.

Jace had never felt so appalled. With quick movements he stood and seized a thick wrist just as grubby fingers brushed her dress. He saw Penny's body shiver, anger overtook his thoughts. Years of wrestling large animals provided him with the art of knowing how to use his balance and strength. He shifted his feet, twisted the offending limb and with a quick jerk, flipped the man backwards.

The hefty body vaulted over its own shoulder. Arms and legs made a full circle in the air before Jace released his hold. The crude looking Butch hit the floor as a loud crack echoed off the high ceiling. Silence filled the room.

No one moved as Jace re-settled himself on his chair.

He turned to Penny. "I apologize you had to see that, my dear, but I did warn him." Leaning over, his lips touched her cheek. He searched hers eyes, asking for forgiveness. His hand toyed with the silky tresses lying across her shoulder. The wall of his chest felt every beat of his heart. He could only hope it wasn't apparent to the rest of the room. She reached over, laid a hand on his knee, and her face tilted sideways, brushing against his fingers.

The man on the floor expelled the air that had been locked into his lungs with a loud hiss. Greasy hair mopped the floor when his head lobbed from side-to-side in pain. Clutching the elbow of his right arm, he wailed, "My arm! He broke my damn arm!"

"Touch her again and you're a dead man," Jace assured with a nonchalant glance at the injured man. His other hand went to his knee to cover Penny's twitching one. He stared at the front of the room, sending the same message to the man at the podium.

"Sheriff!" Luke yelled and pointed his mallet at Jace. "Arrest that man!"

Stony stares went to the back of the room where Sheriff Wilcox leaned against the wooden frame of the lobby door. Shaking his head, the lawman responded, "No law was broken. I can't arrest a man for defending his wife." He flicked his head and instructed his deputy, "Elliott, take Butch over to Doc Burton and have his arm set."

Jace signaled his thanks to the sheriff with a slight nod as he sized up the man. He was tall, probably about the same height as himself. Silas had told him Tim Wilcox had held the job for over six years. He described him as a fair and honest man.

Receiving a twin response from the relaxed looking form, Jace brought his attention to the men at his side. Elliott Spencer had been around almost as long as the sheriff but he was a bull of a man. The second-in-command stood about five-foot ten and weighed close to three hundred pounds. Silas had suggested the sheriff had possession of the brains while the deputy possessed the brawn. Jace patted the hand Penny had wrapped around his forearm when Luke called for his arrest. Together they watched Spencer perform his task.

The lawman used no tenderness in gathering the whimpering Butch to his feet. Before taking their leave, Elliott tipped his tall, wide-brimmed hat at Penny. "Right happy to hear 'bout your marriage, Ma'am." Giving the injured man a shove forward, he threw Jace a trustworthy grin.

From his stance at the podium, Luke looked at his remaining men. All three avoided his gaze, indicating they were not going to hear a word he said. Pounding the mallet, his face red with anger, he barked another order, "Sheriff, remove Miss Jordan from the room!"

Jace let out an exaggerated sigh. Every eye in the room was on him. Not giving Luke the respect of standing while speaking to him, Jace let his words sound as if he had to explain something for the umpteenth time to a small child. "Her name is Mrs. Owens, and she is not leaving my side." Twisting in his chair, he continued, "Sheriff Wilcox, I could use your assistance in something, would you come up here please."

"Mrs. Owens, I too would like to congratulate you on your marriage." Wilcox acknowledged when he arrived next to her chair. Jace rose to shake hands with the lawman.

"Thank you, Sheriff," Penny responded as she folded her hands in her lap. Her gaze sprinted between the two men.

Jace gave her a reassuring smile before he pulled an envelope from his pocket and handed it to Wilcox. "Sheriff could you please examine this and inform Mr. James what it says."

A smile curved the Sheriff's lips as he scanned the paper in his hand. He nodded to Jace before turning to the podium. "Mr. James," flicking a wink at Penny the lawman continued, "in my hand is a marriage license that confirms one, Jace Owens, and one, Penelope Jordan, are indeed married. It is signed by," Wilcox glanced back to Jace and raised an eyebrow in indication the signature impressed him, "Judge Charles P. Hogan. The license has also been notarized by the United States Supreme Court." A full smile embraced his face as he handed the paper back to Jace.

"I don't care who notarized or performed the so called marriage." Luke rolled his eyes as he bellowed, "I want her removed from this meeting."

"I do care that you understand who she is. *First and foremost, my wife*! Her name is Mrs. Owens, and that is how you shall address her, *if* you ever encounter her," Jace explained with great deliverance. "Now if that is understood?" He waited for Luke to give an ignorant nod. "And as long as you're up here, Sheriff, perhaps you wouldn't mind informing, Mr. James, of what the by-law's of the Cattlemen's Association states." Reaching down he retrieved the book on the chair. With great flair he flipped the thick cover open and paged through a few sheets. "Ah, here it is- membership and meetings." Jace handed the ledger to the Sheriff.

"I must say you are well prepared, Mr. Owens," Tim Wilcox said.

"My brother is a lawyer," Jace admitted for the sheriff's ears only.

Luke was showing his anger. The entire crowd could almost see steam coming out of his protruding, reddened, ears. "What the hell is the meaning of all this?"

Jace let his dislike of the rude man known. "You will watch your language in the presence of my wife."

Sheriff Wilcox cleared his throat and glanced between the two men as the stare off continued. Out of the corner of his eye, Jace saw the lawman place a hand on his holstered gun. He continued to glare until Luke pulled his eyes away. The Sheriff waited a few more seconds, until everyone's attention was diverted back to him, before he began to read.

"'Article B-1, Membership. Members must be the owner of a Dakota Territory Ranch that runs at least five hundred head of cattle and whose yearly dues are in good standings. NOTE: The clause of five hundred head was voted on and added as amendment 102 in August of 1869."

He glanced up from his reading and explained, "It lists the member's names in attendance at that meeting. I won't read those." He scanned the words. "Then it states, 'this amendment may be withdrawn by a quorum of voting members in attendance at an official meeting.'" Showing his ability to read and be observant of his surrounding he continued to shift his eyes. "Let's see what else? Oh yes, here it is, Article B-4. Articles B-2 and 3 talk about quorums and meeting frequencies."

The Sheriff shifted his stance. "'Article B-4' Meeting Attendance. Members must make every attempt to be in attendance at all meetings. Only ranch owners will be permitted to attend meetings. Ranch hands and / or other appointees will not be considered members, therefore not allowed to attend official meetings. Legal documentation of cattle ownership and property deeds will be required and recorded in the official record book before acceptance into the association and/or meeting attendance is permitted. In the event of a public meeting to inform community members of up coming proceedings, special events or additional undertakings that have been duly approved by all members, special community meetings may be held. At which point any Dakota Territory citizen will be permitted to attend.' I think that about covers it." He let the cover slap shut and handed the book back to Jace.

"Just a moment, Sheriff, could you please remind Mr. James of this list of members?" Jace asked as he flipped the pages to the back of the book. He made no attempt to delude his enjoyment of correcting Luke's ignorance. And he could almost understand what Daniel found so potent about trial proceedings. Though Jace would never admit it to his brother, not after all the years he spent mocking his sibling's pompous attitude.

The sheriff glanced down at the list of names that had been recorded and notarized when they became members. He looked back up at Jace and asked, "The entire list?"

"No, that isn't necessary. How about membership number three," Jace instructed.

"The Copper Cow Ranch: Harold Lincoln Jordan and Penelope Rebecca Jordan," Wilcox read.

"Penelope Rebecca Jordan, now known as Mrs. Jace Owens," Jace clarified while rubbing his chin. "And line number thirty-six please."

"The Copper Cow Ranch: Harold Lincoln Jordan,

Penelope Rebecca Jordan and/or spouse when married. It's noted that the addition to the Copper Cow membership was notarized on January 15, 1870."

Jace glanced at Silas and shifted his eyes to Penny. The older man took Penny's trembling hand and leaned over to whisper in her ear. Jace wished he could wrap his arm around her trembling shoulders. Instead, he settled for a look that said trust me. Her answer filtered back to him as her head tipped down and her shoulders straightened. He let out the air from his chest and pointed to the book, "And line number five please."

"The R & S James Ranch: Robert Sheridan James and Susan Leigh James."

"And line number 38 please, Sheriff," Jace said.

"The Lucky J Ranch: Luke Robert James. March 12, 1872."

Rumblings grew louder throughout the room. "What the hell is the purpose of all this?" Luke beat the mallet on the podium.

Jace knew it was time to make a move. He sent threatening glares, flashing them between the three cronies stationed in front of the platform. No one attempted to prevent his approach as he began to walk toward the make shift stage.

"Let me re-phrase it so even the slightest brain can comprehend what the good Sheriff has just stated. First off, the Copper Cow is in complete compliance with all membership standards, which means my wife, as it's legal, rightful owner, can and will be, attending all meetings, regardless of the fact that she is a woman. A fact, which I am very happy about." Throwing a bold, tell all look in Penny's direction, he let a few chuckles emit from the audience before stepping closer to Luke.

"It also appears my deceased father-in-law wanted to be sure his daughter would have the opportunity to voice her opinions of any actions regarding her property even after her marriage. Therefore, he made her future husband- that would be me, a legal member over two years ago. However, it also appears that you, Mr. James, only became a member a mere five months ago. Amazing, you're not as deft as I thought you were. I see by the look of shock on your face that you comprehend, not only has

Mrs. Owens been a member in good standing much longer than you have, but I, as unbelievable as it may sound, have also been a member longer than you." Jace allowed his words and slow stroll to stop at the same time.

The two men stood face to face, due to the fact that Luke was still standing on the wooden crate. Tension filled the room.

Jace continued before the quaking form in front of him found his voice, "I would also like to inform you that in my research of past minutes, there was never an official, authorized vote, nor acceptance of your presidency. In the absence of your father, the presidency should have diverted back to the past president, Mr. Silas Osborne." Jace reached over to retrieve the offending mallet from the other man's stubby fingers.

Luke released the hammer and took a step backwards. One spurred boot searched to find the floor below the crate he had been standing on. After several faltering steps, he managed to find solid footing on the stage. Reaching for the pearl handled, six-shooter strapped to his hip, "Stay back," he warned.

A startled, "Jace!" echoed through the room.

Chapter Eight

The sound of a gun being cocked or the feel of cold steel pressed into his back, one of the two, stifled Luke's attempt to retrieve his weapon. His eyes grew wide and his empty hand halted in mid air.

"Don't draw that weapon, James," Sheriff Wilcox warned. The lawman had made his way around the stage and behind Luke while Jace delivered his speech to the room.

"What the hell are you doing, Wilcox? Arrest that man, he's loco!" Luke exclaimed. A flash of relief seemed to overcome his face when he realized it was the Sheriff holding the gun to his back.

"I'm not crazy," Jace assured. "I'm selfish. And I won't allow anyone to damage or hurt anything that is mine." Placing the mallet on the dais, he turned his back on the other man, making a clear indication of his opinion of Luke's insignificant worth and abilities.

A trembling hand covered her mouth. Penny's gaze met his as he step down from the platform. Her startled squeal had tore at his chest like a hot knife. He saw the hand Silas had used to stop her from bolting to the dais.

Without thought to the room full of onlookers, he opened his arms in invitation. Swift movements glided her body into his embrace. Shaky arms encircled his waist and she buried her face into his chest. He wrapped his arms around her shoulders, and pressed their bodies together.

Murmuring soft words of comfort, Jace stroked the silky tendrils running from the top her head and flowing down her back. His senses filled with her aura. He let his arms tighten around her again and felt warm fluid flow onto his chest. It filled him with a sense of wholeness. The kiss he placed on the top of her head was meant as encouragement, but he wasn't really sure if it was for her or him. Her soft form seemed to melt into his shape. He pondered the sensation for a few seconds before realizing the room was waiting for his next move.

He looked over the top of his wife's head at the crowd; all eyes were focused on them. With a glanced over his shoulder, he said, "Sheriff, could you please escort Mr. James to his seat and clear the room of any none members so Mr. Osborne can get this meeting started?"

"With pleasure," Wilcox agreed. He pulled the firearm out of Luke's holster, slipped it into his own belt, and ushered the grumbling man to the rear of the room. "You men know if you belong here or not. Take your leave if you're not a member."

One arm remained wrapped around his waist as Jace led Penny to their seats. In comfort, her fingers laced with his when they sat down to wait for the meeting to reconvene. His pulse retuned to a simple, steady beat, but an unexplainable glow remained. He squeezed Penny's fingers with his and flashed a wink at her as Silas made his way to the platform.

Penny's heart pounded in her chest. Whether it was from fear of the events at the podium or from the embrace that followed, she hadn't yet determined. But the reassuring pressure of Jace's hand entwined with hers filled her with a security she'd never felt before. She basked in the moment.

There was little complaining, and even less fan fare as the room cleared of those who were not ranch owners. Penny peered over her shoulder and noted Luke sitting in the back row. His lips pulled into a pout as he watched his callous companions exit the room. The Sheriff pulled the door shut and presumed his previous stance of leaning against the doorframe.

Penny pulled her gaze back to the front of the room, careful not to glance at her husband. Her mind wasn't ready to acknowledge reactions to the fear that had overcome her at the thought of him being harmed. She tried to look engrossed in the room's activities as her mind and emotions swirled.

Silas pushed the crate away from the podium with one foot, batted the mallet against the wood and proclaimed, "Alright men, let's get this meeting called to order. Mr. Horn, what is the first order of business on tonight's agenda?"

"I'm afraid, Mr. President, an agenda was never created for this meeting. A messenger burst into the bank this afternoon and informed me there was an emergency meeting being called tonight. The dispatch rider could not, or perhaps I should say, would not, give me a reason for the occasion, other than Miss Jordan's marriage." Edward Horn stood to address the room as he made his statement.

All eyes shifted to Luke who glanced around the room. His self-esteem appeared to have diminished without the burliness of his cronies guarding him.

"Yes, I called the meeting. I was attacked earlier today by Mr. Owens and felt the rest of you needed to know this wild man was claiming to be Miss, uh, Mrs. Owens' husband."

"We've already settled the issue of the legitimacy of their marriage and are not going to have any further discussion on that matter," Silas instructed. "But tell me, Mr. James, where were you when, as you claim, Mr. Owens attacked you?"

"On her front porch!" Luke exclaimed, looking hopeful in his ability to portray the other man's faults.

"Had you been invited to their home?" Silas continued his investigation.

Beady eyes shifted back and forth. "N…no," Luke had to admit.

Penny looked around. She hoped no one in the room would believe he had been invited to the Copper Cow. Including the man beside her. Instinctively her hand clenched his. Long fingers caressed her grasping ones.

"It appears to me this so called attack was nothing more than a man removing a trespasser from his property. We will have no further discussion on that matter either." Silas tapped the mallet against the wood in finalization of the subject. A few snorts and grunts were heard before the old man spoke again, "So gentlemen, as long as we are here, does anyone have specific issues, pertaining to the official business of Cattlemen's Association, they wish to discuss?"

"Yeah," a shout came from the rear of the room, "I

haven't sold a single head of beef in over six months!"

"Me either! Where's the railroad deal that's suppose to be happening?"

"And I want to know where the hell this Lucky J Ranch is, James? You seem to be the only one selling any cattle," another shouted.

"Gentlemen, one at a time!" Silas encouraged with another quick rap of the mallet.

Penny relaxed in her seat. Her interest in the meeting diminished, she or should she say, her husband had succeeded in securing the outcome she wanted. Her mind replayed the day's events. It was almost impossible to believe all that had happened in a mere twelve hours. Minute by minute, she relived the day as the men discussed various issues.

An hour later the occupants of the room began to file out. Concerns had been addressed, and even though no answers had been found, the men seemed confident in having Silas as their president again, in addition to having someone defy Luke and his tales. Several men approached Jace and Penny before exiting, shaking his hand and tipping their hats at her. Satisfied, Penny stood beside him and responded to each of their gestures. Silas stood on the other side of Jace, his hand rested on her husband's broad shoulder.

"He hoodwinked us when he came back from the war with his tales. I guess no one really knew how to stop him. Or maybe we were all somewhat afraid. It appears we have just stood by and watched it get worse and worse," Silas said, not talking to anyone in particular.

"Well Silas, I'm afraid it may get worse before it gets better. He is an angry and spiteful man," Jace commented as all three of them observed Luke still seated in the back of the room.

Silas nodded.

Jace lifted the ledger off the chair and folded his hand around Penny's elbow. As one, they made their way to the door.

"Glad you insisted on escorting Luke and his clan to the edge of town tonight, Sheriff," Silas said as he shook hands with Wilcox.

Peering at Jace, the Sheriff shook his head and

lowered his voice, "I'm afraid I'm only delaying the inevitable. I assume you are aware of the hornet nest you stirred up, Mr. Owens. It could get ugly, real ugly."

"Yes, Sheriff, I was well aware of what I was doing. And I would appreciate your support while I'm cleaning up the mess I made." Jace accepted the warning.

"I'll be glad to provide any assistance needed. Matter of fact, let me know if you need to be deputized. It can make the cleaning up a little easier in these here parts." Wilcox winked at Silas, touched the brim of his hat in dismissal at Penny, and barked, "Come on, James. Let's go."

"That was exhilarating!" Penny exclaimed as she flopped herself onto the bed once Jace had let them into their room. "There were times I thought my heart would beat itself right out of my chest! Did you see how humiliated Luke was?" She bounced herself to the edge and swung her feet to and fro, making the metal frame creak with the movement. She felt so alive.

A click echoed in the room before Jace pulled the skeleton key out of its hole. Without a word, he walked across the room and laid it on the bedside table.

"What?" she questioned his dumbfounded look, "What's wrong?"

He sat down on the chair and began to remove his boots. "You. How do you transform yourself like that? You went from a docile little wife to a...a fanatic in mere seconds."

"A what? I'm not a fanatic. Nor am I a docile little wife," she said. What was wrong with him? They had accomplished a major goal tonight. "But I did enjoy watching Luke be put in his place for once."

"Watching a man being humiliated is not exhilarating. It's dangerous."

Taken aback by his seriousness, she folded her arms across her chest and let her bottom lip protrude with a small pout. She wasn't ready to think about the outcome of the meeting, she wanted to savior in the victory. Why wasn't he more excited?

Bending down, she began to unlace her boots. Her actions stilled, and her gaze followed him when he stood to remove his coat and shirt. A ripple ran across her stomach. His hands moved to untie the string at his waist. "What are you doing?" she asked.

"I'm getting ready to go to bed. I suggest you do the same."

"You're not sleeping in this bed."

"Yes, my dear wife, I am."

"Where am I supposed to sleep?"

"It's large enough for two."

"I can't, we can't...share a bed," she whispered.

"Yes, we can, and we will. In case you have forgotten, less than twenty-four hours ago, I was still drugged beyond comprehension. And even though Singing Dove worked a miracle on my body, it's been a long day. I'm exhausted. Now, get undressed and crawl under the covers while I turn out the light."

"Undress? I can't undress with you in the room."

"Fine then, sleep in your clothes. I don't care if they get wrinkled, nor how shabby you look when we take our leave in the morning." The room grew black as he blew out the lamp.

"Mr. Owens! This is not proper."

Jace grasped her face with both hands and brought his mouth down on her open lips. The kiss ended as quick as it had started. "I told you I was going to kiss you every time you called me that," he reminded her. "Now, scoot over. I need to sleep on the side closest to the door."

Penny blinked her eyes several times. Had he just kissed her? She ran her tongue over her lips, seeking confirmation. Yes, she could taste the salt from his lips. She reeled across the bed and found her footing on the floor on the opposite side. Stunned, she watched a shadowy form flip back the covers and crawl into the bed. Standing in the darkened room, she contemplated her next move.

After several minutes of silence, he begged, "Penny, please come to bed, I need some sleep."

Common sense prevailed. He was right. Her dress would be in shambles if she tried to sleep in the folds of pink material. And she couldn't force him from their room. Not only would it not be fair to him, it would inspire tongues to wave.

"I can't," she said.

"I swear on my mother's grave, I will not attack you. I will not force myself upon your person in any way, shape or form. You can trust me. I'm too tired to do anything but sleep."

"No, it's not that. You're right. My dress will be a mess if I try to sleep in it."

"Well then, take it off."

"I can't."

"Penny," he sighed.

"No, I mean, I can't because the buttons are in the back. I can't reach them."

The blankets covering her side of the bed flipped out of the way. Jace pulled himself across the area. "Turn around and I will unbutton you." His fingers didn't need any light. They found the buttons and deftly released each one, completing the task in record time. Spinning back to his side of the bed, he grumbled, "Now let's get some sleep."

Penny removed the barest of necessities and slipped into the bed. Hugging the furthest corner of the edge, she rested her head on the pillow, convinced sleep would never come.

****

Bold light forced itself against her eyelids. Penny snubbed it and tried to bury her face into the coziness of her nest. She sought the comfort she had snuggled into throughout the night. Finding nothing but empty space, her lids fluttered open.

Recollection of the previous day came flooding back. With a start she sat up, brushed the tangled masses of hair away from her eyes, and searched the empty room for any signs of Jace. With effort, she untwisted the layers of undergarments restricting her movements and climbed from the bed.

The shine of the sun, which was high in the sky, blazed into the room. "Oh my," she mumbled and moved to the table to observe her small time piece. "Ten o'clock? Why I never!" She continued to mutter to herself as she began to prepare herself for a day that was almost half over. In short time, she made use of the fresh water in the pitcher, plaited her hair into a neat braid, and retrieved her dress from the wall hook. The pink material fell into place while her mind continued to wonder. Where was Jace? Had it all been a dream?

Foot falls sounded in the hall. The heart in her chest flopped. She retrieved the key from the small table, unlocked the door and opened it just enough to peer out. Deflated, she recognized Mrs. Larsen, the hotel owner's wife, outside her room. A fake smile formed, "Excuse me, Jeannie May, but could I ask for your assistance please?"

"Good morning, Penny, I mean, Mrs. Owens," the woman greeted. "What can I help you with? Your husband carried fresh water up before he left. He asked that I watch to be sure no one disturbed you this morning. He explained you had had a long day, yesterday." Jeannie May looked at Penny with a knowing smile in her eyes.

Penny drew her brows together, searching for the meaning of the other woman's stare. When nothing came, she shook her head and held the door open in invitation. "I am unable to fasten my dress, could you please help me?"

The older woman entered the room. "Why of course, dear, and then we can go down and have a cup of tea. I'm sure Mr. Owens will be stopping in any minute, to see if you have awakened yet. He's been busy running errands all morning, but stopped in every half hour or so to check on you. What a treasure you found for yourself in that one. Half of the ladies in town are talking about how lucky you are, and of course the other half are talking about how they wished they had found him first."

"Oh, really?" Penny questioned. She stepped away when Jeannie May signaled the job was complete and mumbled a soft, "thank you," as she made her way across the room to collect her dress boots.

"Oh yes. The dining room was an absolute buzz this morning; folks were praising that man of yours up and down. Did he really break that ruffian's arm just for touching you? And the way he organized the Cattlemen's Association, I hear it was magnificent. His brother is a lawyer you know, and he is a veterinarian. Well, of course you know that."

Noticing Penny had completed her tasks, Jeannie May continued, "Come along now dear, I have to get down to the kitchen. I'm sure we are going to be just as swamped for lunch as we were for breakfast. Why, we haven't been this busy, since…well, the restaurant has never been this busy before. Maybe that time those folks from England were here, but…"

Penny stopped listening to the prattle, and followed the other woman out the door, along the hall, and down the staircase. Just as her feet stepped off the stairs, the front door opened. Her heart did a somersault. The light filtering through the opening haloed a tall form. She clutched the banister for balance against her dizziness. It wasn't a dream. She did have a husband and he was magnificent looking.

"Good morning, Sleeping Beauty," Jace completed his greeting by brushing her forehead with his lips.

"Why didn't you wake me?" Penny asked when she found her tongue.

Jace had to touch her. One hand rose and traced her jaw line. "I didn't have the courage," he admitted. His body still held the remnants of the overwhelming sensations that had besieged him during the night. Her sleeping form had snuggled against him. At first his exhausted body relished in the treat, but after only a few hours, the luxury turned into a growing need. When he became concerned he wouldn't be able to keep it suppressed much longer, he had pulled himself from their bed. Tired he sat in the chair, watching her sleep, contemplating the predicament they seemed to be in. The sun had begun to peek over the steep hills surrounding the valley when he had dressed and slipped from the room. Ready to put his plan, with new goals, fully into motion.

Her words broke into his thoughts. "I find that hard to believe, Mr., uh, Jace." Her cheeks grew rosy. "From what I have heard this morning, the whole town thinks you are the most courageous man they have ever encountered."

He folded her arm through his and guided her toward the dining room. Pride entered his chest, she was so pretty, so vibrant. "Really?" he asked, "A real knight in shining armor?"

Her feet stopped in their tracks. "Whom have you been talking to?"

Jace gave her a sly wink and with a gentle tug convinced her to continue their jaunt. “Come on, my dear wife, let’s have some lunch before we head for home.”

Penny tossed him a shy smile and fell into step as he made their way to an open table.

****

Jace paced the floor, stopping every now and again to glance out the office window. A faint telltale plume of dust caught his gaze. His heart pounded and he stared until it formed into an image. Anger replaced apprehension when he strode from the room and it rose to a boil while his booted feet pounded the dirt as he made his way to the center of the yard to watch her approach.

“Where the hell have you been?” One hand grabbed the leather strap of Midnight’s bridle as soon as it came within his reach.

Strict orders had been left with everyone. She was not to leave the compound without an escort. For over an hour he had looked for her and tried to not let his fears override his common sense.

“Where have I been? How dare you ask me that?” Penny exclaimed as she flipped her leg over the saddle horn. “As if you care!”

Dropping to the ground, she pointed a finger at him in annoyance. “If you must know, I have been out checking my land, checking on my cattle, running my ranch! A feat you believe I am incapable of. A feat that in all actuality, you are incapable of doing!”

Taking two steps forward, she pounded the finger into the center of his chest. “Where the hell have I been? Where the hell have you been, Mr. Owens? For three weeks you have left this house before the sun rose and came home after it set. You have left specific instructions for every person around here to make sure I don’t leave the yard. For three weeks I have been cooped up like a…like a prisoner! Who the hell do you think you are Mr. Owens?” Her words screeched with frustration.

Tilting his head back, Jace closed his eyes and took a deep breath, searching for self-control. “Watch your language, Penny.”

“What?” A puff of dirt rose to float around their legs as her feet stomped the ground. “Watch my language?

You can't tell me what to do. You are not my father. You are not my guardian. You have no control over me!" she yelled.

Jace felt his anger faltering. He couldn't blame her; he was the one who was being unfair.

His silence seemed to infuriate her more. She ripped the leather gloves from her hands and threw them at him. "You make me so mad!" The gloves bounced and floated to the ground. Tears glistened in her eyes and her hand slapped against his chest. "You are nothing to me."

Jace grasped her fingers as they brushed against his shirt and secured the hand to his chest. He caressed the softness. Warmth from her palm penetrated the cotton covering his torso. Looking down at her upturned face, he released a sigh of relief in knowing she was safe.

Her enticing features filled his senses. In anger, the gold flecks in her green eyes danced at him. But there was something else just beneath the fury, something raw and alluring. Damp lashes dipped to brush against her flushed cheeks. Soft beams of sunlight glistened off long, shimmering tresses haloing her face. His hands itched to run through the curls that flowed over her shoulders. Her chin quivered, and the pout of her lips lessoned as a pink tongue darted out to moisten them.

"I'm your husband." His self-control slipped and his lips bore down to absorb hers. Three weeks of avoiding her was wearing on him. The days were getting harder to get through. His taxed mind feared the sight of her upon waking each morning, yet his throbbing body longed for a mere glimpse of her every second of the day. His want of wrapping her in an embrace was stronger than anything he had ever known.

Releasing Midnight's rein, he allowed his arms to swallow her small frame. He relished the taste, the feel, and the sensations of every fragment of her mouth. His hand wandered down her spine, searching, feeling, until it fit into the soft curve above her hips, slight pressure brought her closer. Her pelvis pressed against his thigh.

Her arms wrapped themselves around his neck. With intensity a tiny hand clasped the back of his head. He took it as an invitation and deepened the kiss, forcing her mouth to open beneath his. When his hand pressed her curves tighter, she wrapped one leg around the back of one of his, fusing their bodies into one. He savored each moment of the embrace. Vibrations flowed through every vein in his body.

The kiss began to weaken, but then grew with passion again. Neither wanted to separate, neither wanted the moment to end. They were locked into a trance stronger than any outside force.

Midnight whinnied, his head brushed against them. She pushed the animal away and re-wrapped her arm around his neck. Her head tilted, providing him with another opportunity to plunge deeper. Time stood still as three weeks of built up obsession overtook their senses. The embrace grew with enthusiasm.

In the distant, Jace heard someone cough, signaling an impending approach. With censure he waved a hand to discourage whoever it was from disturbing them. Replacing his hand around her waist, he lifted her into his arms and turned their occupied bodies away from the sound.

"'Scuze me, Mr. Jace, but youz gotz some men folkz here to see ya." Henry tapped him on the back. "Mr. Jace? Miz Penny?"

It was several moments before the words penetrated his mind. Unwillingly, Jace brought the kiss to an end. He lifted his lids to discover two tiny dimples, created by her content smile, highlighting her features. They made her face even more delectable.

The knuckles of one of his hands rose to caress a soft cheek. Sooty eyelashes fluttered before tugging themselves open. His thumping heart skipped a beat when her grin matched his. He pulled her head to his chest and sighed as she brought her hands down from his shoulders to wrap around his middle. Her cheek nestled into his torso. He placed a final kiss on the top of her head just as a voice interrupted his thoughts again.

"Mr. Jace?" Henry repeated.

"Yes, Henry?" Jace responded as he turned their bodies to face the hired hand. Looking beyond the old character's shoulder, he spotted three men. They must have ridden into the yard during the embrace, because they were dismounted and stood a few feet behind he and

Penny. The reason he had retuned to the ranch this afternoon became clear in his mind.

"Silas. Right on time, I see," Jace greeted. Penny's body grew stiff as a board. He increased his hold on her, wanting to protect her from any form of embarrassment. Glancing back to the hired hand, he instructed, "Thank you, Henry. Uh, please stable Miss Penny's horse."

"Iz already did." The old man jostled with laughter as he ambled off to the barn.

"Oh, right, yes, well, thank you." He needed to buy a little time. His body was wound tight. Right now his legs would not be able to climb the steps of the porch. Glancing in that direction, he spied Mary Alice, mouth agape, and Singing Dove, boasting a bright smile, standing at the top of the stairs.

"Mary Alice, will you please show our guests into the house, perhaps they would enjoy some lemonade. Penny and I will join you in a moment." Jace glanced back to Silas and sent a pleading look, asking the man to understand.

The old man let out a laugh that rolled across the prairie. Showing empathy for Jace, he started for the house. "Mary Alice, you look wonderful. How have you been? And Singing Dove, it's good to see you again." With a wave, Silas invited the other men to follow him.

"Thalo' Hunka." Singing Dove smiled at the older man.

Silas turned to the men, "That's my Lakota name, it means our adopted relative who raises beef."

Jace watched as the men nodded and climbed the stairs behind Silas. He also caught the way Singing Dove nudged Mary Alice to remove her gaze from he and Penny and acknowledge their guests.

"Uh? Oh yes, yes. Silas Osborne, how have you been? How's Sue Ellen? You gentlemen come on in now," Mary Alice greeted the men and stepped back to hold the door open for them to enter the house. She continued to send worried glimpses toward her niece.

"Here let me." Silas took the door and motioned for the two women to enter first. Turning to follow the group into the house, he glanced back to where Jace and Penny stood, and chortled, "Go ahead and take your time."

"Oh," moaned Penny. She had yet to raise her head from the comfort of his chest, mainly because his hold wouldn't allow her even the slightest movement.

Jace shifted his stance, consented for one arm to remain around her, and used the other to lift her chin upwards. "Hi," he said.

"Hi." Her smile emitted flashes of humor.

A low chuckle discharged from his chest before guilt rose. "I'm sorry."

Her brows drew together. She brought one hand up to stroke his chin. "For what?"

He let his head tilt against her hand, absorbing the caress. "For ignoring you the past three weeks, for avoiding you. For making others hold you captive. For being angry…I don't know, for everything I guess."

"For kissing me?" she asked.

"Y-No, never that." The words were out before he could think. Justification for his reactions came next. "I had to. You called me, Mr. Owens."

"Mmm…" she moaned as her hand reached around to the back of his neck, pressure forced his head toward hers. "Remind me to call you Mr. Owens more often will you?"

"All right," he mumbled and accepted her kiss before giving one of his own.

"I guess we have to go in now." Her mouth moved against his.

He tasted her words and pulled back. Tilting his head to the bright shine of the sun, he sought for more coherent thoughts. "Yeah, they are waiting for us."

"Who are the two guys with Silas?"

"They're from the stockyards in Yankton. We're working out a deal for the Cattlemen's Association." Jace allowed his hands to roam up and down her arms. He didn't want to let her go.

"Oh, were you ever going to tell me about it?"

Glancing at the house, Jace questioned himself, his thoughts. He felt her slipping away from him. It had gone on too long. He framed her face with his hands, forced her to remain in front of him. "Penny, I'm sorry. I couldn't tell you."

"Why? What did I do for you not to trust me?"

"You didn't do anything. It was me I couldn't trust. It was all me. I had to keep my distance from you. I was trying to find a way to control-uh- my lust for you."

"Your lust for me? I don't understand."

Taking a deep breath, he tried to explain, "Penny, when a man has been without a woman, in a, uh, intimate way for a long time, it's…well, it becomes more and more difficult for him to, ah, function or behave in appropriate ways."

"You've been avoiding me, staying away all day, everyday, because I make you horny?"

Jace swallowed the lump in his throat and glanced around to assure their privacy. "Penny! Where did you hear such a word?"

"From Candice." She shook her head. "That's it? You're horny. Now I really don't understand."

"Penny, I'm trying to explain. Good grief it was hard enough seeing you flouncing around the bed in layers of pink. But that next morning, here at the ranch, when you came down," he pointed at her attire, "in those. Where on earth did you ever find men's clothes that fit you like a second skin? Never mind I don't want to know. It was just more than my, my loins could take."

"I understand that part," she insisted. "I don't understand why you were avoiding me. I am your wife." She placed a hand on his chest.

Her slightest touch made the blood throb in his loins. "Penny, you don't know what you're saying."

Nodding her head, she declared, "Yes, I do."

He had to shuffle his stance, relieve some pressure. "No, you don't"

"Yes, I do. I'm your wife, you're my husband, and I want us to know each other, in every sense of the word. As a husband and wife should."

"Penny," he sighed. Shivers ran up his spine, and he gave a sickening glance at the house. "We don't have time for this right now. They're waiting. We need to go in."

Penny shrugged. Her feet joined his as they started to the house. "Okay, but I'm not going to let you keep on avoiding me. Goodness sakes, I can't even answer one of Candice's letters until we do it."

"What?" His feet stumbled.

"She assumes we have consummated our marriage. I can't write back until I have all the details she keeps asking about."

Jace couldn't help the look of shock that overcame his face. He would never be able to understand a woman's mind. "You want to make love, just so you can write to my idiotic sister-in-law about it?" A wave of emotion came over him. He wasn't quite sure what it was.

"Don't call her idiotic. She is my best friend." Glancing up she smiled, "Harebrained, yes, idiotic no." She followed him up the steps and continued, "I have to write to her about it. Her letters are so full of how Daniel makes her see fireworks-when they are in bed together-I have to have something to retaliate with."

Stopping on the wide porch Jace pulled her to him. "Promise me something?"

"Of course," she agreed.

Chapter Nine

"Don't ever, ever show me her letters." Jace said.

Glancing to the door, knowing this time alone together was almost over, Penny stretched on her tiptoes and pressed her lips to his. "Okay, Mr. Owens." She was ready to promise him the world if he was to ask for it. Being in his arms was an occurrence she wanted to experience again, over and over. It was exhilarating. And all Candice had promised it would be.

Leading the way to a very passionate embrace, she increased the pressure of her lips and forced him to participate in a kiss that left her body tingling from head to toe.

Several moments later, with her fingers entwined with his, they made their way into the office to greet their guests.

Silas finished a tale he was sharing before acknowledging their presence. "Jace. Penny, my dear." He stood to grasp Jace's hand before embracing her. "Good to see you two getting along so well," he admitted for their ears only. Turning to the other men he made the introductions of Art Reins and Bill Casper.

Mary Alice excused herself as Jace led Penny to the couch. Settling down beside her he made his intentions clear. Without a word he had assured her as well as the other occupants that she was an essential part of their meeting.

Penny participated in the assembly, providing her opinion when asked. She was intrigued by the knowledge Jace demonstrated. He was educated on exactly what the Copper Cow was willing to offer and in need of. She couldn't help but wonder where his information came from or how he had gathered it. They had barely spoken since the night of the Cattlemen's Meeting.

The deal was completed and the guests were invited

to stay for the evening meal, whereas Silas declined. Insisting Sue Ellen would have a meal waiting for them back at their ranch.

"I'll have Henry retrieve your horses," Jace offered.

"Mind if we join you?" Bill Casper asked, "We both noticed the unusual design of your barn earlier and would like to have a look at it."

"Of course, pardon me for not offering a tour earlier." Jace turned to Silas, "do you want to join us?"

"No I'll meet you outside. I need to speak with Penny," Silas said.

Jace glanced at her. She nodded in answer to his silent question. He leaned down and placed a soft kiss on her cheek. "Alright then," he said to Silas before directing the other men, "gentlemen, right this way."

She watched them leave. Silas waited until the door shut before he spoke, "So you do love him?"

"Excuse me?" she questioned.

"I wanted to believe the whole meddling sister-in-law story, but I have to tell you, I had my doubts. That is until I rode into the yard today. That was some kiss, little lady."

Feeling every once of blood rush to her cheeks, Penny buried her face in her hands. Between her fingers she proclaimed, "Silas, a gentlemen would never say such a thing!" Her pulse quickened as she imagined what he must have saw.

"I'm glad I saw it. With all the time that young man has spent away from the ranch, I was afraid you two weren't getting along." Grasping her hands, he took a deep breath before continuing, "I let you down Penny. When you needed me, I let you down. I feel real bad about that. I just want to say I'm sorry. And that it will never happen again."

"Oh, Silas, there's..." she started.

"No," he interrupted, "let me finish. "Jace made me realize how alone you had been out here. How everyone had deserted you. I all but pushed you into Luke James's arms myself. I need you to know how sorry I am about it all. I need to know that you forgive me."

Looking into the old man's face, Penny saw tears glistening in his eyes. Compassion filled her. "Oh," she sighed, "of course I forgive you." Clutching his rounded form, she laid her head on his shoulder and was engulfed into a bear hug. After a few minutes she pulled away to kiss his cheek. "And thank you, Silas."

"For what?"

"For making me send…uh, find Jace. Don't you see? If you had run to my rescue, I would have never listened to Candice and found Jace."

He appeared to mull her words over in his mind. "Hum, you have a point there, my dear, don't you?"

Nodding her head she agreed, "Yes, I do. Now come on, you better head for home or your supper will be cold." She took his hand and together they walked out to the front lawn where her husband stood with the other men who were already mounted.

Jace handed him the reins and Silas pulled himself into the saddle. He gave a parting wink to Penny, turned and said, "Oh, Jace, I forgot to mention, but I did send a message to some of the other members letting them know we will be discussing that branding idea of yours at the meeting next week."

Her husband gave an acknowledging nod and watched as the riders took their leave. "Silas seems to enjoy his role as president," he commented as she stepped closer to his side.

"Yes, he does. He's almost back to the man I use to know. I didn't even realize how much I missed him. He's a good man." Placing both hands on her hips she asked, "What branding idea?"

"I, we, Silas and I think it would be best for everyone concerned if we reconfigured the branding regulations of the association."

"Really?" She took a step back to put some distance between the magnetism that drew her to him, like a bee to pollen. "Look, Jace, this is still my ranch. I need to know what's going on around here. That deal you- that we just made with the stockyards is for a significant amount of cattle. Information I needed to know before the deal was made not during. I need your help, your assistance. I don't need you to take over my complete operation." Frustration grew as the words flew from her lips. Kicking at the dirt she glared at him. "Oh, you make me so angry!"

"Penny, calm down. I'm not trying to take over your complete operation. I was going to tell you about everything I've been doing." He tried to reach out to her.

She stepped further out of his range. "When? When did you plan on telling me?"

"Today. But when I got here you were gone. I didn't know where you were. I didn't know where to go looking for you."

"Stop right there! Don't you dare try turning everything around and make it all my fault!" Flouncing forward she pushed on his chest with both hands. "I don't need another man trying to rule my life!"

He absorbed her assault with little movement. "I'm not trying to turn anything around. But you can't just go riding off whenever you want." He grasped her hands as they shot at him a second time. "It's not safe for you to ride around by yourself." He pulled her closer and forced her gaze to remain locked onto his.

"Hey, you two! Don't start that again, come and eat before your supper gets cold!" Mary Alice shouted from the porch door.

Jace nodded in compliance at Mary Alice before looking back down. "Penny, I was going to tell you everything before they came, but you weren't here and that's the truth. Let's go have our supper and then we will have a good, long talk."

She pulled her arms from his grasp. "I have a right to know everything that's going on. Everything!" Penny turned to make her way to the house. He made her so mad. Marriage was just as she thought it would be, one more man telling her what to do. But he was the worst, telling her what she was doing after he had already done it. She wouldn't stand for it.

****

One, two, three, four…Penny counted the peas on her plate and pushed the small green orbs around with her fork. The banter and laughter surrounding the table made her ill. How had Jace found the time to interact with everyone else in the house except her? She rose with the sun, yet he would have already eaten his breakfast and left on some errand or another. A quick glimpse here or there was all she had caught of him. Waiting up late into the night, was no better, she rarely heard him come home.

But, Mary Alice, Singing Dove, even Henry, had built strong friendships with her husband. It was apparent, as those three conversed non-stop with him during the meal. Didn't he know how bad she wanted him with her? How she longed to see his smile or to hear his voice? She was the one he was supposed to be assisting. She was the reason he was there.

Under her lashes she studied him. He had filled out. The weight he had lost during his illness had been replaced and honed into muscles that rippled down his arms and chest. Tingles ran up her fingers as she recalled their exploration of his chest earlier in the day. The remembrance of their embrace caused warm liquid to flood her system. Butterflies took flight in her stomach. Her fork landed on her plate with a clatter.

All eyes flashed her way. "Sorry." She gave a nervous smile, retrieved the utensil as well as her knife and pretended to concentrate on cutting a chewable slice of her steak.

When the conversation resumed, she continued her appraisal. His shirtsleeves were rolled up to his elbows, exposing his forearms and the skin that had turned a golden bronze from the hours in the sun. She recognized the shirt as one Mary Alice had created for him last week and wondered about the rest of his attire. He must have gone to town and made a few purchases. A partial view of him in jeans, a Stetson hat and western boots, such as he was wearing now, had caught her attention the other morning. But by the time she had arrived in the barn, he and Marion were but a blur on the horizon.

Her mind recalled his afternoon comments about her apparel. Maybe tomorrow she would wear a dress. Perhaps if she started looking more like a wife he would treat her more like one. Reviewing her unused wardrobe, she chose what she would wear the following day. Then began to think of restyling her hair, one long braid couldn't be appealing to a man. A soft tap on her arm made her look up.

"Penny, Jace asked if you had finished eating," Mary Alice said. "Lands sake girl, are you alright? You haven't eaten a thing, nor have you said a word all evening."

"Sorry, I just don't have much of an appetite." She placed her napkin on the table and pushed her chair away from the table. "Yes, I'm finished."

Jace commented on the wonderful meal before he pushed himself away from the table to follow her out of the room.

Penny settled on the chair behind her desk. Her anger had subdued during the meal, but the hurt remained. Which only caused her more confusion. She couldn't understand why or how he could evoke such intense feelings in her.

Maybe you have fallen in love with him.

She glanced around the room. Who said that? Had she thought it? No, she had *heard* the words. But Jace was the only one in the room with her. He stood near the window, with his back to her, gazing into the setting sun. And the voice had been a woman's. She glanced at the door. It was shut. Insignificant, since the voice hadn't belonged to Mary Alice or Singing Dove. Yet, it did have a familiar ring to it.

"Penny? Penny? What's wrong, you look like you've just seen a ghost?" Jace questioned.

"No, uh, nothing is wrong." She closed her eyes for a moment and shook her head to clear her muddled mind. "Other than my husband has been avoiding me and keeping secrets that pertain to my ranch." She pulled her shoulders up straight, laid her arms on her desk and leveled determined eyes. "Shall we begin?"

He coughed and wiped a slight grin from his face. "First things first-earlier today when I apologized, I meant it, Penny. I am sorry for not letting you know where I've been or what I've been doing." He walked away from the window and stopping behind the couch, braced himself by placing his hands on its high back. "Part of me wanted to, part of me was excited to share it all with you. But another part of me couldn't. I know this is hard for you to understand, it's hard for me to understand." He held his hand up, asking her to hold her voice. "Please bear with me for a minute."

She nodded and he continued, "You suggested by staying here I would be getting a second chance. And you were right. I see that. I've been given an opportunity to live again. To help people, you included, and I want to do that. I really want to. And I will. I will not leave here until everything is settled." He started to walk around the sofa.

Leave? The word echoed in her mind as she watched his approach. His nearness made her pulse begin to race. She didn't rebuke his movements when he reached down to clasp one of her hands, nor questioned when he knelt beside her chair.

"Please forgive me, Penny. I should never have let this afternoon happen. I won't let it happen again, I promise. I hope you can understand what I am saying. But I can't be your husband in every sense of the word."

She tried to speak but no words would come out. A few small gasps stilled in her lungs, making it difficult to exhale. A burning sensation filled her chest. She closed her eyes as he continued.

"I hope you can see this isn't just about me. It's about you too. I'm not the husband you deserve. I'm not the husband of your choosing. Trust me someday you'll find that man. You're going to fall in love with him and he with you. You'll want to spend the rest of your lives together." His other hand rose to brush against her face. "I'm not that man, Penny, nor can I ever be him. I can't stay at the Copper Cow forever. I have to return to Philadelphia. I have responsibilities there, just as you do here. Please tell me you understand. I don't want to hurt you. I just want to be honest with you."

She squeezed her eyes, forcing the imminent tears to withdraw. Her mind raced, knowing he waited for her response. You can do this, she silently encouraged.

"Y-Yes, Jace. I understand what you are saying. I appreciate your honesty." Pulling her hand away from his, she clasped both of hers together and laid them on her lap. Deep down she knew it had been too easy. He was too perfect. The whole mail order husband idea, her knight in shinning armor, had been too easy, too simple. Life wasn't meant to be easy. Turning her face away from the soft strokes of his other hand, her heart convulsed. One word stuck. It hurt. Breathing through the pain, she asked, "When will you be l-leaving?"

"Leaving?"

"Yes, when will you be leaving?" she repeated.

"Not for a while, I plan on staying around until everything with James is taken care of."

"You put Luke in his place at the meeting. He hasn't been around since. You have a deal happening for all of the ranchers around to sell cattle and Silas is back in charge of the Association. I'd say you have pretty well completed your part of our bargain." Penny couldn't bring herself to look at him. The wind had been knocked out of her. This confession of his was the last thing she had expected after their passionate encounter.

"Luke may have been put in his place at the meeting, but it is not over. This is more like the calm before the storm. James will retaliate and believe me- it will be severe when it happens. I will not leave until I know you are safe." He rose and began to pace around the room. Several glances came her way.

Her temples began to throb, blood pounded at every pulse point on her body. The noise was so loud in her ears she had a hard time hearing his words.

"Penny, I know it will be somewhat difficult to explain when I leave. I will try to make it as easy as possible. I'll think of something to tell everyone." His back was to her as he stood at the window. "It won't be for a while yet. Rest assured, I will not leave until everything is taken care of." He turned back to the room. "It'll work out."

Their embrace from earlier flashed through her mind. The way her body had molded against his. The way his kisses touched the inner core of her soul. She pushed the thoughts aside and mustered all the courage she had left as pain pulled at her heart.

"Y-yes, I'm sure you are right, it will all work out. I do understand what you are saying. I appreciate all you have accomplished and your commitment to stay on for a while longer."

Pressing three fingers against the pain in her temple, she paused for a moment and tried to force her mind to focus on the ranch. Minutes seemed to have ticked by before she could reposition her posture.

"Perhaps now you should tell me about this branding

issue Silas mentioned earlier. It is imperative I know about everything happening around here."

Jace stopped pacing in front of her desk. Her posture as she sat in the massive chair was stately. She held her head high, chin-up, and looked him squarely in the eye. He knew her self-resolve had returned. His eyes connected with hers. Neither spoke as they observed one another.

The first to pull away, Jace took a seat on the sofa and began, "I agree with what you told me at the hotel, that Luke is behind the rustlings. His new establishment, the Lucky J Ranch seems to have several thousand head of cattle, yet no bills of sales have been recorded with the Association. Nor have there been any recordings of the drives he claims to have participated in. The Lucky J is quite a distance northwest and I suspect a good hiding spot for stolen cattle."

He could tell he had her full attention. "Every ranch around has lost a few head, however the Copper Cow has had the greatest loss. I've suggested to Silas that all of the ranches, which have had significant losses, consider re-configuring their brands. Not the dimensions, but where they place the brand on their cattle. For example, if the Copper Cow was to brand all of our, uh, your cattle on the right front shoulder instead of the left flank, where everyone else places their brands, it will be much more difficult for the rustlers to double brand. Once all of the brands and their locations are recorded with the Association, besides the rustling issue, tracking open range cattle and multiple sales will be much more manageable."

Penny's look was thoughtful as she nodded, "An ingenious idea. How do others feel about it?"

"Very favorable so far. At this point Silas is deciding whom to tell about it, and encouraging them to keep it under their hats until the meeting. We don't want James getting word of it quite yet."

"So when do we start re-branding?" Her hands folded together on top of the desk, they were ultra slim with trim nails highlighting their fineness.

Jace had felt guilty while making decisions about the Copper Cow without her input. But she was so tiny and seemed so helpless and alone. Someone he wanted to protect from the world's harshness. At the same time, a sixth sense told him that if he didn't keep his distance from her, his over zealous infatuation would win the battle it was having with the more sensible parts of his mind and body. He knew he needed to get the situation under control and head back to Philadelphia, before he did something that ultimately would not be in her best interest. "I uh, I sent Sam and Calhoun up to the north ridge yesterday to start."

"The north ridge! Oh my, I forgot all about it!" She leaped out of the chair and strode to the map on the wall.

"Forgot about what?"

"Your first, no, that day when you woke up and Luke followed me home? The day of the meeting, you know." Her eyes fluttered his way.

"Yes, I recall the day."

"I had ridden up to the north ridge, just trying to figure out a way to tell you how you ended up at my ranch. I never ride in the hills. I always stay in open spaces. But that day for whatever reasons, I ended up in the hills." Her brows drew together in thought before she turned and focused on the map in front of her. "I found a branding fire just about right here. Which would make perfect sense if the Lucky J is up here." She pointed to a spot on the map.

"Look," she invited Jace to join her with a wave of her hand. "He could be rustling cattle from just about anywhere, gather them into the north ridge of the Copper Cow and then drive them northwest to his new place." Covering an area of the map with her hand she continued, "There is really nothing throughout this whole area…except…"

"Except what?" Jace saw the way her eyes glazed over. "Penny?"

"Except the four farms that were attacked. One was right here, but the other three were over here. Two in this area and one more, the O'Brien's, was more to the north, about here. Their locations made no sense to me before because the James Ranch is over here, south of the first one." She slapped her hand against the side of her leg. "But now I see they were all near the Lucky J. I knew he was behind it all."

"Penny, we can't jump to conclusions. We don't have any solid proof."

"Yet! We don't have any solid proof, yet. It's out there. I know it is. Just like I knew he was behind all of this. I was right." Turning around in a circle, she said it again. "Did you hear that, Jace? I was right!"

"Yes, Penny, I heard," he answered.

Flaying her head from side to side, she mocked words others must have thrown at her the past six months. "Be a good girl and go home now." Changing the tone of her voice to match each statement, she continued her act. "You don't know what you're talking about, girl. Penny why don't you marry Luke? He's asked you several times." Making a grimace, she whirled back to him. "No one believed me." She tilted her head and looked him in the eye. "But you believed me right off. That first night in the hotel room, you believed me. Why?"

Jace nodded his head, having watched her transformation take place again. There were more sides to her than a marquee-cut diamond. She would forever fascinate him with each and every one. For some reason he thought how it felt to be useful. These past weeks he had created goals and was making great strides in meeting them. He had once again found satisfaction and purpose in his life- he understood her excitement at being right. His hands itched to encompass her into an embrace, to share her victory. He squeezed them into fists and released them several times. She was waiting for his answer. It was simple. "Because of your conviction. I believed you, because you—believed you."

"Oh.... Well, thank you." Her head bowed. "Jace, if I told you something else I believe, would you believe me?"

He was afraid, fearful of what she was going to say. His emotions were raw. But he knew he had done the right thing. Or at least he had to believe he was doing the right thing. A life back East waited his return. He would help her get everything settled. Then leave her, unsoiled, so when she found the right man, she would have a husband who could love her, as she deserved to be loved. He had resolve, but he needed her help to be able to control his desire for her. This was more difficult than he had imagined. He wouldn't be able to resist the words she was going to say. That she believed she loved him. He didn't want her to love him. He couldn't let that happen. "Penny, I-uh,"

"Luke killed my father," she interrupted in a whisper. Her frame whirled around and buckled onto the couch.

Shocked, he stood still. Relief and foolishness flowed through his loins as his mind accepted a declaration that was nowhere close to his thoughts. Concern followed. "Penny, I said before, we have no proof of anything."

Her body was motionless. The need to comfort her was strong. He wanted to wrap her in his arms, but fought the urge.

Her hands rose to cover her face. "I don't need any proof. I know it. I know it in my heart." She pushed on her eyelids with two fingers. He knew she held in tears. "Dad figured out Luke's scheme. I knew he knew something, but he wouldn't tell me."

Jace didn't know what to say. He thought James was behind her father's death too. He was the one who found the ether rag. For the second time in his life, he felt hopeless; there was nothing he could do to ease her pain. Just as there had been nothing he could do for Karin. He hated the feeling.

Her hands fell to her knees. "Want to know what else I think? I think Luke made his own father sick. He would have killed him too, but Susan Leigh figured it out and took Bob to Europe. She's not Luke's real mom. She died years ago, but I don't remember much about it. I think her name was Olivia or something like that. I'll have to ask Mary Alice, she might remember..."

She's rambling now, he thought, *she's becoming overwrought.* "Penny, I think you've had enough for one evening. I'll ask Mary Alice to help you prepare for bed."

Holding one hand up, she declined his offer. "I don't need any help getting ready for bed. I've been going to bed by myself for many years now. " Her cheeks puffed as she blew the air from her lungs. "And will continue to do so for many more." She rose from the couch and sidestepped his vicinity, to study the map. "What I do need- is to know why. What was Luke hoping to gain from all this?"

"Greed," Jace surmised.

"No," Penny disagreed, "well, yes, Luke is greedy, but there is more behind it than greed. How do the Lakota play into all of this? He's doing more than just trying to pin the blame on them."

Jace twisted to look over her shoulder. Searching to give her an answer, he studied the map until his eyes blurred. His brain felt tired.

"Oh well," she turned and skirted around him. A friendly slap hit his shoulder. "You're right. It has been a long day. I'm tired. Good-night, Jace."

Speechless, he watched as she glided from the room.

Chapter Ten

Jace couldn't breathe. Dead air locked his lungs. Try as he might, he couldn't expel it. One hand clawed at his throat in an attempt to massage the air out. The other clung to the back of the hall chair for support. His eyes bulged and refused to blink. He felt as if he might pass out any second...

A hard slap on his back forced the air out with a loud swoosh. He gasped for fresh air, which caused a coughing spasm that brought tears to his eyes.

"Looks pretty good, don't she?" Sam stated, having been a few moments behind in following Jace through the front door. "Hi ya, Princess!" the old man greeted the woman at the top of the staircase.

"Hi, Sam," Penny answered and she began her descent. The disbelieving look on her husband's face was just the reaction she'd been engrossed in creating. Her handiwork had taken all of the morning and half of the afternoon. The bellows of her lungs were forced to take small, short breaths, due to the unrelenting corset constricting her ribs. But if she was reading his coughing spasm right, it had been worth it. "Hi, Jace," she let his name curl off her tongue.

Jace waved a hand in a slight greeting, it was clear he still attempted to restrain the coughs tearing out of his throat and chest.

"Want me to get the buggy instead of the horses you had Henry saddle?" Sam asked her husband.

Overhearing the question, Penny intervened, "I've ridden in a dress before, it shouldn't be a problem."

She felt the way his blue eyes scrutinized the breasts she had arranged to reveal all the cleavage they had to offer. Jace quivered and shook his head. "No! Y-yes, get the buggy, Sam." Under his breath, she heard him whisper, "Where the hell did they come from?"

Her face felt warm with embarrassment as Sam's laughter floated in the air before the old man exited. He must have heard the comment as well. She was somewhat fearful the orbs might pop out of the decadent neckline, but excitement filled her with the knowledge that Jace had noticed her female attributes.

Penny took her time, sliding down the stairs one at a time. Now very confident in the image she had produced. Bringing her chin up, she caught her husband's uncontrolled stare and gave a slight toss of her head, letting her hair catch the rays of sun from the open doorway.

Her long tresses hung in spirals down her back. The front sections had been pulled back and secured with delicate, silver combs at her crown, leaving minuscule amounts of wispy tendrils to form alluring corkscrews in front of each ear.

She wore a dress of the darkest navy blue, which transformed to shades of purple and black as it caught the faintest bits of light. The bodice formed a second skin over the shape-forming corset and extended down to form a deep v between her hips. At her waist the skirt flowed out from beneath the v and allowed yards of the magical fabric to flow around her ankles. Tiny white ruffles peeked out near her toes and around the bottom of the sleeves as they ended at her elbows, and along the bare cleavage of her upper body.

She glided to a halt in front of Jace and purred, "Honestly, I don't mind if you prefer to ride."

He started coughing again.

"Mary Alice, will you please bring Jace a glass of water? It appears he's swallowed a bug," Penny instructed toward the closed kitchen door.

Jace shook his head and nodded at the same time. Pulling his eyes from her, he seemed to collapse onto the chair he had been leaning against. He took the proffered glass as soon as it arrived and gulped the contents.

"Lands sake, Jace, don't you know you can't walk around with your mouth open?" Turning to Penny, Mary Alice fussed like a mother hen. "Here dear, I've pressed the strings of your bonnet. Let me put it on for you." Glancing back at the stoop of Jace's back, her aunt questioned, "Doesn't she look magnificent, Jace?"

"Yes," his voice was a slight whimper.

Penny hoped she hadn't gone too far. She wanted to have his full attention, but he appeared to be in pain. After the bonnet was settled on her head, she asked, "Shall we go? Henry just pulled the buggy up."

Jace handed the empty glass to Mary Alice, and rose to his feet. Penny flashed him a coy smile. His face was red, and his arm quivered when she wrapped her elbow through it. At a slow pace, they exited the house and proceeded down the steps. Breathing seemed to be as difficult for him as it was for her.

Mary Alice babbled farewells as they climbed onto the leather seat of the carriage. Penny gave her aunt and Henry a departing wave and settled into her rightful position next to Jace.

It took the better part of an hour before a cold stone voice spoke. "Aren't you afraid you'll catch a chill?"

Holding up a piece of folded fabric, tempting him to look her way, Penny answered, "I brought a shawl along."

"You're not playing fair, Penny."

"Excuse me?"

"You heard me."

You haven't seen anything yet, Mr. Owens, Penny thought to herself as she ignored his statements.

She had lain awake, long after leaving the office that dreadful night a week ago. Reflecting upon their conversation. At first her thoughts had been filled with Luke, her father, the Lakota, all the worries that had encompassed her life the past months. Then she had heard the voice again, the words. *Maybe you have fallen in love with him.* She tried pushing them aside, ignoring them, snubbing them, but nothing work. The voice kept repeating the words over and over.

Giving in she tried conversing with the voice, asking questions, demanding a response. At first there was nothing. Then it came again, but she was a little girl and it was singing to her. Visions had floated around her. She recognized the woman with long, blond hair flowing in the wind as they danced together in the tall prairie grass. It was her mother. Whether, she was asleep and dreaming, or awake and envisioning, she still didn't know. Didn't care. Charlotte had come to her every night since. Together, they reviewed, evaluated, conspired, plotted, and resolved Penny's life.

Everything else would now take the back seat to her, no- their plan of making her husband fall in love with her. Luke James, the Copper Cow, the Lakota, the Association, everything except Jace's love, seemed insignificant to her.

Deep in thought, scrutinizing the execution of her handiwork and savoring the forth-coming victory, Penny didn't comprehend Jace's words.

"Excuse me?" she questioned.

"We will be talking about the railroad at the meeting tonight."

"Oh?" She attempted to sound interested.

"Yes, one of my investments is the Northern Pacific, my friend Charles, the judge, wired me the most recent report. The government sent out a survey team to route the track through the Dakota Territory earlier this year. It will go through Fargo and up to Bismarck. I'm afraid folks are not going to respond to my findings very well. Not after all of James's talk."

"What about the Southern Dakota? The tracks into Yankton were completed this year. It will continue west, won't it?"

"For a short distance, but then turn and run north, connecting with the Northern Pacific. The survey team discovered the most practical place to cross the Missouri River would be at Bismarck."

Jace never removed his eyes from the road, but Penny could see how the corner of his eyes continued to float to her breasts. She was now fairly confident the tight corset wouldn't allow them to be jostled out of her dress as the buggy rolled over the rough road. She let her shoulder brush against his as he steered around a deep rut. He all but leaped from the wagon at the contact. His large frame pressed against the small metal seat rail. His look sent daggers her way.

She rolled her eyes to the sky and settled back against the seat. "Yes, well, I guess that is understandable. It will be disappointing for the town to hear though. Luke's tales were quite promising."

Jace wiggled against the backrest. "James was foreseeing a cow town. I know you've heard of Abilene, Kansas. The cattle enterprise there turned a peaceful little town into hell on earth overnight. The whole town became nothing but saloons, gambling houses and brothels. Wild Bill Hickok was hired as the marshal after their first lawman, Tom Smith, was murdered. Hickok settled down the gunplay, but didn't do anything to clean up the town. It wasn't until earlier this year, when the completion of additional railroad lines caused Wichita and Ellsworth to be more favorable shipping points that things began to calm down for the citizen's of Abilene."

"Yes, I believe I have heard of Abilene." She was trying to be interested in what he said, but it was difficult. Her mind was more concerned with how he was reacting to her. It appeared she had frazzled his nerves. Was that a good sign or a bad sign? She looked at how the toes of his high boots tapped against the floorboard. Her eyes wandered up the long legs, over the lean torso and onto his profile. His cheek was twitching. A confident grin covered her face.

The look he tossed her was one of distrust as he continued his tale. "Things are better there now. A man by the name of T.C. Henry has planted a new derivate of wheat near Abilene. He's decreed it 'winter wheat' and it appears to be very successful. He proclaims the deserts of Kansas will soon become the breadbasket of the nation. Actually, I think, w-, uh, you, uh, the Copper Cow would be proactive in researching and investing in this winter wheat crop. The plants would thrive on these plains."

"Really?" Penny tried to make her voice sound demure and fluttered her lashes as she spoke, "You certainly are a knowledgeable man, Jace."

He rolled his eyes at her. "Being a veterinarian is much more than healing sick animals. It also includes knowing how to keep them healthy. To guarantee environments and foods are providing them with the nutrients, vitamins and minerals they need to thrive. It is also important to stay current on all aspects of society, everything that happens influences the world we live in," his words trailed to a stop as if his train of thought had left.

"Yes, yes, I see what you are saying. It's all quite complex isn't it? Truly amazing even."

"Penny!" He lifted the reins and encouraged the mare to pick up her pace.

"What?" she questioned with faint-hearted ignorance.

"You're…you…never mind."

****

"Mrs. Owens, it appears married life is suiting you very well," Sheriff Wilcox greeted as they walked through the doorway.

Penny's voice twinkled with delight. "Why thank you Sheriff. Yes, I must say, I never imagined married life could be so satisfying."

Jace felt the blood rush to his face as well as other significant areas of his body. Using quick movements, he wrapped an arm around his wife's shoulders and used the span of his hand to pull the material of her shawl together, concealing the focus of the Sheriff's vision. "Wilcox," he greeted as he forced Penny to continue making their way into the room.

"I have had just about all I can take," he growled when they arrived at the front row of chairs.

"What? What did I do now? You've been grumpy with me all evening. Ever since we left the ranch. I was merely saying hello to the Sheriff."

"No you weren't. You know exactly what you are doing, and I…"

"Jace, Penny my dear," Silas greeted them from behind. "I apologize for not making it in time to dine with you. Sue Ellen just wasn't up for a trip to town."

Penny flashed him a coy smile before she turned to the old man, accepted his peck on her cheek and asked with sincere concern, "Oh, is she ill?"

"No, no, just ah, ah, a woman thing." Silas extended a hand in greeting to him.

Jace stalled, his mind swirled. He would have to let go of the corner of fabric he had pulled across Penny's bosom and held in place at her shoulder, to shake Silas hand.

After the long journey to town, he had insisted she cover herself before climbing down from the buggy. The thin material she called a shawl, gave little protection and the slippery fabric seemed unable to stay put. Though he knew he couldn't completely fault the material, his conniving little wife had a lot to do with it.

Her breasts bulged above a tiny stripe of lace, enticing every male eye for miles around to take in the splendor of them. She was stunning and every pour of his body was aware she was a woman. A woman he couldn't touch.

"Please give her our best. I was looking forward to visiting with her." Penny's words were sincere, and snapped Jace back to the present. He brought his eyes to the older man and with regret, let go of the fabric to clasp the other man's outstretched hand.

"I will my dear." Silas answered Penny, turned to him and continued, "Son, would you take a look at tonight's agenda for me?"

Jace nodded and waited until Silas stepped up on the temporary stage to make his way to the podium before assisting Penny onto her chair. "You stay right here and don't move a muscle!" With both hands he pulled the material tight around her shoulders and thought about folding it into a knot across her bosom. Instead, he grabbed her hand and mandated her fingers to grasp the corners together.

Penny let out an exaggerated "humph," as he left her side to join Silas.

They spent several minutes in conversation about the order of the meeting when the older man quit responding. Jace observed eyes that were all but popping out of Silas's head. Following their gaze, he witnessed his wife conversing with two ranchers.

Her shawl, once again fell of her shoulders, and now the ends covered nothing more than her elbows. It took a hard nudge, harder than he approved, to redirect the old man's eyes. "Silas, start the meeting!" he ordered.

The clap of his boots gathered the ranchers' attention and they took their leave before he arrived at his wife's side. "Damn it, Penny!"

"What?" she matched his hoarse whisper with one of her own.

"Cover yourself and don't you dare let that material fall off your shoulders again." When her lips opened to speak, he shook his head with frustration. "No, don't say a word. And don't give me that look. If I see an inch of skin again I will ban you from this meeting myself."

With both hands, he pulled the material around her upper body until the large triangle of the back of the shawl was over her bosom. Then gathered both ends in one hand and held them in place in the middle of her back with a firm grasp. He ignored the way her lips pinched together as she held her protest.

It was several long minutes before his mind and body could focus on the meeting at hand.

****

"But Mr. Owens, it's really storming out there. The missus has a room ready for you and your wife," Mr. Larsen insisted as Jace propelled Penny across the lobby.

Annoyed, Jace pulled the front door open. It took both hands to force it shut again in order to protect the room from the sheets of rain hammering against the outside of the building. "How did you orchestrate that?" he grumbled and escorted Penny to the hotel desk.

Without another word, he took the key from the smiling Mr. Larsen and registered their stay. Irritation ate at him as he led her up the stairs and into the prepared room.

"You know your little game could back fire!" A haphazard toss forced the key to land on the table with a loud clank after he locked the door. Trying to control his anger, he stomped to the window and drew the curtain back. Long flashes of lightening highlighted the torrential rain.

"I don't know what you're talking about." Her voice came from where she stood positioning her bonnet and shawl on familiar wall hooks. "I've ridden in the rain before. If you insist that we proceed home tonight that's fine with me. I won't melt."

Jace refused to look her way. His pounding loins couldn't take much more. "And have the whole town talking about my mistreatment of you? I don't think so, my dear. You've already sent enough tongues waving with that outrageous get up you're wearing."

"I'll have you know this dress is the top of fashion."

"Brothel fashion maybe!"

"Mr. Owens!"

"Don't! Don't even go there, Penny!"

She crossed the room and struck a match to light the lamp on the table. Several minutes later he sensed her approach the window. The air around him filled with sweet scents. He could hear her breathing even before she whispered a shy request, "Could you please unhook me?"

"No, you can just sleep in the damn thing." He refused to pull his attention from the storm.

"Jace, I couldn't possibly sleep in it. I can barely breathe in it. Please."

Her words did sound sincere. Compassion filled his chest and letting out a deep sigh, he turned to make quick work of the small hooks that formed a long trail from her shoulders to her hips.

"The corset too, please."

His fingers throbbed, refusal formed in his throat, then he noticed deep red lines the constraining garment had made below her exposed shoulder blades. Without further complaint, he found the strings near her waist and untied the undergarment. He heard the air leave her lungs with a satisfying flow as he continued to loosen the interlacing cord that criss-crossed up her back.

"Oh, thank you!" Her gratitude was sincere. She walked to the far side of the bed and sat down to remove her shoes. When done she said, "Please douse the light."

Exhausted, Jace followed her instructions and waited for her to remove her outer clothing. Flashes of lightening highlighted her scantly clad body as it climbed between the sheets. Tension tore at his muscles. He looked about the room. A stiff backed chair, hard wooden floor, or soft mattress, he did have a choice. The top of his head tingled. He rubbed against the sensation. Keeping his guard up, he crossed the room to place his stiff frame on top of the quilt.

"Aren't you going to undress?" Penny asked.

"No!"

"Well, could you at least crawl under the covers? Your weight is pulling them off of me."

He felt like a cork had just popped and flipped off the bed, "Penny," he started.

"Now what?"

Standing in the darkened room, he shook his legs, one at a time, hoping to relieve some pressure. He couldn't stop his voice from quivering as he forced the words out. "I'm not going to make love to you just so you can write Candice about it."

"I don't want you to make love to me *just* so I can write to Candice about it. I want you to make love to me because I am your wife."

His legs almost buckled. He ran a hand through his hair. This was almost more than he could take. He was close to breaking, his mind searched for realism. "No, no, I am not your husband. We may have a piece of paper that says we are married, but it's not authentic. It is valid, but we are not really married. It is a situation we were both cajoled into. Believe me, it's not what you want. It isn't what you think you want. And I won't be enticed into making love, so please stop this game you are playing."

It was several moments before she responded, "I am exhausted, Jace. Could we please just go to sleep?"

She was crying, he could hear it in her voice. *Well good for her!* Throwing the covers out of his way, not caring that they landed on her in a heap, he crawled into the bed. He tried hard to stay angry, but he hadn't meant to make her cry. And lying next to her, made his blood pressure rise with something far from anger. He flipped onto his side and wrapped a hand around the corner post of the headboard. The other one, he used to clutch onto the bottom of the mattress. With optimism he prayed for sleep.

****

Jace pulled the delicate, supple form closer into his embrace and nuzzled silky hair with his chin. Inhaling the sweet scent he indulged in the sensations as the morning light began to waken his conscience.

His eyes fluttered as visions filed across his mind. They popped open and another body part jolted. He looked down at his predicament. Penny's body enveloped his. Her face pressed against his right shoulder. Breath flowing between pink lips tickled his skin. One arm stretched across his torso and soft fingers cupped his opposite shoulder, which allowed her breasts to be plastered onto his chest. His arm was wrapped about her shoulders, beneath the long tendrils of curls that flowed across both of them. One of her silky legs draped across his trunk and her folded knee lay directly atop his manhood, while the other wrapped around his knee.

Her body tumbled across the sheets as he jolted out of the bed and stumbled to the chair.

"What, uh?" Startled, Penny pulled sleepy eyes open. "Oh, is it morning already?"

"Yes, the storm is over. We need to head for home," he said while trembling fingers tried to hold the high leather boots still enough for his feet to slip into. He snatched the key off of the table and added, "I'll send Mrs. Larsen up to help you dress."

Within minutes, he loaded his wife into their buggy and set the mare on a quick pace. The ride home was quieter than the ride to town had been. Thankfully, after several attempts at conversation, Penny gave up and left him in peace. His mind had enough to deal with, without answering her frivolous questions.

****

Two weeks later Penny pleaded, "Please, Singing Dove, I've tried everything I can think of." The two women knelt, a few rows apart, harvesting the final remains of vegetables out of the garden beds.

"Hiya," Singing Dove once again shook her head and declined Penny's repeated request.

On her hands and knees Penny crawled across the ground and stalled the other woman's digging. As tiny tears of frustration fell from her eyes she admitted, "I don't know what else to do. If you know of another way, tell me. If not, please give him the *phejuta*. Just a little bit. I know that's all it will take."

Singing Dove drew her body into a sitting position and used the corners of her apron to wipe the dirt from her hands. Penny watched as the light brown hands rose to brush the tears from her damp cheeks. Silently, she pleaded again.

A sigh left Singing Doves lips as she framed Penny's face. She felt her eyes grow wide with shock as her stepmother murmured, "O han."

"O han? Okay?" Penny questioned and translated the answer.

"Han." Singing Dove nodded. "I give *Maka Wichasha* the *phejuta*."

"Yes, you will give Jace the medicine?" Penny interpreted Singing Dove's words. She wrapped her arms around the other woman with elation. "Thank you! Thank you!" Her lips placed a quick kiss on Singing Dove's cheek before she scrambled to her feet and ran toward the house. Stopping mid-way she used her thumb and finger to demonstrate size. "Remember just a little, he will only need a little. Oh, and can you do it tonight?"

"Han," Singing Dove acknowledged before she resumed her digging.

****

Jace felt his defenses rise as soon as he entered the kitchen. Penny was once again dressed to the hilt in another outrageous, shameful, absolutely stunning gown. At least this one was modest enough that he didn't need to fear any insignificant movement would expose something. He refused to meet her gaze as he turned to the other woman in the kitchen.

For a moment he wondered about the way Singing Dove refused to acknowledge his entrance, but brushed it off. "Mary Alice, I informed Sam and Jim that they will be joining us in the house for their meals from now on. It's getting too cold for you to continue carrying plates to the bunkhouse. It appears we may have an early winter."

"Alright, Jace. I'll set the extra places. I always enjoy when winter arrives and there's time for visiting after the evening meal," she said as she rearranged the settings already situated on the long table. "But don't let this old Dakota weather fool your eastern senses. There is still plenty of autumn ahead of us."

Hours later, he felt a great sense of relief as he made his way up the stairs to his bedroom. For all of her personal preparations, Penny didn't seem to have an alternative motive this evening. All occupants of the ranch had shared an enjoyable meal followed with animated conversation, in the back parlor, before calling it a night.

He was aware of her plan of making him fall in love with her. It was as apparent as if she had printed it in the weekly newspaper. Part of him was honored. To have her love would be a privilege few men could compare with. Part of him was miserable, for her plan had worked. Not only was in love with her, but also loved each and every part of her being from his deepest core. He'd even be willing to surmise her plan hadn't been needed. He'd fallen in love with her weeks ago. The exact moment was branded in mind. It had happened at that first association meeting, when she had rushed to his arms after he had dethroned James. At that moment, the wall around his heart had crumbled, and she had filled it to the inner most corners.

Yet, he couldn't act on it. He could never let her know his feelings, nor could he encourage her to fall in love with him.

It wasn't in his bargain. The bargain he had made with himself and with the outside force that gave him this second chance at life. He had promised he would never take another drop of whiskey, promised to walk a straight, narrow, and honest line, promised to help others, and promised to leave her-unscathed. Leave her as untouched as she had been when he arrived. She deserved the opportunity to fall in love and give herself to the man of her choice, not one that had been mailed to her. She deserved a man who had never been broken by life. She had the right to find true happiness.

Deep in thought he entered his room and prepared for another long, sleepless night.

Penny heard heavy footfalls travel past her door. Excitement rippled through her body. She knew he would need a few minutes to prepare himself and also believed he would wait until all of the other occupants of the house retired before coming to her.

The evening's events flashed across her mind. She had sat amongst the other house members; professing interest in the garment she was creating. The number of times she pricked herself with the sewing needle now left her with a sore finger. The final stab had drawn significant blood and provided her with the excuse she needed to retire to her room.

The additional time had been used well. Her hair was brushed until it fell like silk on the sheer muslin that shrouded her maiden form. Several candles were positioned to cast the room in a romantic glow. Propping the pillows of her bed one last time, she climbed onto the softness of the feather mattress, situated each limb to create the exotic picture she had in her mind, and waited for the knock that was sure to come.

Singing Dove's medicine was the best, all of her family talked about the love potion she could create. Penny had heard about it for years, though never once did she ever believe she would be the one to use it. Smiling, she glanced around at the romantic atmosphere she'd produced and sighed.

A grimace formed on her forehead. Did she want it this way? Would Jace's love for her be real and lasting? Or would it end when the medicine wore off? She shook her head and tried to make the thoughts flee from her mind. It was too late to worry about that now. He should be knocking on her door any minute.

Hours later, after climbing in and out of the bed numerous times, she pulled the door open and listened for movement before she slipped into the hall. Light steps scurried her down the walkway to where she stopped and listened outside his door. Her hand shook as she turned the knob. A click echoed into the dark night, she pushed it open. The sound of his deep, even breathing hit her ears. Dismayed, she crossed the room to gape at his sleeping form.

Penny stood motionless, overcome with astonishment. He was stretched out on the bed. The sheet was tossed back and covered only his lower body. His head was supported by both of the feather pillows. One arm was raised and folded over his dark hair, the other strewed across the empty area beside him. Long feet stuck out from below the sheet near the bottom of the goose down mattress. It was apparent he was sound asleep. On tiptoes, she backed out of the room and let the door slip shut.

Once in the hallway, frustration took over. She stomped down the carpeted hall and slammed the door of her room, not caring who heard the loud bang. Flopping onto her bed, the girl, or maybe it was the frustrated woman, within, let pent up tears flow onto the still propped pillows.

****

"Han," Singing Dove repeated while nodding her head.

"Will you quit trying to tell me it worked?" Penny said as she followed her stepmother around the kitchen. "Don't you think I would know if it worked?"

Singing Dove stopped when they were on the other side of the room. "*Maka Wichasha* drank from the wrong cup."

"What do you mean he drank from the wrong cup?" Penny asked, and then shouted across the room, "Mary Alice will you stop that nauseating singing!" Her gaze came back to Singing Dove. "The wrong cup? Someone else drank it? Who? If Jace didn't drink it, who did?"

"*Wichah`cala*."

"Wic..." Penny translated the word in her mind, the old man, before she screeched in disbelief, "Sam?"

Mary Alice looked at the other women. "What about Sam, Dear?"

"Nothing," Penny assured her aunt and turned back to Singing Dove. "If Sam drank it, how can you say that it worked?"

Her gaze followed as Singing Dove looked at Mary Alice who flipped ham slices as they sizzled in the frying pan. Skirted hips swayed to the sound of the love song she was singing.

Realization hit Penny. Her voice wrenched the air. "Mary Alice?"

A fork clattered against the cast iron of the stove with a loud clang before it bounced to the floor. "What?" Mary Alice shot a worried glance their way.

"Oh! Oh, nothing-everything!" Penny exclaimed. Frustrated she stomped to the door and gave it a hard shove. "Get out of my way!" she advised when encountering Jace just on the other side of the door.

Chapter Eleven

An hour later Jace approached his wife as she led Midnight out of the barn. “Where are you going?”

“On a ride.” She settled a foot into the stirrup and flung her body onto the horse.

He grabbed the reins to lead horse and rider back into the barn. “I’ll go with you.”

Her attempts to pull the horse’s head from his grasp failed. “I don’t want you to go with me. I would prefer to ride alone.” Green eyes glared down at him.

“And I would prefer you didn’t ride alone. Besides, I want you to show me where you found that branding fire.” He could tell she was mad about something, but she appeared too tired to fight with him, probably because she’d been sneaking around the house in the middle of the night.

Keeping a close eye on her, he accepted the saddled Marion from Henry and together the horses trotted out of the ranch yard. Without conversation they rode across the prairie and into the hills. The ride was steady and even, she didn’t push Midnight to break away and Jace enjoyed the silent companionship of the trip. An hour or so later she led the way to a small clearing.

He dismounted and explored the hoof trodden ground. The grass had been trampled, not once but consecutive times. “You were right, Penny. It is a branding fire and it has been well used.” Jace looked around, wondering why he hadn’t discovered it during one his many explorations. “It is well hidden from all angles and just as you suggested. The hills form a natural corral.”

“Of course I was right,” she said, but without her usual self-confidence. “Now let’s get out of here.”

Jace studied the way her horse pranced about. With care he approached the animal, making soft soothing noises until he grasped the leather rein running along its black neck. He stroked the horse.

"Penny, what's wrong? You're so nervous your alarming Midnight." Her eyes flashed about, from mound to mound. He placed a hand on her knee, drawing her eyes to his.

"Nothing's wrong. I just don't like riding in the hills, that's all." She wiped her palms, one at a time on the cotton cloth of her pants. "Can we leave, please?"

Jace noted the crack of her voice and agreed. "Okay, we can leave now."

Midnight took off like a bullet as soon as he let go of the leather. With precision Jace threw himself onto his horse and hunched down in the saddle to pursue the pair.

Marion worked hard, but they couldn't gain any ground in catching the other animal. Horse and rider were but a blur ahead. The team leaped over boulders and rushed down the steep declines. Their pace scared him. Even their impressible accuracy failed to offer any relief to his fear. It wasn't until they encountered the wide-open space of the prairie that the duo slowed.

Marion drew closer, and Jace grabbed the rein of her horse to bring them all to a skidding halt. Flipping his leg over the saddle horn, he wrapped an arm around her waist and gave her body a hard tug. Her limber form connected with his. Soft mounds and valleys pressed against him as they landed on the ground between their mounts.

Her hands grasped his forearms as her body slid along his. Her fingers tightened to stabilize her stance when her feet touched the ground after the hard landing. "What are you doing?" she asked.

"What am I doing? What the hell where you doing racing out of the hills like that? If Midnight had barely stumbled you both could have been killed!" He patted her arms and legs and asked, "You are okay, aren't you?"

She pushed his hands away and turned. Shoving her horse aside, she took a few steps, creating distance between them. "Yes, I'm okay."

"You don't sound okay." He followed her. "Penny, why don't you like riding in the hills?"

"I just don't like it. That's all."

"Not a good enough answer." He placed his hands on her shoulders. "Why don't you like it?" He steered her to turn and look at him. Tears streamed down her cheeks. Jace was stunned. He had never seen her cry. She wasn't sobbing or sniffling like other women, she was just crying. Cascading droplets fell from both eyes.

"Penny?" Drawing her to him, he pressed her head onto his chest.

"Don't make me talk about it. Please, don't make me talk about it." The words mumbled against the thickness of his jacket.

There was a flat boulder a few yards behind her. He guided them toward it and asked, "Penny, what don't you want to talk about?"

"That day."

"What day?"

"That day he was in the hills."

"Who was in the hills?" Keeping his voice soft and even, Jace encouraged her tale to come out. Their bodies lowered onto the boulder and he cradled her onto his lap.

"Luke." Her body trembled. She twisted and pressed closer to his form.

"What did Luke do?" He tried to ignore his rising anger.

"He scared Midnight."

"How?"

"He jumped out from behind a rock. We were just walking along the trail and he jumped out and scared us."

"Then what happened?" His hands roamed up and down her back.

"I fell off."

"You fell off Midnight?"

"Yes, he ran away."

"Who ran away? Midnight?" He felt her head move up and down. He swallowed the lump in his throat. "What about Luke? What did Luke do?"

"He jumped on top of me and held me down on the ground." Her sob ripped across his chest.

"Shhh, it's okay, you're okay." When he felt he had control of his fury he asked, "Penny, did Luke hurt you?" Increasing the pressure of his arms, he held her against him as she answered.

"Yes. He, he ripped my shirt. He tore all the buttons off of it."

"What happened after he tore your shirt, Penny?" Rage like he had never known rose from his inner core.

"He said I could become the queen of-of Jamestown." She choked as the last word sputtered out.

Jace offered simple, hushed sounds of comfort. Moments later he continued, "What happened next, Penny?"

"Midnight came back and hit him."

"What?" Confused, he questioned her statement. "How could Midnight hit him?" Her body stilled in his arms. "Penny?"

She pulled her face away from his chest and looked at the horses standing nearby. "Midnight reared up and brought his front hoof down on his head. Luke rolled off me. I thought he was dead for a minute. Then I heard him moan. I got up, climbed on Midnight and rode away."

"Penny, are you sure? Did Luke do more than rip your shirt?" He ran a knuckle down the side of her face.

"No. No, he didn't rape me. I think he was going to, but Midnight saved me."

"Did you tell anyone about his attack?" Using a finger he pulled her face around to his.

"No."

"Why not? You should have told the sheriff."

Her eyes grew wide. "And said what?" She climbed off his lap and used her hands to dry her face. "It would have been Luke's word against mine."

Here comes the rest of the transformation. Jace watched as her indescribable strength returned. It wasn't anything he could see. It was more a presence he could sense. "You could have told your Dad or Sam," he suggested.

"My father had already been murdered. And telling Sam would have just put him in greater danger. He would have gone after Luke, defending my innocence." With a fake laugh she added, "Luke would have claimed we had made mad passionate love. Then I would have been forced to marry him."

Jace rose, walked over to her, and placed his hands on her cheeks. "I'm sorry."

Green eyes searched his face, signaling thoughts fluttered in her mind. He felt frustrated, he didn't know what she was thinking and was startled when her words came out. "Am I that repulsive?"

"Repulsive? What makes you say that?" Her question confused him.

"You."

"Me?" He stroked her cheeks and shook his head. "I don't think you're repulsive."

"Then why-why don't you want me? As a man wants a woman, as a husband wants a wife?"

Jace felt like a stranger watching two lovers from afar. He could predict each movement. Every next step and he had no control over it.

"Oh, Sweetheart, if you only knew," he whispered as his mouth descended on hers.

Her arms grasped his coat and she pulled her body to his. The gesture thrilled him and when her lips opened, encouraging more, he gave it. His mouth devoured hers. Liquid fire filled his loins. Mind and body gave into the immense desire.

Needing to feel her warmth, the pounding of her heart, he unbuttoned her jacket and let his hands run where they may. The buttons of her shirt slipped open. His fingers had a will of their own, searching for the firm mounds of her breasts.

His heart tumbled when her hands followed suit. The fasteners of his jacket and buttons of his shirt were undone. Her fingers ran over his ribs, across his chest, down his sides to his waist.

Pressing his throbbing pelvis against her trim hips, he plunged his tongue to search the hidden sweetness of her mouth. One hand grasped the back of her leg and he wrapped it around his waist as he guided their bodies to the prairie ground. Exploring soft skin, fresh territories, he ran kisses across her face, down her neck onto the edges of her exposed shoulders. His hands tugged at the soft material of her camisole, brushing the thin cotton out of his way. He was as close to heaven as he had ever been. Time was of no consequence as he discovered maiden territories.

Whether it was his conscience that stepped in, or the

cold breeze that brushed his heated flesh as she tugged his shirt from his waistband, he never knew. Either way, something snapped and made him halt his assault of her body. He forced his body to roll away from her searching hands, sweet skin, tantalizing hips, and taste-filled lips. His body shook and ached with unfulfilled need.

They both lay there, on their backs, breathing heavy, starring up at the wispy, white clouds that danced across a blue sky. What was he going to do now?

After a few still moments, Jace flipped to his side and supported his head with a bent arm. "Penny, you know I wouldn't lie to you."

Penny was still in another world and not quite ready to leave it. Her body screamed for more at the same time it luxuriated in newfound awareness. Bright glistening stars had exploded with euphoria, and filled every ounce of her being with an ecstasy so great she still pondered the splendor of it. With regret at pushing the marvelous sensations aside, she rolled onto her stomach and propped her upper body by placing both forearms beneath her. "Uh-huh," she nodded.

"Then believe me when I say I do want you. I want you as a man wants a woman." Jace whispered.

Eagerness rose in her heart, "Then-"

His head moved back and forth, "No, no, we can't act on those feelings, Penny. It will make everything worse. Deep down, I know you know I'm right."

"But..."

He pulled his body into a sitting position. "Deep down, we both want the same thing- the Copper Cow to be prosperous, Luke to be stopped, the Lakota to be able to live in peace. That's what I'm here to help you with. And none of that has anything to do with—with you and I making love."

"I want that too," Penny insisted. Why couldn't he understand? What had she done wrong?

"No, you have Candice expecting you to want it. And I can't be that selfish. I can't make you mine, and then leave. I will be leaving. We both know that. When it's all over, I will return to Philadelphia."

She didn't have a response, couldn't think of anything to say. In slow motion, his hands reached out, took hers and helped her to her feet. Her heart fluttered as his fingers ran up her arms before encircling her shoulders. She laid her head against the steady beat of his heart.

His voice whispered above her head. "When I leave, you will be able to find a real husband. Not a mail ordered one. Someone who will cherish you as you deserve to be cherished." He took a step back and ended the embrace.

Her cheek felt a light pinch as his hands left her shoulders. "Someone you will fall head over heals in love with." Leaning down, he pressed a kissed on that cheek and allowed his lips to linger for several moments. She cherished the feeling.

He pulled away, turned, and walked over to the boulder. Her eyes caught the droop of his shoulders. He started to repair his clothing.

Penny followed suit, her trembling fingers tried to close the fasteners of her shirt and coat, but she never took her eyes from the man as he sat down and covered his face with his hands. Recognition hit her. Her heart constricted. He was in as much pain as she was. How could she have been so blind? Was she that dense, or that desperate?

She pulled her eyes away, blinked against the tears and gave a high whistle. Midnight pricked his ears, whinnied in return, and trotted over to his mistress. After hefting her body into the saddle she stated, "I'm getting hungry, I missed breakfast. I'm going home now."

She waited for Jace's reply. His head nodded as he stood and walked over to stroke Midnight's neck. Marion approached, looking for attention as well. Reaching over, Jace took hold of his horse's rein then turned to look up at her. "Yes, let's go home now. But before we do, would you promise me something, Penny?"

"Yes."

"Promise me you won't go out riding by yourself. Ever."

Penny took in the sincere concern of his eyes. She could still feel the protective cocoon his arms had formed around her. Still taste his lips. *I love you*, she thought. *There will never be someone else. I'm already head over heals in love-with you.* Her gaze lifted to take in the hills on the horizon behind him. Fear of the area no longer filled her. Instead a deep emptiness settled in.

"I promise, Jace." Nodding her head, she repeated the words, "I promise."

****

Penny must be trying a new approach. Instead of plying her feminine wiles upon him, she had become his friend. Treating him as an equal partner in all of the workings of the ranch. Jace wasn't sure how it happened. But was glad it did. Except for the cold dips in the stream that would soon be frozen, he had to admit his life was close to being ideal. Ideal for the bargain he had made for himself anyway.

Their latest trip to town, for another monthly association meeting, had been amicable to say the least. Even the weather had been on his side and though it had been late, they had arrived home safe and sound. Both spent the night in their own beds, just like every other night.

This new relationship also allowed him to be in her company more often. Some days were more difficult than others, but Jace discovered he no longer needed to avoid being around her. Instead he found a form of fulfillment in being with her. Simple pleasures in completing tasks together seemed to be abundant.

He was amazed at her stamina. She worked as hard as any hired hand. Whether it was pitching hay, roping steers, or shoveling manure. Her jeans could get grubby and her hands blistered, but she never complained. Instead she would go in the house, change into some simple, but alluring dress he almost always admired and be on to anther task. Most evenings they would relax together in the front parlor. The light banter that had nurtured between them was becoming a form of entertainment for all.

She knew every animal on the Copper Cow. How old they were, where they were born, what their lineage was, and what they were worth. Right down to the chickens in the back yard. She was the most self-sufficient, tough, and independent women he had ever known. Yet, he also knew she was the most insecure, forlorn, and apprehensive girl he had ever met. It all made Penny the most alluring, fascinating, charming, and loveable woman he had ever encountered.

Jace removed his Stetson and used his forearm to wipe the sweat running down his forehead. The vision of his thoughts held his gaze. Together, Penny and Henry were loading the wagon with the various tools and supplies needed for the exhausting day of branding. Twinkling green eyes caught his. He threw her a playful wink. She stuck her tongue out at him. A chuckle rumbled in his chest as he finished dousing the flames of the small fire and walked over to help them.

After the wagon was loaded, his hand ran over the hub of the wooden wheel, inspecting it for cracks or deterioration. The sun would soon slip behind the hills. All day an eerie sixth sense had surrounded him. He wanted his wife safe at the ranch before it became dark.

Walking to the side of the buckboard, he placed both hands on the soft mounds of her hips and aided her climb onto the wagon seat. The small amount of weight she had gained had settled into all the right places. "It won't take us long to finish up here. We should be home within the hour." He settled her on the seat and added, "Please don't eat all of the biscuits before I get there."

Penny pulled the front of his Stetson down over his teasing eyes. "You beast! I don't eat half as much as you do."

He flipped the brim of his hat up and tugged on the long braid streaming down her back. "Maybe not as much, but you always make a pig of yourself when it comes to biscuits and raspberry jam."

Penny laughed. "Alright, I'll try. But I can't promise anything."

"I'm sure you can't." Several thoughts ran through his mind as he gazed at her. His eyes weren't searching, nor scrutinizing, they just looked at the best friend he would ever have.

She broke his trance by giving the bandana tied around his neck a soft jerk. "Don't work too much longer. There's always tomorrow."

"I know and we won't." Jace took a step back. "Drive carefully Henry, there's some deep ruts after that first knoll," he instructed the driver before he flashed her a parting wink.

"Iz know. Iz the one that drove dis wagon out here," Henry reminded with his open banter. "Giddy up now, wez got to get Miz Penny home." He brought the long reins down across the back of the horses. With a jerk, the wagon jolted forward, to roll behind the buckskins across the prairie.

Penny gave Jace a final wave and turned to watch the scenery ahead. Her heart felt full. She cherished each and every moment she spent with her husband.

The wagon rambled over the ground, covering the distance home at a steady pace. A bright orange globe was making its way behind the hills to the west and the long ride gave her time to contemplate the contentment that filled her life. Her relationship with Jace had progressed to a new level, one that filled her with pleasure, and a bliss she hadn't believed possible.

"Gonna be a long, cold winter," Henry's prediction interrupted her thoughts. "Iz can feel it in my bones."

"Do you miss the winter of the south?" The warmth of Jace's playfulness had worn off, and she pulled the collar of her thick jacket up to block the late afternoon wind as a chill touched her spine.

"Some timez Iz do," the old, black man admitted.

The tingle grew deeper, turning into a sensation of being watched. Investigating the feeling, her eyes scanned the dead, brown grass covering the hills. Scraggly trees and large boulders covered the steep slopes that reached into the sky. She thought she caught a movement and continued to watch until recognizable shapes formed.

"Henry, it looks like we have company." Alarm filled her voice.

Emerging from behind the small rise on their left, four riders directed their horses straight ahead, making a beeline for the wagon. Feathers and colorful blankets decorated the men and their horses.

Throwing a look over her head, Henry barked, "Iz those injunz, Miz Penny?"

"Whatever they are they don't look friendly. Go, Henry, go!"

The old man whipped at the horses. Shod hoofs tore deep into the ground, sending clods of dirt into his face as he focused on controlling a fierce pace. "You best get in da back and liez down!"

Penny reached below the seat and pulled out a heavy pistol. One hand wrapped around the board of the bench, holding her in place as she fired the gun into the air. Two quick shots emitted and sent an echo to roll across the plains and bounce off the hills. Turning in her seat, she attempted to take aim at the oncoming group. The gun spun about in her hand as the wagon bounded across the buffalo grass. Small mounds and hills of dirt felt like huge boulders as the wooden wheels careened over them. The gun bounced about aimlessly.

An arm swung around and hit Penny in the chest. "Iz sorry, Mz Penny, but you gotz to getz in da back!" Henry yelled.

Backwards, she flipped over the wagon seat and landed in the bed. The rough ride caused her to jostle this way and that. At last her thrashing fingers grasped a hold of the back of the seat.

Penny pulled herself up enough to see where the riders were. An arrow whistled just above her head. A scream tore from her throat. She crouched down and searched for the gun she dropped during her tumble. Her fingers grasped the cold metal, with both hands she balanced the firearm, took aim over the side of the wagon and fired. One of four shots managed to hit its target. The first man in line toppled onto his saddle horn. But she must have only wounded him, because he didn't fall from the horse and all four goons continued their assault of the wagon.

"Faster, Henry, faster! They're catching us!" An arrow stuck into the side of the wagon with a loud thud, and accented to her scream.

"Iz know Mz Penny! Don't you fret now! Henry won't let them hurt you! Just liez down!"

Penny searched amongst the tools in the wagon with difficulty. Everything tossed about. Boxes and tools slammed into her from all sides. Even her body seemed to bounce a foot off the bed and made painful collisions against other cargo as it slammed back down.

Her fingers grabbed a hold of a long handled pitchfork, and she hunkered down, holding it so the sharp metal tines were unnoticeable as they stuck out over the side of the wagon. She braced her legs against thick boards and her back against a heavy crate, forcing her body to remain as motionless as possible.

Deep snorts from horses grew louder as they closed in on the wagon. Penny peered over the edge and watched as a long, brown nose of one of the massive beasts drew along side the wagon. Its nostril flared from the strenuous run the rider forced it to maintain. She waited for the right time, squeezed a tighter hold on the wooden handle, and prepared for the attack.

The horse squealed in fear as the rider crowded it against the noisy wagon. She knew the rider was preparing to leap into the buckboard.

With a grunt, she leaned forward and shoved the pitchfork at the booted foot stretching toward the sideboards. With all her might she forced the boot away from the wagon. A quiver vibrated her spine as the man screamed. Using the entire weight of her body, she twisted the fork as the foot kicked and flayed. With renewed strength she pressed it tight against the animal, squeezed her eyes shut and held on.

An unexpected break of contact sent her and the tool flying backward. Her head hit something hard, stars flashed at the sides of her eyes. Gunfire penetrated the ringing in her ears. Rolling onto her belly, she tried to crawl back to the edge of the wagon.

One of the wooden wheels hit the unforgiving surface of a large boulder. Momentum carried the wagon over the rock and the back of the buckboard flew upwards. She grabbed the brace holding the driver's seat in place and tucked her head below it as the front of the wagon came down at an angle. A loud crack split the air when the long, singletree wagon tongue hit the ground and snapped like a toothpick.

Frenzied horses screamed as they reared and struggled to free themselves from the vehicle. The strength of the team of buckskins was great. With little effort they tore the hitch from the buckboard, and driven by fear, flew across the ground. The action caused the wagon to flip onto its side. Penny held on as it toppled and continued to slide on its side. Dirt and clumps of grass flew past her.

"Henry!" she screamed, hoping he wasn't being drug by the frantic horses. With desperation, she peered out from beneath the bench. The wagon still skidded across the ground, but she caught a flash of the horses. The buckskins fought against one another as they raced away from the wreckage, long leather reins slapped at the earth behind them. "Henry!" she yelled again.

The wagon vibrated and rumbled beneath her clutching fingers. The long base bounced high as it careened over the rough terrain and caught air. The energy initiated a new force. The back came forward. It was about to flip end over end. Heavy wooden boards bore down at her.

Screaming, Penny scrambled from under the bench. With a hard shove against the wood, she propelled her body out of the way just as the buckboard flipped and crashed to the ground. It stilled for a moment, then flipped and started to roll across the prairie. She covered her head with both hands as stiff boards broke into pieces with each tumble. Fragments and rubble shot through the dust filled air. Small pieces bounced off her as it scattered the ground.

****

Dry grass and clumps of dirt flew from beneath Marion's charging feet. Jace fired his gun again. Knowing the riders were out of range, he hoped the gunshots would alarm them enough to relinquish their attack. They surrounded the wagon and one appeared to be trying to jump into the back of it. The trigger clicked beneath his finger, his rifle was empty. He let it fall to the ground, pulled the pistol from his waist and fired it just as the four riders separated from the wagon.

His relief was short lived, for as soon as the assailants divided, the buckboard started to tumble. Terror crawled across his body as he watched the living nightmare from the back of the sorrel. With renewed vigor, he soared toward the wagon plummeting across the ground. Wreckage flew high in the air. Jace couldn't recognize human shapes. Just dark blurs slamming against the hard ground.

"Penny!" He would never reach her in time.

Adrenalin surged through his body. It started when two faint warning shots flowed into the branding camp and sent his heart into his throat.

He couldn't get to the accident fast enough. In anguish, he kicked the sides of the sorrel, forcing the spent animal to move faster and screamed, "Penny!"

The largest section of the mangled wagon was just a few yards ahead. Jace leaped from the still charging steed. Convinced he could run faster than the horse.

His heart pounded in his ears, he could feel each pump as it gushed fiery blood throughout his body. His legs throbbed as he skidded to a halt.

"Penny!" bellowing, he scanned the area, "Penny!" Blurred sight saw Sam and Calhoun continue to pursue the attackers.

Jace turned back to the wreckage. A wheel protruding out of the jumbled mass spun on its axle. It sent an eerie sound across the prairie as it groaned and came to halt. Jace twisted and started to leap through the debris. His long legs sprinted past and around the heaps of rubble. Bounding over a large stack of broken wood, he saw her. His heels dug into the dirt as he slid to a stop.

She sat on the ground. Fragments of the wreckage littered around her. He forced his raw cords to whisper her name, "Penny?"

Henry lay in front of her, his head on her lap. Her fingers applied tender strokes to the short, gray curls that surrounded the old man's face. Sad, green eyes looked up at him. "Why, Jace? Why?"

He approached them. Noting the blood on her face and hands, his eyes scanned her for acute injuries. His hands framed her face, she was cut and bruised, but didn't seem to be critically injured. His gaze drifted to the old man.

"Why did they have to kill Henry?"

His heart clenched. The burning sensation behind his eyes peaked. He squeezed his lids against the pain. Twisting around, he situated his body behind hers. With a gentle touch, he encouraged her to let his solid frame support her swaying one. His arms encircled her chest to hold her while she said final good-byes to a life long friend.

"Henry never hurt anyone, Jace." She sunk against him.

He sent a protective, invisible armor to surround her. "I know, Sweetheart," he murmured, kissing the top of her head.

"He wouldn't even kill a spider. He would just carry them outside and tell them they needed to go live some where else." Affectionate touches continued to move across Henry-his hair-his face-his shoulders. "He caught a baby rabbit for me once." Her lungs gulped for air in-between each word.

"We named him Snuggles. I had him for years. He lived in the barn, didn't need a cage or anything." She shook her head. "Henry trained him to come when I called." The tears rolled down her cheeks. "He taught me how to train Midnight too, to come when I whistle." Her eyes closed. "What am I going to do without him, Jace?"

"He loved you, Penny." Jace was at a loss for words. He didn't know what to say to comfort her.

"I loved him too. I'll love him forever." Her face lifted to the sky and pain ripped through him like a knife as her heart-wrenching, "Nooooo," mingled with the moan of the wind before sobs engulfed her body.

Chapter Twelve

Jace nodded his head at Henry's inert form, a signal for Sam and Jim to remove the lifeless body from Penny's lap. He knew the evildoers must have disappeared amongst the rough terrain of the hills when the two men arrived at the accident site.

When the weight was lifted, Penny twisted and buried her face into his chest. Wrapping her arms around his torso, she clung to him in agony.

A few minutes later, Jim Calhoun broke the thick silence, "Must have been a hunting party."

Penny stiffened. Her head shook, but didn't lift. "We were not attacked by Indians."

"Old Henry might say differently, if he could still talk," Jim stated.

"Calhoun." Jace let his voice carry a deep warning.

"Well, he's got an arrow stuck right through his heart," Calhoun justified his thoughts aloud. "The heathens shot him in the back!"

"Damn it, Jim, sometimes I really want to punch that smart mouth you've got," Sam declared as he shook his balled fist at the younger man.

Penny lifted her head to glare at the cowhand. She shifted her weight forward and pick up a pitchfork. The long handle had been snapped in half. The prong end of the tool waved in front of Calhoun.

Stuck at the base of the sharp tines was a metal spur. The tips of the silver disk had been filed to razor sharpness. One of its frayed leather straps fluttered in the wind. "Indian's don't wear spurs," she declared. Letting the fork fall back to the ground, she wearily laid her head back against his chest and explained, "I ran out of bullets."

"Calhoun go find the buckskins, I'm sure they didn't go far," Jace ordered as he gathered his wife in his arms and rose to his feet. "Take them straight to the barn. We'll clean up this mess tomorrow."

"Jace, you go ahead and take Penny up to the ranch. I'll-I'll bring Henry home." Sam looked off into the distance, blinking at the water in his eyes.

Jace knew how much Henry's friendship had meant to Sam. He nodded in agreement, turned, and strode to the sorrel. Darkness loomed as he climbed into the saddle, settled Penny on his lap, and started for the ranch. The evening sky continued to provide him with some light, and he scanned the hills with persistence, watching for any show of movement.

"Oh..." Penny groaned. Her head shifted. "Jace, my head hurts." The whispered words reached his ears just as her body went limp.

"Penny? Penny?" Jace cupped the back of her head as it drooped over his arm. He pressed it to rest against his chest. Warm liquid flowed between his fingers, and his heart jolted as he glanced at his hand. The horse came to a halt. He ripped the bandana from around his neck and with gentle pressure placed it against the gaping wound on the back of her head. With renewed urgency, he heeled the sorrel into movement.

Mary Alice ran down the steps when Marion entered the yard. "Singing Dove said Penny's hurt! Is she? How bad is it?"

Jace brought the horse to a stop and pulled Penny's flaccid body with his as he jumped to the ground. "She needs a bath, Mary Alice. Can you please prepare one for her?"

"Of course! So- she is okay?"

"She will be," Jace declared. Pressing his lips to his wife's forehead he carried her to the house and whispered, "She will be." He refused to believe otherwise.

He climbed the stairs, two at a time and shouldered his way into his room. Jace lowered Penny's motionless body to the bed. He felt for her pulse before rolling her onto her side to untwist the long braid and get a better look at her injury. Frustrated beyond belief, he lit the lamp on the bedside table and turned back to Penny.

A soft glow filled the room and with diligence, he cleared every strand out of the way. His hands trembled as he examined the gash. It was jagged and ran down the back of her head. He grabbed the towel from his washstand, soaked it in water and placed it over the area. It wasn't life threatening, but it would be painful for several days.

Concentrating on each inch, he began to run his hands down her arms and legs, searching for any hint of damage. Finding no serious ones, he eased her on to her back and continued his assessment. Her clothes made the examination difficult.

"Mr. Owens! What are you doing?"

Jace jerked upright to stare at the woman in the doorway. He felt like a small boy who had just been caught with his hand in the cookie jar. Pulling his eyes away from Mary Alice and back to Penny's half naked body, his daze cleared. "Help me get her undressed!"

"I will not help you! You get out of here. I'll undress her by myself." Mary Alice tried to pull on his arm.

"I will not leave. I need to examine her for injuries." He shook the hand from his forearm.

"Singing Dove can do that," Mary Alice insisted.

"I will do it! I'm a doctor."

"You're not a doctor! You're a veterinarian!"

Jace brought annoyed eyes down on the woman who once again grasped his arm. "I am her husband!"

"You are not. Well you are, but not-not that w…"

"I'll help him." Singing Dove stepped up to the bed. She handed a small leather pouch to Mary Alice. "Put this in her bath water." Her brown eyes flashed toward the door.

Mary Alice let out a loud "Humph!" and marched out of the room.

"Thank you," Jace said as he turned his eyes back to the red welts and long scratches marring the pink skin of Penny's arms. "I'll need a sewing needle to stitch her head wound. It will heal much faster." His voice broke.

"It's ready," Singing Dove answered as she pulled the shirt he had removed from beneath Penny's form. She then began to remove dirty boots and torn jeans.

Gathering his resolve, he began his appraisal again, running his hands around her waist. Dark bruises were already starting to form. He felt for any breaks in her rib cage. “I'll need you to boil it.”

“I did.”

“I'll need you to...”

“I know.”

Jace looked up at the Lakota woman. She did know. Probably knew more than he did. In silence, together, they treated each injury before Jace carried Penny's limp form to the brass tub filled with herb-scented water.

****

The faint smell of smoke woke him. He slipped his arm from beneath Penny's neck to slide out from under the covers and off the bed. Without a sound, he crept across the room and lifted the curtain away from her bedroom window. Rays from the morning sun were starting to peek in the eastern sky and provided just enough light to recognize Singing Dove in the back yard. She'd built a small, but smoke-filled fire.

“She's contacting her family.” The voice came from behind him.

He turned, smiled at her drowsy form and greeted, “Hi.”

Her gaze started at his head and ended at his bare toes, her lips formed a sweet grin. He knew he must look a site. His hair was ruffled, and he wore nothing but tan cotton pants, which looked like he'd slept in them. He had.

“Hi,” Penny responded.

“How are you feeling?”

Her eyes grew shinny with unshed tears, “It wasn't a dream, was it? Henry's...”

He crossed the room. “Shhh, don't think about it right now. You took a hard hit to the head.” Climbing beneath the heavy quilt, he leaned back against the pillows lining the headboard. One arm reached around her neck and shoulders pulling her to him. “Go back to sleep, Sweetheart. It's early,” Jace whispered.

“You've been here all night haven't you?”

“Mmm...” Not admitting anything, he settled her head on his shoulder, leaned his head back, and closed his eyes.

She had awakened a number of times during the night, if only to cocoon her body closer into his embrace.

Trembling limbs had clutched onto him when he had crawled into the bed beside her, after carrying her from the bathing chamber where Mary Alice had clothed her in a soft, flannel nightgown once the dirt, grim and blood had been washed from her body and hair. Singing Dove had made her drink a strong herbal tea. They all had hoped it would relieve her pains and improve her chances of sleeping.

Several times he had felt warm tears fall onto his chest and had felt her anguish with each droplet. Remembering them, he tilted down and kissed the top of her head.

The palm of her hand lay on his bare chest, right on top of his heart. She nestled her head against his shoulder and sighed, "They will be here by noon."

"Who will be?" He laid his left hand on hers and wrapped his fingers around her elfin ones. Holding her was a feeling he loved. It filled him to the most inner core. His right arm once again flowed around her shoulder and beneath the covers permitting his hand to cup the curve of her side. All night he had held her like this, not allowing any pressure to be put on the long jagged cut that ran down the back of her skull.

"Singing Dove's family," she answered.

"How do you know that?"

"I can smell her fire. She's signaling them. You should be watching. It's amazing. Using a blanket she will send puffs of smoke up into the morning sky and by this afternoon, they will be here."

"Really? Why is she signaling them?"

"I don't know for sure. But my guess would be to ask them about the Lakota arrow that- that shot Henry. The Lakota didn't kill him, Jace."

Tension crept into her body. "Shhh, I know the Lakota didn't kill Henry, Sweetheart. Don't worry, I won't let any one blame them for it," Jace made the words sound soft and comforting, trying to force her anxieties to decrease. "Let's go to sleep for a little bit, we both need some rest." He knew she would ignore her own need for sleep, but would support his if he said he needed some. She was always more concerned about others than about herself. He felt her soft sigh more than heard it.

"Yes, let's. You must be exhausted," she agreed sleepily.

A smile crossed his face as he felt her breathing deepen. He opened his eyes, and stared into space. How was he going to be able to leave her? The thought of going on living without her was unbearable. He must be sadistic. Like torturing himself, because that was just what he was doing. Falling deeper in love with her each and every day. All the while knowing, that soon he would have to leave her forever.

****

Jace felt that unknown sixth sense and held up his hand. "Excuse me a moment, please, Sheriff?" Without waiting for a response, he rose out of the desk chair and scurried across the room to open and peer out the office door. His heart jumped. "Penny. What are you doing? You should still be in bed!"

Rushing to the staircase where she made her way down to the final few steps, he swept her into his arms, turned and placed his foot on the bottom stair.

"No, I don't want to lie up there…thinking any longer." She stopped his steps as she wrapped her arms around his shoulders. Her fingers locked behind his neck, and she laid her head on his shoulder. "Please don't make me."

His eyes caught her pleading look. He understood. "Alright." He placed a kiss on her forehead before he carried her into the office.

With a glanced at Wilcox, Jace asked, "Would you please get a pillow off of the divan in the back parlor? Second door on the left."

Tim Wilcox rose from his seated position, and appeared to be somewhat stunned by his request. "Oh, uh, certainly."

"Grab the quilt off the rocking chair too, please," Jace instructed as he lowered his wife onto the couch. With care he positioned her torso in the corner and raised her legs to stretch along the length of the hide covered lounger.

Wilcox returned. A broad smile covered his face. Without comment, Jace took the pillow, placed it behind Penny's shoulders and covered the length of her blue skirt with the quilt.

"Thank you, Sheriff," Penny acknowledged.

Jace motioned for the Sheriff to take the chair behind the desk as he placed himself on the sofa next to Penny's feet. He laid an arm atop the blanket over her legs, and with a gentle touch, patted her knee. "How do you feel? Do you want me to ask Singing Dove to make you some more tea?"

Penny shook her head. Her face flushed red. "No, no, I'm fine, thank you." She flashed her eyes back and forth between he and the Sheriff.

"The Sheriff and I were just..." Jace started.

"Discussing the attack that killed Henry?" Settling her eyes on Wilcox, Penny clarified, "They were not Lakota, they were not Indians at all. They were white men."

"Your husband has suggested the same thing."

"We are not suggesting anything, Sheriff. We are telling you a fact." His wife threw Wilcox a stone cold look. "They had painted their faces and decorated their horses with feathers. Two wore blankets as ponchos, and two wore animal skins with head coverings, but they had on wool pants, tall western boots and spurs."

Jace almost felt a twitch of sympathy for the lawman; he knew the instant she had spoken that she was armored. That invisible force she could expel from her core was intact. "I was just about to show you, Sheriff," he nodded at the desk top, "one of the attackers was wearing that spur lying on the desk in front of you. My wife tore it off him with a pitch fork during the raid."

Wilcox leaned forward and picked up the object. The metal jingled as he turned it during his investigation. "With a pitch fork?"

Jace arched one brow as he looked at Penny and nodded. "She ran out of bullets."

Wilcox wiped a hand across his bushy mustache, covering the smile, but not a fleeting laugh, "I always knew you were a resourceful woman, Mis- uh, Mrs. Owens." Once again growing serious, the man flicked the round disk with his finger, causing it to rotate on its tiny axle. The sharpened tips glistened as they caught small shafts of light. "Only a cruel man would wear spurs this sharp."

"Or a ruthless one," Penny supplied.

A knock on the other side of the door interrupted the Sheriff's reply.

"Come in," Jace answered the request.

Sam pushed the door open, glanced into the room and smiled as he pulled the hat from his head. "Hi, Princess. How ya doin'?"

"I'm fine, Sam. How are you doing?"

"I'm good." The two of them shared a solemn, private look, before he turned to Jace. "Could I talk to you for a second?"

"Of course. Excuse me, Sheriff," turning to Penny he added, "I'll be right back."

She nodded and gave him a slight smile.

Jace followed Sam into the entranceway and pulled the door shut behind him. "What's up?"

"Nothing, well, nothing bad," Sam supplied. He rubbed a hand across the thick, gray whiskers covering his chin and nervous eyes glanced around the empty space. "I, uh, I guess, I'm here to ask your permission, to, uh." He replaced his hat upon his head, only to remove it again, and tap it against his thigh.

"My permission for what?"

"Well, Ole, Henry, he's, he was after me for years to, uh, marry Mary Alice. I figured since the preacher will be out to lay him to rest day after tomorrow, I'd see if Mary Alice and I could get married after the funeral. Figure Henry would, well, he'd like it that way."

Jace was taken aback. "Shouldn't you be asking Mary Alice for permission, instead of me?"

"Oh, I already did that. She said I had to ask you. You being the man of the house now, and all."

"Well, if it's okay with Mary Alice, it's okay with me." Jace slapped the man on the back in friendship while offering his other for a handshake. "Congratulations!"

Shaking the pro-offered hand, Sam let a smile cover his weathered face as it became covered with a slight red tint. "We were hoping you and Penny would stand up for us."

"Does Penny know about this?" Jace glanced at the office door.

Sam's brows pulled together as he shook his head. "No, we have tried to be very discreet about it." A small cough emitted before he added, "Over the years...I uh-asked her before you know. Right after she arrived here. But her husband had just been killed in the war. Then after awhile—well it was just never the right time, until now."

Jace understood all too well.

A hand reached out and grasped his arm. "We, Mary Alice and I, were hoping you'd be the one to tell Penny. Explain it all to her. You being her husband and all."

Jace fought hard not to laugh at the disillusion of the other's statement. He thought of Mary Alice, and the anxiety she must be experiencing over trying to explain she and Sam's long-term relationship to her niece. Jace had figured it out right after his arrival, but knew Penny was oblivious to it. "And all," he said while nodding his head. "Tell Mary Alice not to fret, Sam. I'll explain -it all-to Penny."

Sam settled his hat on his head with a deep sigh. "Thanks, Jace. I'm much obliged!" Removing his hat once again he wiped the sweat from his forehead and then replaced it. "I'll ask the Sheriff to let the preacher know. I talked to Reverend Harper about it this morning when I rode in to tell him about Henry."

"Alright," Jace replied and turned to the door. He placed a hand on the handle and glancing back over his shoulder said, "I think Henry would approve of it, too, Sam."

Sam smiled and nodded before he turned to the front door.

Curious, Penny watched as Jace re-entered the office. He gave her a reassuring smile and extended a hand to the other man. "Thanks for riding out this afternoon, Tim. We will be appreciative of anything you are able to do."

"You're welcome and if you don't mind, I'd like to ride out to attend Henry's service." The Sheriff stood to shake hands with Jace and accepted a nod of approval. "No, please, don't get up, Ma'am." Shaking his head at her, he picked the spur up off the desk. "Mind if I take this with me?"

"I'd prefer to never see it again. Nor its twin." Penny

supplied as she tried to resettle her sore body on the sofa.

Wilcox slipped out of the room as Jace tended to her comfort. In slow motion, he removed the slippers from her feet and reprehended, "You should still be in bed."

"No, I'm getting stiff from lying around." She had awoken to a room that was much too empty. Instantly, she had missed his presence and wanted to be near him. He was the only thing that seemed to ease her pain.

"Your body is bruised from head to toe. You'll heal much faster if you take it easy for a few days." He sat down, lifted her legs, and scooted his body under them. Draping the limbs across his lap, he adjusted the quilt to cover her toes before he looked at her with mock seriousness. "When were you going to tell me what *Maka Wichasha* meant?"

Penny had to pull her thoughts from the comfort his nearness provided. She made her eyes pop open, clenched her teeth into an odd smile, and tried to hide a giggle. With a false look of shock, she asked, "Who told you?"

"A member of Singing Dove's family," Jace said in a low voice.

She could tell he was doing his best to act hurt or embarrassed. She reached up and patted his cheeks, like comforting a child. His words registered her mind. "Singing Dove's family? Two Bears? Is Two Bears here?" Excitement rose with the image of the brother figure she hadn't seen for a long time. She attempted to pull her legs from his grasp, wanting to climb off the lounger.

Jace refused to allow her to rise. "No, he's not here. They already left. He did go up and look in on you, but you were sleeping."

"Oh, I would have loved to have seen him. It has been so long." She continued thinking aloud, "He is so wonderful!" A pained look crossed Jace's face. She wondered about it, had Two Bears questioned him about their marriage? "He's the big brother I never had." She patted his hand. "You should have awakened me."

"It was the opium." Jace covered her hand with his.

"What? I didn't take any opium." Penny felt his warmth penetrating her skin. The heat ran up her arm and into her chest.

"Not you, me. The reason I stunk. It was all the

opium Candice had been feeding me."

"Oh," she nodded. "It was quite a fitting name for you, then." She tilted her head and sniffed the air. "You smell much better now." With a grimace she continued, "But I'm afraid the name has kind of stuck."

"Yea, well, I guess it grows on you. It does have a nice ring to it, if you don't know the meaning of it." A glum look covered his face as he grunted the words, "Skunk man."

Then allowing his voice to frame the name with dignity, he recited, "*Maka Wichasha*." A gleaming, proud smile showed pearl white teeth. "See what I mean?"

"Yes, I see what you mean." Penny took in every feature, from the wide forehead, down the curve of his nose, across lean cheeks to the point of his chin. Her heart fluttered. He was the image her mind had created when she had read fairy tales as a small girl. He was a knight in shinning armor. Her knight. She lost control of her hands. They separated themselves from his and rose to frame his face. Her fingers brushed against the fullness of his hair. "Hmmm," she leaned her body toward his and whispered, "perfect."

"Hmmm, what? What's perfect?" Jace asked as his hands came up to caress hers.

"You," she sighed.

"I'm far from perfect, Penny." Jace shook his head.

Penny stifled his movements with a firmer grasp and nodded. "Close enough to perfect for me." The words were a slight whisper as she allowed her lips to merge with his. The kiss was soft, not powerful or passionate, but gentle and simple. Just right. It ran through her body like liquid fire, even though neither of them pushed to make the encounter stronger. She savored the feeling and the encompassing connection.

"You're making me forget how ill you are," Jace murmured against her lips. His hands moved to form a frame around her cheeks.

"I don't feel ill at all." She leaned closer, wanting a second taste.

Jace nodded his head, not quite breaking their faint merger. His lips continued to brush against hers as he spoke. "Yes, you are." With a deep sigh, he leaned forward and gave one final full kiss, before separating them. His hands slipped from her face. He used them to pull her legs closer to his body. His spine straightened and he leaned against the back of the sofa.

He sucked in a deep breath of air. She could see his heart beating beneath the blue of his shirt. After a few moments, he let the breath out and gave her a side ways glance. She didn't even attempt to remove the smile that his kisses had placed on her face.

Warmth flushed her system when his luscious lips smiled back at her. He pulled his head upright and leaned toward her again, but not close enough. Not nearly close enough. Her heart beat against the inside wall of her chest in anticipation.

With a secretive voice he playfully whispered, "You're not the only one who can keep a secret. I know one too."

Penny took in the teasing light of his eyes, the broad smile on his face and the overall silliness of his charisma. *God, I love this man.* The proclamation was silent, but solid in her mind. She, along with the apparition of Charlotte who continued to come to her daughter's aid whenever called upon, had given up on their mission after recognizing distress in the form sitting on the bolder following their ride in the hills. Realization had hit her then, she couldn't force him to love her, nor did she want to be the cause of his pain. She loved him too much for that.

When comprehension of just how much she loved Jace had set in, she also ascertained that loving him meant seeing him happy. Which also meant she was destined to let him go.

She felt as if she had plucked him from his roots, like a spring flower someone wanted to enjoy. They could put it in water, preserve it for a short time, but soon it would wither and die, for its lifeline had been destroyed. She loved him too much for that and wanted him to have a full and lasting life. If that meant consenting to his return to Philadelphia then that is what she intended.

Mentally she had put herself in his shoes and remembered what it was like living out East. Though she had had many enjoyable occasions, she had longed for her home on the prairie. She had longed for its familiarity, for its comfort, for the companionship of her family, the wide-open spaces and the wind in her hair, all the core parts of her life. The things that provided the nourishment she needed to live.

Yes, she could have survived in the East, but she would never have been able to live her life to its fullest. It must be the same for him. She didn't want to be the reason he didn't find the bliss he was ordained to experience.

Knowing it would be hard, probably the most difficult thing she would ever have to do, she became determined to accept her fate with resolve. And she didn't want his time at the ranch to be melancholy. She prayed years from now, when he would think of his time at the Copper Cow it would be with joy. He would remember her as a kind, thoughtful, considerate, loving person, someone he had enjoyed spending his time with.

After that day several weeks ago, she had reshaped her goals and focused on being his friend. Treating him as a welcomed guest in her home and cherished every moment she was given to spend with him.

"You can't read my mind so quit trying," Jace whispered, breaking her chain of thoughts.

Penny let out a nervous laugh at his interpretation of her scrutinizing look. She thumped the top of his head. "I know. Your skull's too thick." Then in a low voice she leaned closer and pried, "What is it?"

"What's what?"

"Your secret?" She could feel the warmth of his breath on her face. Butterflies fluttered in her stomach at the thought of those lips touching hers again.

"Oh, that. Someone's getting married." He raised and lowered his eyebrows teasingly.

She was confused. "Someone's getting married? Who?" Her mind took a moment to process his words. "Oh, I know. Jeanie May Haws. She must have convinced Matt Long that he can't live without her."

"Who?" Jace asked with a bemused look. Shaking his head he held up one hand. "Are you the only woman in the Territory who doesn't have two names? Jeanie May, Sue Ellen, Ann Marie, Mary Alice, Singing Dove..."

Penny let out a giggle then put a hand on her ribs.

"Oh, oh, don't make me do that. It hurts to laugh." She rolled her eyes and answered, "I don't know, I've never thought about everyone having two names before. Now don't try and change the subject again, it is Jeanie May isn't it?"

"Are you okay?" he asked with concern. His hands reached to touch her ribs, but stopped and settled on the blanket covering her hips. "You do have several bruised ribs." When she assured him that she was okay, he went on. "No, it's not Jeanie May Haws and Matt Long, well, it might be. I don't even know them. But they are not who I'm talking about."

"They're not?"

"No." He shook his head and lifted his brows up and down again before giving her an-'I know something you don't' look.

"Then who? Whom are you talking about?" She enjoyed their game. Enjoyed sitting with him like this.

"Mary Alice and Sam."

"What!" Penny screeched.

Chapter Thirteen

"Shhh," Jace pressed a finger to her lips. They both glanced across the room as they heard feet scramble away from the other side of the closed door.

"Mary Alice and Sam?" Penny whispered.

"Yup."

Penny recalled the *phejuta* she had begged Singing Dove to make for Jace. The love potion she had been convinced would make him come running to her bed. The medicine that Sam had drank by mistake. Singing Dove had said that it had worked, and Mary Alice... "Oh, my. What have I done?" Penny covered her face in shame.

He pulled her hands away. "You didn't do anything."

"Oh, yes I did." She nodded her head up and down and drew her face into a serious, dreadful grimace.

"No, you didn't. Haven't you ever wonder why Mary Alice was so intrigued with the marriage by proxy concept? I think she was trying to figure out a way to marry Sam without his knowing it."

"Mary Alice is curious about everything, Jace, for heaven's sake! Mary Alice wouldn't, Sam wouldn't." Penny couldn't believe what she was hearing, what she was thinking.

"Yes they would and they did. That's what Sam needed, to uh ask my permission. Henry had been after him to wed Mary Alice for years. So they decided they would like to do it right after the funeral." Jace was careful in choosing his words and tone. She could tell he was worried about upsetting her with memories of Henry's passing.

Years of living at the ranch entered her mind. A chuckle started to rise as hidden memories floated in and out of her mind. Soon it became a soft giggle. With reservations at the complaints of her bruises she tried to stifle a full-blown laugh.

"Oh, that is precious. No, it's wonderful! Henry would love it." She tried to pull her legs off his lap, but stopped when the pain became too strong. "Will you help me up? I need to go congratulate them." Her heart filled with happiness.

"No, I will not help you get up. But I will go get Mary Alice and have her come in to see you while you stay right where you are," he said as he slid out from beneath her knees and off the couch. With caution he repositioned her legs.

She instantly missed his warmth. "Will you get something for me first?"

"Of course. What do you need?"

She pointed to the desk. "In the bottom left drawer there is a doe skin bag that Singing Dove made for me. Would you please give it me?"

Jace did as asked. He set the decorated bag down on her lap and without saying a word turned to leave.

"Wait," she stopped his exit. "If you don't mind, I'll have you put it back." Penny opened the drawstring and began taking items out one at a time. "It was my treasure finding bag when I was little, but now has become my, well, my keepsake bag. This was my grandmother's bible, and this, my grandfather's pipe. Here's my dad's pocketknife, an eagle's feather from Two Bears, and a medallion that Sam gave me. Candice gave me this necklace, but the clasp is broken," she rambled as she pulled each item out. "Oh, I forgot about this." She held up a small skeleton key. Unshed tears stung her eyes.

"Henry gave me this. I wanted to use my mother's chest when I was leaving for finishing school, but the key for it had been lost years before. Henry said that my grandfather gave him this key. It was for the shackles that were on his legs when Grandpa bought him. Grandpa gave him the key to unlock the leg irons and told Henry he would never have to wear them again. Henry said he threw away the shackles, but kept the key. He said it was his key to heaven on earth. It worked for the lock on the trunk and he told me to keep it. Said he no longer needed it, he was already in." She let the words slip away as a tear rolled down her cheek.

She glanced up. Jace stood in front of her, listening

with intent to her tale.

"Would you give it to him for me? I would like him to take it- to his new heaven."

Jace cleared his throat before answering, "Yes I will see that he has it." He took it from her outstretched hand and caressed the steel before slipping it into his pocket.

Shaking her head to clear her thoughts, she reached into the bag again, feeling for the smooth sides of a gold wedding band. "Here it is. It was my mother's. I'm sure Sam didn't think of a ring. I want to give this one to Mary Alice. Here, hold it please, while I put this other stuff back in the bag."

Jace took the ring between his thumb and forefinger. It glistened in the light as he examined it. "Penny, are you sure? I mean, if it was your mother's, maybe you would like to use it, to have it when, when…"

"No, Jace, I want Mary Alice to have it. I will never need it," she stated her true feelings, pulled the drawstring closed on the bag and handed it back to him, taking the ring in exchange. "Thank you. Please send Mary Alice in now." Her look ended any chance of him arguing with her decision or declaration.

****

A slight breeze stirred the chilly air, but the sun shining down on the gathering was filled with immense delight. The bright rays bounced off the iron fence that encircled the small cemetery and sent sparkles to dance amongst the mourners.

Penny watched as the carefree twinkles landed on the headstones that marked the graves of her parents. She said a small, silent prayer. At the same time Jace's hand massaged the small of her back. She flashed him a smile. He seemed to be able to read her innermost thoughts. They both turned to give their full attention as Reverend Harper began his sermon. The service was as she instructed. One that would send Henry on his journey with the great respect he deserved.

She had shed buckets of tears in private, and though they fought to be released again, she refused their intrusion. Her public good-bye to Henry would be filled with the love and laughter he had showered her with, her entire life.

It appeared that most of Elm Creek and journeyed out for the service. The kitchen overflowed with an array of bowls, platters, and baskets of food to be shared by all between the two services.

The hours slipped by fast and Penny was blessed with a deep feeling, knowing it was just the kind of day Henry would have wanted.

Still somewhat amazed that Sam and Mary Alice had been in love for so long and she hadn't realized it once again brought a smile to her face. It did explain many curious moments that had been ignored over the years. She felt an overwhelming happiness for them. The sparkle in Mary Alice's eyes and the twinkle in Sam's was all she needed to bring warmness to her heart and a smile to her lips.

She stood next to the bride, filled with joy as the Reverend read the wedding vows. Her eyes snuck a peek at Jace. His midnight blue ones were already on her. Their gaze connected and remained focused on one another as the other couple shared their promises. When the instructions of the wedding kiss came Jace gave her a slow, sensual wink. Her heart fluttered and her eyes closed on their own accord, almost as if her subconscious accepted his playful action as something more.

The afternoon sun had long since disappeared when the owners of the Copper Cow, stood on the front porch to watch the last of the trail of the wagons roll down the lane. Penny allowed her head to lie against the side of her husband's chest as the dust began to settle. A soft sigh escaped her, and his encompassing arm massaged her shoulder.

"Excuse me, Mr. and Mrs. Owens." A tall, lanky lad with red hair and freckles, appeared at the bottom of the stairs. "Could I speak with you, please?"

"Certainly, Cody," Penny agreed. She lifted her head and waved at him to join them on the porch. "Jace, have you had the opportunity to meet Cody O'Brien? His family has a farm just north of here."

"Yes, I did earlier today." Jace removed his arm from her and offered it to the young lad in a handshake. "What can we do for you, Cody?"

"Well, sir, I hope I'm not being too forward in asking,

but I was wondering if you would need a new stable boy around here, now that, well, considering the circumstances." Cody tried hard, without much luck, to hide his nervousness.

"How old are you, Cody?" Jace asked.

"Fourteen, Sir."

"Are you still in school?" his questions had a stern, but friendly tone to them.

"No, Sir. I graduated the eighth grade last spring."

"Cody, doesn't your mother need your help at home? I know your father is still recovering from the injuries he received during the fire," Penny interrupted the questions Jace tossed at the lad.

"No, Ma'am. I mean, yes, Ma'am. My father is still recovering, but there isn't much left there to take care of. My little brother Jake can do the few chores there are." The boy's feet shuffled again. "What we really need is the money, Ma'am. If I was to find a job, why we might have enough saved up by spring to rebuild the barn." His spine stiffened with pride as he answered with honesty.

Penny knew without a doubt, how much a job would help the boy's family. She looked over to Jace, her eyes pleaded with him to understand. She felt the connection and with slow motions closed her lids. When her lashes lifted, she saw his smile of understanding and accordance. Happiness filled her and she glanced back to the boy.

"Cody, we do need a new stable man," Jace stated, "but, I would like to talk to your parents about it. I will ride over tomorrow morning and if we can all agree on an arrangement, the job will be yours."

"Thank you, Sir, Ma'am. Thank you very much. My folks and I will be expecting you tomorrow morning. I will do a good job for you, Sir. I promise." The young man offered a farewell shake to Jace and a quick wave to Penny before he flew down the steps.

"I had Calhoun ride over and hire him this morning, to help out with all of the guests. He's done a very good job today," Jace explained to Penny as she watched Cody enter the barn.

"I know," Penny answered with a smile. Turning toward the wide double doors she added, "He will be paid a full man's wage, for his work today and in the future."

"Yes, dear," Jace mocked with affection as he followed her into the house.

****

"It's probably safe to go upstairs now, if you're ready," Jace said later that evening after he and Penny had spent a few hours lounging in the back parlor.

"Jace, what a terrible thing to say!" Penny scolded as she looked up from the letter in her hand.

"They are newlyweds." He folded the newspaper he had been staring at instead of reading and laid it on the table beside his chair before he rose to prepare the fireplace for the night. Seeing the blush on Penny's face, he changed the subject to the mail that had been brought from town. "So what did my dear sister-in-law have to say? It appears to be a very lengthy letter."

"You made me promise to never show you her letters," she reminded him as she refolded several pages of fine linen paper.

"Just an overview of the news will be fine," Jace said, ignoring her reference to another time, another place.

"It will bore you. It's all about Victoria Woodhull."

"What's the reason Candice suggests for Mrs. Woodhull's failure to win the presidency? I'm sure her report is much more interesting than the newspaper article I read about the election."

Penny let out an exaggerated sigh and with a playful flair began, "If you must know, Candice claims Victoria was forced to disclose an affair Reverend Henry Ward Beecher was having. She writes that Victoria had tried everything, but members of Beecher's family, namely a Catherine Beecher and a Harriett Beecher Stow, were making all kinds of accusations against Victoria. They were proclaiming she was having affairs with married men. They were even calling her a witch and a prostitute. It was quite a scandal, to the point where the Woodhull's, Victoria and her husband, were evicted from their home and literally became homeless for a night. Candice states it all with audacity, I might add." Her eyes sparkled with delight as she mocked Candice's seriousness in the tale. With exaggerated flair, her hands and eyes acted out the story she was reciting.

"Really, sounds like things got pretty ugly," Jace

commented as he lifted the patch-worked quilt from her lap. He pulled his face into a grimace before grinning at her delight of story telling. Her clean, fresh aroma filled his senses as he leaned down, grasped her elbow, and helped her rise to her feet.

Muted darkness filled the room when he extinguished the final lantern. He placed a guiding arm around her waist to aid her through the dark room. Slight tremors slither across her body, or was it his? "Poor Victoria," he commented, trying to bring his thoughts back to the present as they exited the room.

"Oh, it gets worse," Penny assured. Leaning her frame into his, she accepted his aid. "It seems Mrs. Woodhull wrote about it in her paper. She revealed the Reverend was having an affair with Lib Tilton, the wife of Beecher's best friend, Theodore Tilton."

They began to climb the stairs together, and Jace didn't even pretend to cover his laughter. "Did she really think that was going to make them stop attacking her?"

"Yes, and so did Candice. But it appears they made a grave mistake. Victoria was arrested for sending obscene literature through the mail, and ultimately ended up spending Election Day in jail. Candice was, still is, at least when she wrote the letter, livid. She is the president of 'Victoria's Leagues', you know and claims they will continue to fight the outrageousness of it all." Penny had to giggle at her own imitation of Candice's theatrics.

When their laughter waned, Jace became serious, "I'm sorry, Penny."

"For what?" Her face drew together with a confused look.

"I know you were a supporter of Mrs. Woodhuff's."

"I wouldn't say I was a supporter of hers. I declined to send Candice any money for her campaign. But I do admire the woman. Her thoughts on political reform, fair wages, and an eight-hour workday all seemed like wonderful ideas to me. I also respect her for standing up for equal rights as she did. This is such a man's world."

He nodded in agreement, "Yes, she has some great ideas. Some I hope will eventually make it to Washington. But I am afraid you're right. We do live in a man's world. A world, which isn't ready for a woman to be president."

He stopped their journey outside of her bedroom door. “And probably won’t be for a hundred years yet.”

“A hundred years?” Penny asked with contrived shock. Her laughter twinkled in the air as she predicated, “More like a hundred and fifty years. It will take at least that many generations to break down the pig-headed domination of you men.”

Seriousness seemed to overtake her lighthearted mood as she patted his cheek. She stretched onto her tiptoes, and he felt lips brush against his face as she whispered, “Thank you for being with me today, Jace. I’ll remember it forever.” Those lips traveled toward his mouth and gave him a soft, fleeting kiss before she pulled away and turned to enter her room. A soft, “Good-night,” filtered into his ears.

Jace felt her slip from his arms. His heart tightened in his chest as the door closed on his face. He placed one hand on its handle, placed the other on the doorframe and laid his forehead against the solid wood. He stood there for several long, agonizing minutes. It would be so easy to walk in, to gather her in his arms, to... He stalled the distressing thoughts and using his arms, pushed his body away from the door, forcing his legs to balance his weight. A sense of helplessness encompassed him as he walked down the hall to his own room, where he could wallow in his own misery.

****

Snowflakes swirled in the air, not the big, fluffy kind, but the tiny sharp ones. The variety that bit any open skin and found a way to creep into every tiny crevice. Jace pulled the collar of his coat up around his neck and tipped the front of his hat down. Thin dustings of the white flecks had started to settle on the low areas of the brown, dormant ground of the prairie.

“I’m glad we will be home soon, this could turn into quite a storm,” Sam commented as he steered the buckskins, pulling the new buckboard, down the long road between Elm Creek and the Copper Cow.

“Me too,” Jace agreed from the seat of his saddled mount. “I’m also relieved my supplies came in when they did. I had almost exhausted all of Doc Burton’s. The ones I could use as a veterinarian anyway.” He glanced at the bags and boxes lining the wooden bed. “I was surprised to get the message they had arrived and it was good to be able to refill Doc’s cabinets before winter sets in.” He trotted his horse up even with the driver again. “You did a fine job on the new wagon. How’s it pull?”

“Like she’s brand new!” Sam boasted with a grin. “I’ve built a good dozen of these over the years. I guess practice does make perfect.”

Jace didn’t answer. The scene on the gray horizon mesmerized him and fear entered his frame.

“What the hell?” Sam exclaimed when he too noticed the soft puffs rising into the air miles ahead of them.

“It’s the ranch!” Jace shouted, with his knees he jolted the sorrel into gallop.

“Jace, don’t go running off in a rush, Singing Dove might just be signally her family about the weather!” Sam yelled.

Jace didn’t have the time to respond, he had to get home. He had to make sure his wife was safe.

He flew into the yard and pulled on the reins with brute force. Marion’s hoofs slid across the gravel. Without waiting for the animal to catch his footing and come to a halt, Jace leaped from the saddle. His hands braced his sideways hurtle of the small fence encircling the yard before he took the stairs three at a time.

Barging through the front door he bellowed, “Penny! Penny!”

Mary Alice ran from the office, tears streamed down her face. “She’s not here, Jace!”

Goosebumps covered his body. Every hair follicle stood at attention. The words burnt his throat as he growled, “Where is she? What happened?” His eyes flashed around, trying to catch sight of long red hair.

“I’m sorry, Mr. Owens. I didn’t see him! I only saw Jim.” A voice came from the doorway of the office.

Jace turned to look at the young boy. Solemn eyes held back tears with great determination. He took a deep breath and tried to control his fear with desperation. Taking two steps forward, he grasped Cody’s thin arms with both hands. “Who! Who didn’t you see?”

“The *Zuzeca*.” Singing Dove’s words floated to the doorway from where she stood, next to a prone body on the couch in the office.

"James? James was here?" The horror he feared had come to life. "He took Penny?" He didn't need an answer. He knew it had happened. Jace pushed Cody out of his way and strode to the couch.

"He caught me from behind, Owens," Calhoun moaned. "He must have been hiding in the barn." Jim attempted to sit up, but collapsed back to the cushions. "He knocked me out cold."

"Knocked you out cold! What the hell kind of a solider are you?" Hands that had been clenched at his sides rose and grabbed the cowhand by the front of his shirt.

"Jace, calm down." Mary Alice stepped forward and placed her hands on his arms, preventing him from shaking the other man. "It wasn't Jim's fault. Luke snuck up on him." When he let go, she smoothed the material of Jim's shirt back into place. "Besides he's not a solider, he's a ranch hand."

Jace stepped away from the couch and turned to gaze at the fire blazing in the stone fireplace. He pulled the hat from his head and rubbed at the pain etching across his forehead before running his fingers through his hair. "He's not a ranch hand. He was deployed out here by the United States Army to investigate all of the stories Luke James was sending to Washington about Indian raids." He spun back to the couch and glared down at the man. "I don't know how anyone could have thought you were competent enough for such an assignment. You can't even watch over one small woman. One that just happens to be my wife!" Jace's final words came out with such force they echoed off the walls.

Fury poured from his body; he could almost hear it in the deafening silence that filled the room. His lungs sucked in a huff of air and he exhaled with a slow even pace. "I now tend to believe the other story I heard. General Brewster sent you out here to get you away from his daughter. Not caring one way or the other if you succeeded in your mission," Jace seethed and he turned his back on the man.

"I tried to stop him, Mr. Owens. Honest I did," Cody announced. The lad's body trembled and signified his fear at the wrath Jace emitted.

Disgust at scaring the boy, forced some sense of substantial thought to enter his rage-filled mind. He sent a look of apology at the quivering, gangly frame and noticed a long red line that ran down the side of the freckled face. The skin wasn't broken, but it was marred and showed the hard hit the lad had received.

Comprehension of how the Cody must have got it rolled up his spine. Compassion for the lad filled him. He crossed the room and laid his hands on thin shoulders. "I'm sure you did, Cody. I know you would try to protect Mrs. Owens. Thank you." Jace squeezed the flesh beneath his fingers with kindness. "Now, tell me exactly what happened."

"I was in the tack room when I heard a loud noise. I looked around a bit before I found Jim. He was in the hay of one of the stalls. I tried to wake him, but couldn't. I saw blood coming out of the back of his head so I ran up to the house to get help. Mrs. Owens came back out to the barn with me. Mr. James was out there then, I hadn't seen him before, anywhere. He grabbed her as soon as we stepped into the barn. I tried to make him let her go, but he hit me with a board."

Cody shuffled his feet and blinked his eyes several times before he continued, "I must have blacked out for a minute. 'Cause when I woke up, he had her wrapped in a blanket and was putting her on his horse. I tried to catch them on foot, but couldn't. So, I ran back up here to the house to find Mary Alice or Singing Dove. I told them what happened and that I was going to saddle a horse and ride after Mrs. Owens." He lowered his face in shame, "But they wouldn't let me, they told me I had to stay here."

Jace's whole body trembled. With contained control he credited the child, "And it's a good thing you did. They needed you here and now I need you. Cody, do you feel well enough to ride?"

"Yes, Sir!" Red hair tossed about as the boy nodded his head.

"I need you to ride to town and get Sheriff Wilcox. Tell him what happened and tell him that I went after Mrs.- Mrs. Owens." He almost choked on her name, realizing that is how he thought of her, Mrs. Jace Owens-his wife. "Then I need you to stay in town. The weather is getting bad out there and I need you to stay in town until it blows over. Do you understand, Cody?"

"Yes, Sir!" The boy had slipped from his fingers and was already shrugging into his coat. "I won't let you down, Mr. Owens! I promise," Cody vowed as he scrambled out the door.

Jace watched the door close behind the lad. A thousand thoughts flashed through his mind. He glanced down to his side and asked, "Where did he take her Singing Dove?"

Wet tracks ran down the woman's cheeks. Her shoulders lifted and she stated, "Northwest."

Light reflected off the key she held up for him, without a word he took it and headed for the closet that housed Harold Jordan's gun collection.

Minutes later, Jace pulled the flap of his collar up and ran across the yard to the barn. Weary brown eyes looked his way as he threw open the door. Cody must have led Marion out of the snowy wind. Crusted hair, caused by their hard ride home, covered the horse. "I'm sorry, Guy. It couldn't be helped." Rubbing the long, sweat coated neck he looked around for another mount. A thrashing noise come from the paddock and grew loader with each clatter. Jace walked to the back of the barn and opened the door.

Midnight's front feet crashed against the wide boards of the corral. His ears were laid back and steam rose from nostrils that flared with irritation. Jace let out a sharp whistle.

Long strands of his flowing mane waved in the wind as the beast turned, squealed, and made a wild dash toward the sound. Sliding to a halt within inches of him, the horse used his flat face to give a hard nudge to Jace's shoulder.

"Come on, Boy, let's go find her," Jace made a verbal pact with the stallion.

Singing Dove walked into the barn just as Jace mounted. In silence, she filled his saddlebags with foodstuffs and a blanket. Her fingers motioned for him to lower his head. She tied a thick scarf over his hat and around his neck. One hand gave his cheek a soft pat before she nodded at the horse.

"We'll bring her home safe and sound, Singing Dove. I promise. Safe and sound!" The decree left his mouth and the horse soared out the barn door.

As the icy wind slapped his face, Jace heard the mournful sound of the chant the Lakota woman started to sing. It carried with him for miles.

Chapter Fourteen

Blood pooled in her head, made her dizzy, and caused the raw bile in her stomach to rise. Penny swallowed against the threatening eruption. She tried to lift her head, but the force of their speed was too strong. The piecing pain in her hip was intolerable, and she couldn't find a way to brace against it. Her feet were numb, whether from the cold, or the lack of circulation, she could no longer tell.

It seemed like hours had ensued since Luke had tackled her. A crude dark cloth had been flung over her head as she walked through the open barn door and someone knocked her to the ground. With panic she had fought to pull the binding material from her body. There had been a thud and a cry of pain. Instantly, she had known Cody had been struck.

Her restrained struggles had been no challenge against strong arms. With quick movements her attacker managed to twist the putrid smelling blanket around her head and body. Unforgiving hands had secured the cover with a tight rope around her waist and arms before binding her shins with another. The sour blanket's only saving grace was the moth eaten holes that continued to allow her to receive small bits of fresh air now and again.

One of those openings had also provided her with a quick glimpse of her attacker. Fear had encircled her body as Luke dragged her to the side of the barn where he threw her over his mount and climbed on behind her. Leaving her draped over the saddle horn, he'd kicked the horse with sharp spurs and raced away from the Copper Cow at a treacherous speed. Her head bobbed and joggled until she found an area in front of his knee to brace it from the perilous snapping. But she was still unable to find a way to keep her legs that hung over the other side of the animal from being offended. A thick knee smacked her dangling feet continuously as the horse's legs lifted high in a precarious gallop.

Forced speed made the ride rough and unstable. Without mercy the saddle horn dug into the thin skin covering her hipbone. The animal's gait was uneven and wild, so every painful blast was unexpected. Try as she might, she was unable to find a way to brace herself enough to absorb the intrusions.

Their pace slowed as the trail started to ascend. Her fear mounted when she realized they were now in the hills. She tried to force the panic away. She wasn't about to give the *Zuzeca* any additional power over her. The uphill ride forced her body to shift against her attacker. The movement provided some relief to her battered hip, but caused the bile to rise again in her throat at the thought of touching his person. Swallowing the offensive taste, she focused on attempting to track time and direction. She needed to pinpoint their location, as well as their destination.

The horse jolted to a standstill, its sides heaved from the strenuous ride. Penny let her body go limp for a moment and mandated her tense muscles to find a moment of reprieve.

"Get up!" Luke's snarling tone came from above her. "What the hell are you jackasses doing lying around? Anyone could have rode up that trail and you wouldn't have seen them!"

"Sorry, Boss. The weather got so bad we had to build a fire to stay warm." The answering voice came from her right side. She twisted and tried to see through a peek hole.

"Put that damn thing out. We have to ride!" Luke yelled.

Her legs knew temporary relief when the rope binding them was removed. It was short lived. Within moments it felt like a hundred, red-hot needles stuck her as blood flowed to where the tight bindings had been.

A slight whelp of fear escaped her throat when Luke grabbed her waist and lifted her bound body off the saddle. Without care or tenderness, he attempted to force her body to straddle the saddle. Thick fingers dug into her thighs and the deadened weight of her stiff legs were forced to spread apart. Harsh movements mandated her tender hip to slip into the narrow space in front of him and into the high swells of leather. The skirt of her wool dress bunched up, exposing her pantaloons and socks to the elements.

The taste of blood trickled onto her tongue as she bit her lips to absorb the pain without a sound. A couple tears slipped from the corners of her eyes when she sensed a knife enter the blanket covering her head. Renting of material reverberated in her ears as the blade slit a hole in the rancid wrap. Crude jerks pulled her hair through the jagged cut. The blanket tore further and slipped down to her shoulders. Freezing air nipped at her face and stung her skin with tiny bites of ice.

His hand clutched at her crown as if he was revealing a prize to the four rough riders around the fire. "When a man wants something done right, he does it himself!" Luke boasted before he let go of her tresses, wrapped a crude arm around her shoulders and forced her back to press against his chest. "Now saddle up! We have to ride!"

"Boss..." A tall, filthy looking man with chiseled features took a step toward them. "I don't think Butch can ride. That leg of his has gotten real bad."

Penny peered down at the heavily built form lying near a small fire. His left foot and ankle were wrapped with a dark mass of rags. Swollen toes, black with dirt and infection, protruded out of the crude dressing. His right arm was bandaged near the shoulder with similar looking material.

Luke leaned his head next to her ear and hissed, "The bullet in the arm and the gashes on his leg are both your handiwork, my dear."

Penny turned away from the scene and his words. He pulled his head from hers. She sucked in a gulp of cold air and tried not to gag at the lingering scent of his breath.

"Butch, can you ride?" Luke bellowed.

The man groaned in pain, "I don't think so, Boss."

An unexpected noise made both Penny and the horse jerk. The ringing in her ears was immense. Smoke encircled her face and infringed her lungs. She stared at Butch as his body bucked from the bullet's aimed entrance and synchronized exit. Blood gushed from the center of his chest. She squeezed her eyes closed, not wanting to witness the scene.

"Now, let's ride!" Luke ordered.

She felt his movements as he holstered the pistol back on his hip and hit the horse with the metal disks on his boots. The mount leaped forward and almost knocked one of the other gang members down before it began to race away from the small campsite.

The other riders caught up with them and the wind picked up velocity as they rode through the hills. Penny refused to let her mind relive Butch's murder. Instead, she searched the lay of the land and made mental landmarks for her return journey. Luke must have sensed her mission because they paused long enough for him to pull the offensive blanket back over her face.

She accepted the protection against the cold and concentrated her sense of direction on creating a map. The wind gushing across the land echoed in her ears and heightened her vibrations of dread. When they stopped, she wiggled her head and searched for a hole in the blanket. Darkness had set in and she couldn't tell if she was seeing the dark sky, or just the crude covering.

Luke slid to the ground and without warning ripped her from the safety of the saddle. The blanket fell away from her head. Freezing wind and tiny bits of ice slapped her face, making it difficult to decipher the layout of their destination. She did catch sight of a crudely built cabin as he threw her over his shoulder. Her head hung down his back. It was impossible to see anything except the white blanket of snow that now covered the ground.

Luke kicked open a door and barked an order at his men before entering the cabin. He stomped across the room and dumped Penny onto a lumpy bed. The legs of the cot creaked with protest as her body tumbled. Pain slapped at her left temple when it hit something solid before she could stop the irregular movements. With her arms and hands still tied against her sides, she used her legs and feet to find enough balance to still her body from thrashing about.

"Not so high and mighty are we now, Miss Jordan?" Luke growled. The glow of the match he struck against the edge of the table flickered across his face. His vulgar features were displayed. He cupped the flame and used it to light the wick of a glass lantern on a table in the center of the room.

Penny knew he wanted her to rant and rave, to beg for kindness and comfort, or to ask for forgiveness. She wouldn't give him any of it, while ignoring his words, she twisted further from the edge. Scooting across the mattress, she forced her dress to flow down and cover her ice-cold legs. Her pantaloon and socks were stiff with ice from the long, cold ride. Shivers entered her body, both from the cold and from her capturer, but she refused to let panic overtake her.

Dust filled her nose, she sneezed at the intrusion and a rude guffaw from Luke filtered across the room. She shot him a cold stare. Light from the lamp filled the room. Her gaze took in their surroundings. It was a one-room shack. The bed was against one wall, a table with four chairs around it, sat in the middle, and a large wood-burning stove adorned the wall opposite the bed. The entrance was in front of the table and an uneven built cupboard stood along the wall across from the door. The only window was behind the bed. *The Lucky J*, her mind comprehended.

Snapping noises echoed off the rough-hewn walls as he broke small twigs apart and threw the kindling into the door of the stove. Penny ignored his open display of power as she estimated the circumference of the panes of glass beside her-*too small to crawl through.* Her gaze continued to roam the room, searching for an escape route or for anything she could find to create a makeshift weapon.

When smoke began to fill the room, Luke slapped the side of the dented stovepipe. Penny heard the creosote let loose inside the ventilation pipe, it fell into the flames with snaps and crackles. The room filled with heavy smoke and the smoldering air caused tiny tears to form in her eyes. She closed her lids against the stinging and forced the droplets to recede before anyone could mistake them as tears of fear. Luke let out a loud curse and opened the cabin's door. The smoke became mingled with cold, but fresh, night air. Penny opened her eyes after she heard the door close and sensed the room had been somewhat cleared of the offensive cloud.

His wicked stare bore on her. An evil grin crossed his face. With slow, showy movements, he pulled a knife from his belt and began to walk toward her. The blade glistened as it caught the flame of the lamp while he strolled past the table.

Her heart slapped at the inner wall of her chest. The room seemed to shrink in size with each step he took. Penny pulled her body into a fetal position. Her mind began to recite the Lord's Prayer.

Dirty fingers reached out and grabbed the front of the soiled blanket. With two hard tugs Luke pulled her to the edge of the bed. His hand rubbed across her breasts before he reached down to pull on the rope that circled her waist. He brought the knife up to her face and twisted it for her full view.

A low chuckle rumbled from his chest before he lowered the blade to the rope and with one fast upward motion he attempted to cut the twines. The knife caught on the stiff hemp. Her body jerked forward at the intrusion. He shoved her back on to the mattress and holding the rope with one hand, forcibly sawed at the coiled twines. One by one they began to unravel and let loose. She could sense his anger as it rose with each frustrated grunt and willed her body not to tremble. When the frayed ends finally lay at her sides, he twisted her legs over the edge and once again grabbed at the front of the blanket. Pulling her upward, he forced her into a seated position and knelt eye level with her.

His grotesque breath blew onto her face as he pulled his thick lips back to bare yellow teeth. "You could have had it all, Miss Jordan. You could have been the queen of Jamestown!" He let go of the blanket with a jerk and straightened his stance.

Penny stilled her body and pulled the offensive blanket closer to her bosom. Now thankful for the small amount of protection it might provide her. She had seen pure evilness in his eyes and at the moment felt true fear.

He threw the remnants of the rope onto the table. "There will be gold streets leading up to my mansion. The train tracks leading to my establishments will be made of gold. Footmen and doormen will be available to wait on me hand and foot. Diamonds and jewels will decorate my house, right down to the handles of my knives," he proclaimed as he flashed the blade around. "But don't fret, my darling-uh- Mrs. Owens, I might take pity upon a lovely, lonely widow."

Beady eyes stared into hers. Watching, waiting for uncontrollable, frightened reactions. When she didn't expel any of the reactions she knew he wanted, he pulled his gaze and turned away from her. She let a sigh of relief emit through pursed lips, her terror had been close to boiling out.

"What's the matter Penny, cat got your tongue?" With his back to her, he laid the knife on the table and sauntered over to the stove. Using the corner of his coat to protect his hand from the hot metal of the handle, he opened the hinged door. "Well, that is fine by me. Your voice can get a little annoying at times," he said before he filled the flaming area with several sizable logs.

A gust of frigid air filled the room as the cabin door flew open again. Three men, covered with icy snow, filled the opening. Each tried to be the first one in, which only caused all three to become wedged in the narrow opening. After several moments of arms and legs that pushed and shoved, the middle one broke loose and stepped forward. The other two followed, slapping at each other with disgust.

The first one, a round, short, tub of a man had snot frozen to his bushy mustache. Penny stifled a gag when he began to melt it with his lower lip and tongue.

"Shut the door, damn it!" Luke screeched.

Penny watched as the latter two scrambled to do as instructed. The way they stumbled over one another, she wondered if they would ever manage to get the door closed let alone latched. They did, but not without grumbles and fists thrown at each other.

"What the hell do you three think you're doing?" Luke asked after they had settled themselves on the chairs around the table.

"We stabled the horses, Boss. Just like you said," a tall, lanky, gang member admitted.

Luke crossed the room and slapped the table with a thick hand. "One of you still has to stand guard!"

"But you said Owens was in Elm Creek," the mustache sucker said.

"He was, but so was I- then! Ace, get out there and stand guard." Luke turned to the third man.

Ace was of average build and height, with facial skin that was ruddy and pock marked. His eyes were almost gold in color and Penny noticed how the left one wandered about.

"Aw, Boss, it's awfully cold out there. Besides no one could have tracked us here. There's a blizzard out there. That wind is so cold, I..."

"Get out there!" Luke interrupted the man's whine by grabbing the front of Ace's grubby coat. Stains, of who knew what, were splattered across the front of the tan colored wool. "Of course they would try and follow us! We captured their queen!" He turned to Penny and provided her a look of pretend concern as he continued, "But they will probably freeze to death trying to find us."

"Boss, you said they wouldn't be able to blame it on us. You said we all have alibis," the tall one reminded their leader.

This one was at least six and half feet tall, but Penny thought he couldn't weigh much more than she did. His shoulders and knees were so bony they almost popped out of the raggedy material of his denim coat and pants. His face was gaunt. Narrow eyes were sunken into deep sockets below a chiseled forehead and above a very crooked nose. Penny questioned the health of his skeletal frame. Her empathy for the three men almost outweighed her fear of them.

"You are the stupidest bunch of rough riders I ever met!" Luke declared with hatred. "Slim, we do have alibis," he assured the tall man before he turned to Penny. "You see, my dear, a delectable little filly back in Elm Creek led me down the street and up the side steps of her- uh- establishment. Everyone in town saw it, including your husband and the fine Sheriff. She will remain there all night, in her locked room, refusing to let our love nest be interrupted. And tomorrow when they come asking she will insist I was with her all night. Making it impossible for me to have kidnapped anyone. Including you." He pointed to the table. "My men, of course, have similar alibis."

"But, Boss, no girls led us down the street," mustache sucker professed. His back was to her, so it was impossible for Penny to see his face. Which was fine- once was enough.

"Ticker!" Luke bellowed and the mustached man jolted his chair back onto all four legs from his reclined position.

"Yea, Boss?" Ticker asked as he grabbed the edge of the table to halt his forward motion.

"Do you have your watch?"

"Of course!" A mangled timepiece was pulled from his chest pocket and held up for view. He twisted in his chair to give Penny a proud examination of his prized possession.

Luke pointed to the watch and let his finger bounce in the air as if it was walking around the face of the clock. "You keep track. In one hour Slim will relieve Ace. One hour after that you will relieve Slim and then one hour after that Ace will come out and relieve you. We will keep doing this all night. Understand?"

Ticker nodded his head and held the watch in front of the other two. Penny couldn't believe her eyes. She almost had to laugh at the intelligence of Luke's gang. Were these the same men she had been so fearful of?

Luke's angry bellow interrupted her thoughts. "Now, Ace, get out there and take your turn!"

Grudgingly, the man stood to take his leave. His wandering eye caught Penny. It attempted to hold her gaze for a moment before he stomped to the door. She wondered if he had tried to intimidate her or if he just blamed her for his job duties. Luke slammed the door behind Ace's exit with force and finalized the watch plan conversation.

****

Midnight refused to acknowledge any control his rider commanded. Jace gave in and lessened his hold on the leather strap, which dictated the pressure of the bit in the horse's mouth. He let the horse determine the pace of their quest. His silent admission that the animal knew better than he, what its limits were.

The cold fragments of frozen snow that bit the

exposed skin of his face no longer registered pain. The horse's infinite speed had numbed the flesh while they flew across the wide-open country. Jace tucked his head behind the long, black neck stretched out in front of him and they began to climb a steep hill.

Any filtered sunlight had long since faded and the muted shine of the moon was incapable of penetrating the stormy skies. Jace gave his trust to the animal as they glided over boulders and around hairpin turns. His hands flew to grasp the saddle horn when Midnight suddenly became startled and brought his massive body upward in a vertical rear. Hoofs pawed at the swirling flakes in the air.

The steed's front legs hit the ground with a jolt. Jace stared down at the corpse lying on the icy ground beside them. Subdued light revealed a body that wasn't as snow covered as the ground around it. It was evident heat had trickled out of the man as the ice crystals fell on him and the cooler earth in his vicinity. Warm blood had turned the flakes into water and caused a thin, now frozen, stream of red to highlight the bullet hole in the center of his chest.

Jace swallowed at the fear in his throat. "Let's go, Boy." He nudged the horse back into movement.

Hours later the animal slowed his gait. With caution he selected his route through the inches of snow that covered the ground. Jace picked up on Midnight's heightened senses. "What is it, Boy? Are we close to Penny?"

The horse tossed his head in answer and came to a halt. Jace lowered his stiff body from the saddle and began to lead the animal forward. "Shhh, don't make a sound."

Midnight shook his head and bumped Jace in the back with his thick skull, undoubtedly to inform the whispered warning was unnecessary. They made their way through the snow and slipped into a small grove of pines.

Between two of the needled trees, the swirls of snow cleared long enough for Jace to capture a picture of the compound. A small cabin with smoke circling above it was built down in the bottom of the valley. Another larger building stood to one side. A dilapidated corral ran along the space between the cabin and collapsing barn. *The Lucky J*, Jace determined.

Movement brought his attention to the left. A few yards further down the ridge he made out the familiar shape of a man. The sentry stretched and pulled his body from a huddled position to stand in the clearing. Slipping back into the trees, Jace and Midnight picked a muted trail and cautiously stalked their prey. A few yards behind the man Jace stopped and unhooked a coiled rope from the saddle horn. He wiggled his fingers in order to force the blood to flow and provide him with the nimble control he needed.

The other man took a stance near the steep edge of the hill. Jace recognized the movements and sound as the man began to relieve himself. Steam rose from the ground as a stream landed in the snow.

Twirling jute made a soft whistle as it flew through the air and swished over the man's head and shoulders. It encircled the unsuspecting chest. Jace gave it a hard tug and with quick movements wrapped the other end around the leather horn on Midnight's back.

The guard hit the ground hard. The bandana tied around his lower face for protection against the cold wind muffled his shocked yelp. His struggles stilled as a Jace knelt beside him.

With quick movements Jace pulled the rag from the man's face, balled it with his fist and forced it deep into the man's mouth. After he tugged the scarf from his own head and neck, he slit it in two with his knife. His agile fingers secured half of it around the man's jaw, further protection against any sounds. The other half was tucked in his pocket for future use.

Still crouched beside the prone man's form, Jace retrieved a hat that had fallen to the ground. With a demented whisper, he dropped it onto the man's crotch. "Wouldn't want stubby to get frostbit." He glared at the man with hatred. "Move so much as an inch and Midnight will make you wish you hadn't."

The horse took a step backward, the rope tightened. The bound body slid a few inches across the frozen ground, proving the point.

Jace nodded to the horse. “He will take off in a full run, dragging your sorry ass behind him. Over the rocks, through the trees, and down the hill, I suspect that really could be harmful to your little, exposed friend.”

A wandering eye flashed in all directions, fear of his promised fate was visible. The man nodded his head in understanding. Terror gripped his body, apparent by the trembles that overtook it.

“Keep the rope tight, Midnight,” Jace issued as he straightened his knees.

The horse tossed his head and the movement pulled the body a slight degree backward. Anxiously, the quivering man attempted to use the tips of his restrained hands to hold his hat over his manhood. His distressed muffles tried to assure his capturer of his agreement to remain still.

Jace glanced to the trail that led to the cabin. It was steep and out in the open. He turned away from the path and began to creep along the edge of the valley wall, in search of another route.

He made his way along the ridge and began to descend behind the barn. The hairs on the back of his neck rose in warning as he inched near a pile of boulders. With caution he pulled a gun from his holster and stilled his movements.

“*Maka Wichasha*,” whispered words caressed his ears. Jace stared as one of the boulders unfolded itself into a human form.

“Two Bears?” he questioned with disbelief at the transformation he witnessed.

The slam of a door made both men glance down at the cabin. Two men stomped across the frozen ground, away from the structure.

Two Bears slapped his own chest and pointed to the men, with the other hand he pointed at Jace and whispered, “*Wichincala*.”

Jace understood. Two Bears would go after the men. Jace was to find the young woman- Penny.

****

Penny’s continued search for a makeshift weapon had revealed a long crack along the top of the wooden board that stretched across the length of the headboard of the bed. Discreetly, she scooted close enough to try and pry off a long sliver. When positioned just so, behind her stiff spine, nervous fingers began to work their way into the crack and forced the wood to split.

Uncontrollable movements made her arm flay against her back as the wood let loose. A muffled crack was sent throughout the room. Blood pounded in her ears as she waited for the sound to be detected by the others. A sigh of relief exhaled as she realized the men were engrossed in Luke's tale and didn't notice the sound or her movements.

Trembling fingers examined then slipped her newfound weapon beneath the folds of her skirt. It would do- a piece of jagged wood approximately eight inches long and about two inches wide at one end. The long shaft tapered to a stiff point at the other end. Satisfied with her find, she scooted forward and once again balanced her frame on the edge of the bed. Demurely, she folded her hands on her lap and waited for the right time.

Luke's tale was long and growing with hateful insults. It would soon be difficult not to let her body demonstrate the waves of turmoil his words flogged her mind with. His eyes glistened with confidence as his listeners encouraged the fictional account.

"The poor Easterner, Jace Owens, froze to death while searching for his wife in the Black Hills during a blizzard. Papers across the nation will pick up the story. Especially when it is discovered Mrs. Owens was kidnapped by renegade Injuns." His delight flowed as he continued to create the tale aloud for his audience.

Enchanted, the two men at the table smirked and snorted in agreement with their pack leader.

"The distinguished Luke James, and his band of gallant men, rescued the beautiful Penelope Jordan in the nick of time. Bravely James and his men pursued the murdering pack of heathens through the dangerous hills. With a surprise attack the fearless James Gang sent dozen's of Lakota's to their final resting grounds, saving Miss Jordan from her dismal fate of rape and murder!" Luke took the final swig of brown liquid from the bottle he had been waving in the air and tossed the empty container on the floor. It bounced off his foot. He attempted to kick it out of the way as he retrieved another from the warped cupboard. The container rolled across the floor and wedged itself against the leg of the woodstove.

"The Army will then see the danger of allowing the Lakota to remain in the hills. And will drive the heathens all south. Allowing thousands to die on the way!" Pulling a small pouch out of his pants pocket, he turned and tossed it at Penny. "Which, my dear, will leave the land for me and my men to claim." He nodded at the pouch. "Open it, go ahead and see what I will be claiming!"

Penny didn't even glance at the bag that landed beside her. Nor did she allow her eyes to focus on the incensed man demanding her attention.

"I said open it!" Luke stomped to the bed, drew his hand up and brought the back of it across her face. "You will obey me, Bitch!"

Penny's head flew backward with a snap. Her lip ripped open from the thrust of his knuckle. She ignored the blood that began to trickle from the laceration and demonstrated an unyielding demeanor with boldness. Even with the knowledge her rejection of his authority would increase his fury, she held on to her resolution and refused to give him any domination of her person.

Luke grabbed the pouch and loosened the drawstring. With the other hand he clutched her cheeks and shoved the bag within inches of her nose. Abusive force made her observe the contents of the pouch. "Look at it! It's the finest you will ever see. Much finer than anything that comes out of California!"

The muscles in her neck strained against the hand that clutched her face. But she forced herself not to fight against his brutality. Instead she closed her eyes and discreetly allowed one hand to begin to make its way from her lap.

Her indifference infuriated him. "You two get out of here!" Luke ordered the men at the table. His feet kicked her legs apart. "I know something you can't ignore."

Spittle from his lips sprayed onto her face. Fear vibrated up her spine. Beneath her skirt, her hand found what it searched for. Trembling fingers wrapped around the thick end of the jagged piece of wood.

"But, Boss, Ace's time ain't up," Ticker argued.

Luke let go of Penny's face and threw the bag back onto the bed. Furiously, he twisted around and grabbed Ticker by the throat, forcing the man to come to his feet. "I said get out of here! And don't come back in until I say."

The two men scrambled to leave the room, knocking chairs over on their flight out the door. Luke grabbed the lantern before it tumbled to the floor from the rocking table and set it on a crooked shelf of the cabinet. The glow of the light made his eyes look red as he glared at her.

"Now my dear, Mrs. Owens, let's see how a real man compares to that city boy you are so proud of!" He began to unbuckle his belt as he stalked toward the bed. His fingers reminded her of claws. She knew they were itching to tear her apart.

The buckle seemed to be on her side and wouldn't let loose. A growl rumbled the room as he quit fumbling with it and lurched at her. Those unbearable hands grabbed at her protective cover. The moth eaten blanket shredded as the claws dug in. Strips of material floated onto the bed. Luke let out a laugh as he reached for the front buttons of her woolen dress.

Fear like she had never known encrusted her body. She tried to force her mind to remain coherent. Her fingers tightened on the dagger, and she pulled it from its hiding place. As the tips of his fingers touched the front of her bodice, Penny flipped her body sideways and stabbed the sharp end of the long scrap of wood deep into Luke's neck. She pushed hard, plunging the dagger deeper and deeper into his flesh.

He screamed in pain and grabbed at the arm driving the shaft into his skin. Incensed by her fight, he threw his body onto hers. His hand clutched on to hers, twisted her arm, and forced her to let loose of the weapon. He began to slap and punch at her.

Hands flayed and fists tore at the softness of her flesh. Rage poured from him. He opened his mouth and brought his teeth down. Penny tried to roll away but his teeth sunk into the thick part of her arm, right below her shoulder. A scream tore from her throat as the sharpness of his fangs broke through the wool of her sleeve and into her skin.

She fought against his brutal strength. Kicked and scratched at anything within her reach. But his body was pressed upon hers and wouldn't allow her enough movement to make any dire contacts. His knees held her dress tight to the mattress below them, which was being forced to form a deep cavern between the rope stays, stifling her struggles even more.

Jace peered in through the frosty window. He made out Penny's form as she battled against her attacker. A scream entered his ears. Enraged, he flew around the cabin. The door was no kind of barrier to his charge. With a piecing war cry he let his authority penetrate the room.

Penny scrambled to corner of the bed as he ripped Luke's vulgar body away from her struggling arms and legs.

"Jace?"

Luke flew through the air and landed on the table with a thud before he rolled onto the overturned chairs. His body flipped to his hands and knees and scrambled under the wooden structure. Blood dripped from a wooden stake protruding out of his neck.

Jace didn't even glance at the sound of his name. Rage seized him and caused him to be blind and deaf to everything except the *zuzeca* that slithered across the floor. He threw the table out of his way. It slammed against the open doorway and he grabbed the neck of the offensive snake. Lifting it high in the air, he flung the creature across the room and drove it to land on the hot iron of the blazing stove. A scream faded from its throat as it coiled into a pile on the floor.

Only then did the sweetest sound penetrate his senses. "Jace?" Tiny hands encircled his waist. "Jace?"

He turned to crush her against him. Her body still trembled from the terror of her attack.

"Yes, Darling, it's me. Oh, Sweetheart, are you okay, did he hurt you?" He had to find out. His hands roamed her body as the words rushed from his mouth. His blurred mind tried to comprehend if she was truly unscathed. Horror filled thoughts had not cleared enough to fully believe she was alive.

His gaze followed his hands and finally rose to peer at the most beautiful site he had ever seen. He brought his lips down to ravish hers. Her hair, her neck, her cheeks, everywhere they could reach, anywhere. He couldn't seem to touch her enough, to taste her enough.

She clung to him. Grasping and patting as if she was making certain he was real. He felt her fear diminish as their embrace grew and knew the moment her mind accepted his presence. The moment man and woman surged together to become one.

An intrusive sound- a scream or perhaps the unmistakable sound of a pistol trigger as it locked into firing position- penetrated their reception.

His body twisted in front of hers as Jace turned to the sound. Snow swirled in through the open doorway. The oil lamp, balanced precariously on edge of the crude cabinet cast an eerie shadow onto the ceiling.

Luke took a step toward them. His feet staggered. A gun leveled on Jace's chest. "This just gets better and better," he gasped for air as he attempted to push the words from his guts. An evil laugh emitted and he concluded, "I now get to kill the husband myself!"

Jace reached for his six-shooter, but the sound of a gunshot cracked the air before it was out of his holster.

Penny's terrified scream mingled with the blast. Both sounds ricocheted off the walls and into the night air. Shocked, Jace stared straight ahead.

Chapter Fifteen

"Hate to shoot a man in the back, but sometimes it just can't be prevented." Sheriff Wilcox strode into the room. With a booted foot he tapped the arm of the body lying on the floor. "Elliott, drag the body outside and then let's see if we can put this door back on its hinges before we all freeze to death."

Half an hour later, Penny sat on the cot with the blanket Singing Dove had packed wrapped around her shoulders. Two Bears sat beside her.

Jace fought to keep a little green monster from overtaking his spent emotions as he took his seat on her other side. He'd felt the jealousy emerge when he saw the way her eyes lit up as the handsome brave entered the cabin. The man she claimed to love like a brother had crossed the room and wrapped his massive arms around her. Jace had left to help Elliott then, afraid his over zealous emotions might rip the brave from her embrace. After he re-entered the cabin, he had settled her on the mattress and wrapped the blanket he'd retrieved around her shoulders.

Now, his arm encircled her waist, tugged her closer to his frame and began to massage her uninjured hip. Jace felt joyous when she snuggled closer and rested her head on his shoulder. His other hand reached over to caress her cheek, and lightly touch the nasty split of her lip before it lifted her chin. They gazed at one another and it was evident to anyone who would have cared to look that they both enjoyed the view. His lips descended and pressed against her forehead.

The heart in his chest raced, his prayer of her safety had been answered. He couldn't remember ever being more thankful than he was at this moment. Lifting his lips, he gave her a quick wink and glanced to the table. His hand slipped from her face and followed the length of her arm until it found her trim fingers. Their hands entwined as he settled them on his lap. In unison they brought their gazes back to the table and joined the other occupants of the room listening to the Sheriff.

"James's parade down Main Street had been a little too obvious. As soon as Jace and Sam left for the ranch, I went to investigate. His uh- little associate, Lori Beth, refused to open the door to her room, it took sometime before we got a key from her landlord. Lori Beth claimed not to know where he went or the reason why she was to pretend he was with her. She just kept saying we will all be sorry when she becomes the Queen of Jamestown."

Penny's spine straighten, her entire body quivered. Jace pulled her tighter into his embrace and placed a kiss on the top of her head as Wilcox continued.

"Elliott and I left for the Copper Cow immediately, knowing his alibi had to be the cover for something. We caught up with Sam just as Cody O'Brien came flying up the road. We stopped at the ranch and Singing Dove told us Two Bears had arrived and rode out right after Jace. We grabbed fresh horses and followed the trail. Sam stopped at the top of the hill to untie Ace from Midnight before the horse killed him. Elliott and I saw Two Bears and his friend capture the other two, so we headed for the cabin. I could see Luke climbing to his feet through the open door way, I yelled, but I guess you couldn't hear me, with the wind hollowing and all." He added the last with a smile before growing serious again. "He was going to kill you, Jace. I had no choice but to shoot him in the back." Wilcox shook his head with disgust.

Sam sat in a chair across from the Sheriff, he threw a look of disgust toward the three bound and gagged men propped against the entranceway. The door had not only been ripped from its hinges, but also broken in two. Without a hammer or nails to be found, the only way to keep the cold air at bay was to physically hold the wood over the opening. A job that seemed fitting for the gang members. Sam stared at the man in the middle.

"I wasn't trying to save his sorry carcass, I was afraid Midnight might injure himself the way he was pawing at the ground around the idiot. I had just untied the rope when the horse heard Penny's scream. He tore down that hill like lightening shooting across the sky."

The older man turned toward Penny and sighed, "I'm sorry, Princess, but when I- we put the horses up for the night we found the remains of Tom and Jake."

Her eyes closed as she nodded her head. Jace caressed her trembling body as she accepted the news.

Elliott pulled his thick frame forward and leaned his elbows on the table the men sat around. "We also found several of Two Bear's braves, which explains the Lakota arrows and stuff found at each of the barn fires."

Two Bears nodded in agreement.

The deputy scratched his head and glanced at Penny. "No offense, ma'am, but I still don't comprehend what James was after."

Wilcox shrugged his shoulders, showing that he didn't have all the answers either.

Penny sat up and pulled out of Jace's embrace to reach around to the back of the cot, between she and Two Bears. Her hand lifted a small pouch into view. With a flick of her wrist, she lobbed it at the table. It landed in front of the Sheriff with a thump. The rounded bottom teetered before tipping onto its side. Several rocks tumbled out.

"Gold, gentlemen, Luke found gold in the Black Hills," she said.

Small flecks covering the pebbles glistened in the lamplight. The wind that howled and slapped at the outer walls of the cabin mingled with the snap and crackle of the woodstove as all eyes gazed at the shinny nuggets.

It was several minutes before the Sheriff scooped up the glittering stones and placed them back in the bag. He pulled the string tight, stood and handed it to Two Bears. "This is yours," he said.

Two Bears shook his head and refused to take the pouch. He turned to whisper to Penny.

"Two Bears says the Lakota have no need for it," she translated after they had conversed in his native tongue for a few moments.

"If you don't mind, Mrs. Owens," Wilcox began, "ask him to take it and to keep it hidden. Ask him to please, keep those shinny rocks well hidden from the white man."

Penny did as the Sheriff asked as Jace assumed the

rest of the room's occupants were doing just as he, envisioning the disasters and devastation that was sure to come. Eventually it would be made known...There's gold in the Black Hills of the Dakota Territory.

Two Bears rose and tipped his head at the other brave who stood near the bed. "Han," he said and offered his hand to the Sheriff.

"He says, yes, they will keep it well hidden. For as long as possible," Penny explained as she looked at Jace. Sadness covered her face. Her eyes went back up to Wilcox and she continued, "Two Bears and Red Eagle will be leaving now."

When the Sheriff started to protest, she stopped him. "The rest of his party has built a camp nearby and have gathered the remains of their brothers that were found with Jake and Tom. They will spend the night there and return to their families tomorrow. He would like you to move the ugly men away from the door."

Elliott rose to take care of the prisoners. Movements were limited by their bindings, but they managed to balance the door between the three of them while the deputy stood between them and the departing men. He offered his hand in farewell to Two Bears and Red Eagle and after the braves exited he ordered Ace, Slim and Ticker to replace the door and sit back down in front of it. The deputy added wood to the stove before he walked back to the table.

"Well men, Ma'am, I suggest we try to hunker down and get a few hours sleep. The sun will be up in a few hours, by then this storm should have played itself out and we can be on our way home," Wilcox suggested.

****

A few hours later, Penny watched as the deputy flopped Luke's blanket wrapped body over the back of his horse. She found herself thinking she almost wished he were still alive. Just so he could feel the pain and humiliation of having to ride a horse across the Territory in such a way. Disgust overcame her. She let out a deep breath, sent a silent plea for forgiveness and shook her head to clear her mind.

Her heart fluttered as Jace flipped into the saddle behind her. His lean fingers adjusted the blanket she was cocooned in before he guided her hips to rest upon his. His hand applied slight pressure on her stomach and brought her back against his chest.

She could feel his protective armor encircle her and complied. Her head snuggled beneath his chin and she prepared for the long ride home. The sun was shining and the bright, white snow gave everything a fresh, new look. She didn't even glance behind her, didn't need to. She would never have to worry about Luke James or the Lucky J again.

The ride home was long in miles, but short in time for Penny's mind. As the miles flowed beneath Midnight's even gait, a great sorrow formed in her chest. She realized she now had to face an even larger nightmare- Jace's departure. Her worse fear was upon her- it was time for her to let him go. Would she survive it?

That night, lying awake in the comfort of her own bed, she relived every moment in his arms. Recalled every time she saw a smile cross his handsome face, tasted every kiss of his lips, and heard the soft tune of his voice saying her name. She could almost feel the contours of his body beneath her fingers, and basked in the memory of his fresh masculine scent. In a way she was torturing herself, but the thoughts wouldn't quit. In another way, she was sealing him in her mind. Where he could live forever.

****

For two weeks she walked around blurry eyed and mindless, trying hard to accept her fate. This time she just couldn't seem to muster up the strength she needed.

Penny stood at the office window and watched her husband shake hands with the Sheriff before he turned to make his way to the house. The curtain flopped into place as she pulled away from the glass and stumbled to her desk. The middle drawer was pulled open and her eyes stung, the envelope holding the paper she had prepared was still there. A part of her wished it had somehow disappeared.

It hadn't.

The time had come.

Jace strolled across the front lawn and up the porch steps. The Sheriff had agreed with his request. Only the two of them would ever know Wilcox's bullet hadn't killed Luke James. The bullet had just grazed a shoulder. The long, wooden splinter stabbed into his jugular vein is what had brought his demise. Jace felt Penny had been through enough. She didn't need to know she had killed a man.

He bounded up the steps, maybe someday he would tell her. When they were old and gray, and sharing tales of their life together with the grandkids. Jace smiled at the thought of Penny being old and gray. That would never happen. She would always be young and beautiful in his eyes.

"Hi," Jace said as he closed the office door behind him. His light mood left. Sadness floated in the air. He glanced her way. That wonderful, lightly freckled face hadn't peeked a smile since they had returned home from the Lucky J. He missed her laughter and playfulness. He missed her honesty, her knowledge, and the relationship they had built. Everyone was worried about her. When he asked Singing Dove to examine her, the woman had just shrugged her shoulders-she didn't know what to do either.

"Hi," she answered with a monotone voice. "So, it's all over?"

He felt her eyes watching his back as he strolled to the window, pulled back the curtain and followed the Sheriff's departure down the long road.

"Yes. Wilcox said he led them to the gallows himself." Jace turned back to the room. As always everything was spotless, but something was missing. It hadn't dawned on him until now, but in the last two weeks the house had transformed back to what it had been like when he first arrived. Empty, conveying an unlived-in presence. That presence had been there when he first arrived, but had disappeared during the few months he had been here. It seemed that when Penny was happy, the house was happy. When she was sad, the house was sad.

Chilly sensations raced up his spine. He shook them off and pulled the heavy jacket off his shoulders. Draping it over the back of the couch he walked to her desk. "They admitted to killing your father."

Penny tipped her head in understanding, but said nothing.

Jace waited, when it was apparent she wasn't going to comment, he added, "They also admitted to attacking your wagon, to burning the O'Brien's place, to..." He stopped when she held her hand up.

"I know everything they did. I don't need to hear they admitted to it." She placed both hands on her desk and let out a deep sigh.

Look at me, he willed. *Look at me!*

She ran her fingers over the leather top of the desk. "The new hands seem to be working out."

With a sigh, he admitted, "Yes, they are good men. All four of them will serve the Copper Cow well. The extra help is needed now that all of the rustled cattle have been returned. And Dallas is a fine cook, having him prepare all of their meals has taken a load off Mary Alice."

She nodded, "Calhoun took his leaving well."

"Yes." He leaned down, forcing her eyes to find his. "I should have told you about his commission. I'm sorry."

A false smile curved her lips as she shook her head. "I forgive you. I figured it was something. He certainly wasn't a cow hand." Shrugging her shoulders, she pulled her hands from the desk and folded her arms across her chest. "I guess we should be glad he was such a bad solider. I don't want to think about what might have happened if he had discovered what Luke was really after."

"Neither do I," Jace admitted and straightened. "He might have been shifty enough to switch sides." Jace fought his urge to walk around the desk and engulf her in his arms.

Penny unfolded her arms and placed one hand on a drawer knob. "Christmas will be here soon."

Jace drew his brows together. She had been acting so out of character, still was. He didn't know how to reach her. "Do you like Christmas, Penny?"

"Of course, who doesn't like Christmas? Sharing your blessings with your friends and family. Rejoicing in the reason, the birth of our Savior." She made herself smile as she looked at him and attempted a teasing voice. "The wonderful foods and festive songs. Don't you like Christmas, J-Jace?"

"Yes, I like Christmas, just fine." She was not a good

actress. Jace saw the way her hands trembled, heard the way her voice stuttered. "Sweetheart, what's wrong? What aren't you telling me?"

Penny pulled open the drawer and took out an envelope. She gasped for air.

"Penny? What is it? Maybe I can help." He leaned forward.

Her body surged back, away from his, stopping as it hit the back of her chair. "No, Jace. You've already done more than I ever imagined. You-you've fulfilled your end of our bargain."

Bargain. The word felt like a slap across his the face. He had been ignoring the fact that he'd made one, made several in fact. With her, with an outer force, with his inner self, where he had promised to help her and then leave her, untouched.

It wasn't time yet! There was more he had to do. The top of his head tingled. He ran his fingers through his hair and across his forehead. *What more*? She had her cattle back, James and the fiasco's he had been creating were all taken care of, the Association admired and respected her, and she had good, honest ranch hands. Jace felt his body start to tremble. It started at his toes and inched its way upward, like the rumbles of a volcano.

"Here." She handed him the envelope.

"What's this?" He clenched a fist to quell his nerves, before he took it from her hand.

"It's a bank draft. It's your pay, for services rendered," her voice cracked.

Jace pulled his hand away. The paper had singed his fingers. "Damn it, Penny. I don't want your money!"

She watched the envelope float to the desktop. "I, I know we never settled on an amount. If that's not enough, I."

Jace slapped the desk. "I said I don't want your money. None of it!"

Penny stood, folded her arms across her chest and rubbed her upper arms with the opposite hands, as if she had to ward off an icy chill. "If you leave today, you might make it home in time for Christmas. You could spend Christmas with your family." She looked exhausted, deep dark circles had settled beneath her green eyes.

"Is that what you want, Penny?" Jace began to step around the desk, but stopped when she started to back away from him. "Do you really want me to go back to Philadelphia?" *Say the word! Please just say no, and I'll stay forever!* His mind screamed at her.

Time stood still as they gazed at one another. He knew Penny couldn't lie to him. She wouldn't lie to him. She started to shake her head negatively. His heart skipped a beat. Then the shaking stopped and she began to nod affirmatively.

"It's what I need," she whispered. "I need you to go back to Philadelphia." She flipped around and bolted for the door. "Good-bye, Jace." The words floated behind as she ran for the stairs.

Jace started for the door, then stopped. The transformation never came. Tears burnt the back of his eyes. Her amazing transformations, the ones he was so astonished by, one had not come this time. Hadn't come for the past two weeks.

He stepped forward, pushed the door shut, and leaned his head against it. After a few moments, he reached into his pocket and pulled out a gold locket. His fingers were shaking so hard, it took several tries before he got the latch to let loose. He looked at the pictures it held, one of him and one of Daniel. It had been their mother's. Charles had sent it with some of his other belongings.

The plan had been to give it to Penny tonight- along with his love. The words he had heard a few months ago, when he'd entered the barn for the first time, returned to his mind. "We don't need you anymore. She does." It had been Karin's voice. Soft and sweet, releasing him from his lifelong commitment to her. It had taken him months to understand, but now he did and he knew he wanted a life with Penny, a long, fulfilling life. But it's not what Penny wanted. Probably never had been.

All this time he'd thought he had to leave her. Never once had he thought about her sending him away. She didn't want him to stay. She had what she wanted, her ranch and he wasn't a part of it.

He walked to the desk and lowered himself onto her chair. Pulling open the bottom drawer, his trembling hand grasped her memory bag and tugged the top open. As tears fell from his eyes, he kissed the locket and let it slip threw his fingers, into the bag. He tightened the pull string and closed the drawer. With the back of his hand, he wiped the water from his face and stood to retrieve his jacket.

Shrugging into the thick material, he looked around the room. His fingers struggled with the buttons running down his front. His eyes closed. A remembrance flashed through his mind. Tiny hooks of the dress he had deftly unhooked for her. Other visions formed and danced across the closed lids as his ears rang, recalling her laughter.

He could see the smile that made his heart flip when it formed on her face. His fingers tingled as if feeling the quickness of her heartbeat or the softness of her skin and his mouth salivated at the thought of the taste of sweetness from her lips. He could smell the pleasant aroma that lingered in any room she had been in. His eyes opened, and he felt a pain like he had never witness before, grip at his chest. In agony he clutched his right arm and stumbled for the door.

An hour later, Jace mounted the sorrel as Singing Dove entered the barn. She filled his saddlebag with foodstuffs and a blanket then placed a hand on his knee. "*Wakhan Thanka*, The Great Spirit, he guides us, Jace. He does not bargain with us."

Jace smiled, she had never called him by his given name before. Her words echoed in his ears, her wisdom was so great. He reached down and patted her soft cheek. "Then please ask *Wakhan Thanka* to guide me home, Singing Dove. Ask the Great Spirit to guide me home."

"Han," she agreed as he rode out of the barn.

Penny now stood at the window in the office and watched until the long road swallowed him. She had ignored Mary Alice's pleas and demands on the other side of her locked bedroom door while she cried her eyes out. But the thought of one final glance had enticed her to leave her room and join the other household members in wishing Jace a safe journey.

He hadn't said a word to her, just touched the rim of his derby hat as he rode past. He wore the same clothes he had arrived in. She was shocked by how different he looked in the brown suit and squat hat.

Mary Alice's voice had been filled with sobs, "His plan is to leave Marion at the stockyards in Yankton, he'll ask Bill Casper to see the horse is returned to the Copper Cow. After that he will board an Eastern train and should arrive in Philadelphia before the end of the month."

Penny hadn't answered, hadn't even acknowledged she had heard her aunt's words. Instead, she left the others on the porch and closed herself in the office, taking her stance at the window. Through tear-filled eyes she searched the horizon, wanting one more glance.

The heels of tall boots penetrated her ears. They clopped on the floor as someone entered the room. She wiped the tears from her eyes, but didn't turn as the person proceeded to her side. The desire to collapse into the arm that surrounded her shoulder was strong, but she fought it.

"Princess, do you really think you know what you're doing?" Sam asked.

"It was time." The words burned her raw throat.

His hand rubbed her upper arm. "What do you mean, it was time? None of this makes any sense to me."

"We made a deal. He would help me save the ranch then I would let him go back East. I had to keep my end of it," she tried to explain.

"He wasn't here because of any deal you made with him." Sam pulled her around to look at him.

"Yes, he was, Sam." Penny put her hands on his chest; her hard exterior would break if he hugged her. "What don't you understand? I pulled him away from the only life he had ever known and forced him live in a strange new world. I had to let him go back. He has a right to live the life he had chosen. Not one- some woman forced on him by ordering a husband through the mail." Tears became closer and closer to cascading from her eyes.

Sam looked at her. His eyes were wide and a look of disgust seemed to come out as he shook his head. "Did you ask him, Princess?"

"Ask him what?" He was confusing her.

"What his choice was? Now, not when he first got here. Did you ask him if wanted to return to Philadelphia or if he wanted to stay here, at the Copper Cow? Did you give him a chance to make the choice?"

Her head swirled. Why would she have asked him? He had told her all along he had to leave. Hadn't he? She couldn't talk, if she opened her mouth her sobs would be released.

Sam placed both hands on her shoulders. "Penny, did you ever ask Jace if he wanted to stay married to you?"

She shook her head -it was all the movement she could muster. She had never thought of that.

"I didn't think so." He kissed her cheek and then slipped from the room.

The swirls in her mind became stronger. She raised her hand to cover her mouth. Would he have considered staying? "Oh, Good Lord, what have I done?" she moaned as her legs collapsed beneath her. Her body floated to the floor and sobs raked her chest.

****

Jace had to force his legs to move. His feet, one in front of the other, had to make their way down the boardwalk to the train station. One at a time, he thought. Each step should get easier, but they didn't. Because each stride took him further and further away from Penny. All the way from the Copper Cow to Yankton he attempted to persuade himself this was what he wanted. No- what he needed.

Convincing his mind walking away from Penny should be easier than loosing Karin and the baby was farfetched. For it wasn't. He had lost his first wife to death, something that was out of his control. But Penny was still alive and there was no reason why they couldn't be together. He had loved Karin, she had been a wonderful person and their life together had been good. He would have died a happy man having spent his whole life with her. But it didn't work out that way. She had died. And he had met Penny.

Penny wasn't just wonderful she was amazing, no incredible. She filled a void in him that had always been there, just below the surface. She made him complete. He needed her to survive. But she didn't need him. She said she needed him to leave. She needed him to leave.

Jace was so deep in thought he didn't notice the

middle aged woman in the middle of his path until he almost tripped over her. His knee bumped into her side as she was bent over, retrieving the lost contents of her bag. "Oh, excuse me, Ma'am," he apologized.

"I'm terribly sorry, the latch on my bag opened and, oh," she stopped to grab at another piece of paper the winter wind whipped off the ground.

Jace stepped into the street to rescue the paper for her. He glanced at the writing as he picked it up. It was a deed, a deed to the James Ranch. He handed it back to the woman, drew his brows together and said, "My name is Jace Owens."

The woman pulled herself upright and accepted the paper. "Jace Owens of the Copper Cow?" She tucked the final paper into the small carpetbag clutched against her chest.

"Uh-yes." He didn't recognize her.

Her hand thrust forward in greeting, "I'm Susan Leigh James, Mr. Owens. It is truly a pleasure to meet you."

Jace glanced around, looking for any traveling companions she might have. "Is your husband with you? Your daughter?" Jace noticed the tears that came to her bright blue eyes before she blinked them away.

"No, no, Mr. Owens. I'm afraid my husband passed away. And our daughter is with my sister, in Boston."

Jace could sense her sincere sadness. "I'm sorry to hear about your loss, Mrs. James."

"Mr. Owens, I- I hope you don't think this is too forward of me, but might I be able to travel back to Elm Creek with you? I have some business there to take care of and I have been terribly afraid of traveling that far by stage alone." Her nervousness was very apparent.

"Well, uh-Ma'am," Jace stuttered. He was a sucker for a damsel in distress, but he couldn't return to Elm Creek, he couldn't return the Copper Cow. He couldn't return to Penny.... Furthermore, the stagecoach trip to Elm Creek took almost as long as the train's ride all the way to Philadelphia did.

Once again Susan Leigh interrupted his thoughts, "Perhaps, we could have a cup of coffee, and I will tell you my reason for traveling to Elm Creek."

Jace glanced to the train station a mere ten yards ahead of him. Jumbled thoughts of his time at the Copper Cow bounced around his head. Visions, words, and moments—moments he so wanted to relive- but couldn't.

Or could he? What was he really going home to? His partner had taken over the running of their veterinarian business a year ago. Charles oversaw his investments. And Daniel and Candice certainly didn't need him underfoot. There wasn't anything for him to return to- in the East. But in the West, he had a life. He had new veterinarian customers, he had new dreams, and he had Penny.

A loud screech rippled the air as the train whistle sounded and a conductor announced, "All aboard!"

The sound of Penny's voice floated across his mind and muffled the loud street sounds. *"I need you to return to Philadelphia,"* she had said.

Wait…She said she needed him to return, not wanted him to return. Hope rose in his chest…Penny always confused her wants with her needs. His eyes went to the sky above him. Had the sun been shining this bright earlier?

A smile formed on his lips as he glanced back at the attractive woman who stood between him and the East.

"I think I would like a cup of coffee, Mrs. James. Shall we?" He held his arm out to escort her away from the station.

Chapter Sixteen

It was Christmas Eve morning. Penny couldn't help but think of Jace—as if she thought of anything else. Every waking moment was devoted to his memory and every sleeping moment was filled of dreams about him. Each night since his departure, after retiring to her room, she would wait until silence engulfed the house and then sneak into Jace's room. The one she now thought of as theirs. There she would shelter herself in the bed. Cocooned in his lingering presence she would remain until the early morning light interrupted her dreams-dreams of she and Jace living happily forever. Sometimes it was on the Copper Cow. Sometimes it was in Philadelphia. But always they were together.

Butterflies fluttered in her stomach, caused by the remnants of last night's dream that still floated in her head as she made her way down the stairs. A soft melody drifted out of the kitchen and caught her hearing. She smiled, every morning since her marriage to Sam, Mary Alice could be found singing in the kitchen.

Penny pushed the door open and said, "Good morning." Startled, she saw only her stepmother preparing the morning meal. Could it have been her voice filling the air with a soft love song?

Singing Dove crossed the room, patted Penny's cheeks and then gave her a heartfelt hug before she returned to her chores and her tune.

Sam entered through the back door before Penny had a chance to comment.

"Morning Princess. I found the perfect tree. I'll have the men carry it into the back parlor after breakfast." He glanced at the dark green, velvet dress she had on. "You look awfully pretty today, Penny."

"Thank you, Sam. I figured since it is Christmas Eve and all," she explained her mode of clothing with a shrug.

During her plan to entice Jace, she had discovered joy in dressing as a woman. With the extra ranch hands they now had, she found she was no longer needed in the barn or fields as much as she once had been. A grin covered her face as she realized Jace's stay at the ranch had also caused her pants and men's shirts to hang unused in her closet. His short stay at her home had made so many significant changes to her life. Every day she seemed to discover a new one. The smile left. Every day she found a new reason to miss him.

After the morning meal, Mary Alice cleaned the kitchen while Penny helped Sam position the tree to stand in the center of the back parlor. When he left the room, she retrieved several packages of decorations from her mother's old chest. First she placed small candles on several bows and then positioned elegant glass bulbs to dangle from others.

The tree still needed more, so she made a long string of fresh popped corn. While looping it around the huge evergreen, she thought of past Christmases. This one was destined to be lonely. A melancholy feeling grew upon her shoulders, a feeling she'd become accustomed too and continued her work as the heaviness grew in her heart. Singing Dove floated into the room, and Penny glanced over, not really sure if she wanted company. Lounging in loneliness seemed more fitting.

Her stepmother strode across the room and with a bright smile patted Penny's face before she whispered, "*Maka Wichasha.*"

Penny felt her breath catch at the sound of his name. Her hand rose to touch the locket hanging around her neck. She had recognized the pictures as soon as she had opened the gold disk upon its discovery the evening Jace had left. Tears had cascaded from her eyes as she had placed it around her neck and vowed to never remove it.

Now her fingers trembled as they rubbed the pendant. "W-what? W-what d-do," she stuttered trying to get the words out. Singing Dove would only say his name if she knew something about him. Penny swallowed and started again, "Is he hurt? Did something happen to him?" Tears formed in her eyes. Her other hand rose to press against the pain behind her breastbone.

"Hiya," Singing Dove shook her head, "*Wakhan Thanka* guided *Maka Wichasha* home." Her deep brown eyes sparkled with delight as she nodded with affirmation.

"The Great Spirit guided Jace home," Penny translated. A deep sigh left her body. "Oh, he made it back to Philadelphia safely." She nodded and glanced back to the tree. Thoughts came out aloud, "Home in time for Christmas." Tiny tears slipped from her eyes. She wiped at them with her fingers before turning back to her stepmother. "Thank you for telling me, Singing Dove."

The Lakota woman let out a deep sigh and shook her head. With a firm grasp she took a hold of Penny's hand and led her out of the parlor. They entered the hallway just as the front door opened.

Confused, Penny looked from her stepmother to the form that stepped through the door. Her mind had to be playing tricks on her. It couldn't be him. Could it? Blood from every part of her body rushed to her head. She felt faint. Her vision blurred. Her free hand pressed against the wall, steadying her stance and keeping her from slipping to the floor. Or was it to keep her from running to his arms?

A second form appeared in the opening. "Penny, my dear girl, it appears I've startled you!" Susan Leigh said as she stepped in front of Jace. She twisted and tried to see around the woman who handed her winter shawl to Mary Alice. Her view remained blocked as Susan Leigh made her way down the walkway to embrace Penny in a warm hug. "Your darling husband was kind enough to escort me all the way from Yankton." Chilled lips touched Penny's cheek as the woman whispered, "Oh, what a find you have there, my sweet child!"

Penny found her voice and her eyes found him again. He removed his jacket to embraced Mary Alice in a bear hug. "Susan Leigh? How are you?"

The other woman's arms were still wrapped around her. But all she saw was the way Jace's eyes locked onto hers. Then he moved- he was walking toward her. Soon he would be close enough to touch.

With the hand still braced against the wall Penny pushed herself forward and glided out of the woman's embrace. Taking one-step, then another, and another, she moved toward him. Her hands itched with temptation. Her heart fluttered with pleasure. Was it really Jace? Was her mind playing tricks on her? Blood gushed into every point of her body. It pounded in her ears, throbbed in her neck, pulsed down her shins.

He stopped in front of her and placed both hands on her shoulders. "Hi," was all he said. His voice was hoarse, but sounded like heaven to her ears.

"Hi," her voice cracked, one simple word was too much. Her hands snuck out and placed themselves on his hips. She welcomed the flames licking at her palms. Relished at the heat pouring onto her shoulders. He was real. He was here. He was home in time for Christmas.

His head drew down and his lips touched her forehead. She felt as if she might melt. Time stood still as their bodies absorbed each other from the simple embrace.

Mary Alice's voice barely penetrated her ears. "Come along Susan Leigh, let's get some coffee to warm you up after that long ride."

Jace lifted his lips from her skin. *No!* Her mind screamed. She needed his lips so much. His eyes stared down at her. She blinked at the devotion she felt flowing from her own. She couldn't hold it back. A smile formed on his face. She mimicked it as happiness filled her.

He took a step back, but held onto her arms, forcing her feet to follow. When she did, he took another step back, then another. Together they made their way, he tugging on her shoulders, she pushing on his hips, into the office.

Without a word Jace kicked the door shut before he continued to lead her across the room where the couch bumped the back of his knees. Never disconnecting their gaze or touch, he lowered them both onto the lounger.

"I tried, Penny, but I can't do it." He ran his hands down her arms until their fingers could caress each other.

"Can't do what?"

He shook his head, "I can't return to Philadelphia, like you asked me to."

Penny drew her brows together in confusion as she denied, "I didn't ask you to return to Philadelphia."

Jace lifted a brow, "You didn't?"

"No, you said you had to return there."

"I know, I said that I had to return, but that was before…"

Penny shook her head. She had to explain, "That's where you belong. With your family, your friends, your veterinarian practice. That's where your roots are. I took all that away from you when I asked for a mail order husband. I had to give it back to you."

His hands still clasped hers, but he raised one and used his thumb to wipe away the tear that slipped from her eye. "Penny, my darling wife, I belong where my heart is. And my heart's not in Philadelphia."

"It's not?"

"No." He placed her hand on his chest as he shook his head. "It's right here." He laid his other hand on her chest. "And it has new roots that grow from right here."

"But Candice and I, we forced you to come out here. It wasn't something you wanted." Through the warm flannel of his shirt, her palm could feel the steady rhythm of his heart. It felt wonderful. He was so handsome and perfect. Her mind began to take in the words he spoke. Was he saying what she hoped he was saying?

"Maybe not at the time. But it is now." His eyes went to the locket circling her neck. "Penny, I know I'm not the husband you would have found if things had been different. I know I'm not the man you dreamed of marrying when you were a little girl. But if you would just give me a chance, I will try to become that man- the man of your dreams- just as you have become the woman of my dreams. Please give me that chance, Penny."

She saw a single tear slip out of the corner of one deep blue eye as her own began to fall. "You will? I am?" She exhaled the breath that had caught in her chest. Happiness flowed through her veins. "You are."

"I am what?" he asked as he released her hands and brought his up to cup her face.

Her heart skipped a beat. She wrapped her arms around his neck and leaned toward his lips. "You are the husband I always wanted. No-the husband I always needed. You are the man of my dreams. Jace Owens, you are my knight in shinning armor." Having waited long enough, her mouth pressed against his.

Time stood still as their lips touched. When she needed more, she opened her lips and used them to catch the fullness of his bottom one. Her movements lured his and soon they both searched, tasted, owned. The embrace continued until they were breathing heavy from the excursion. Gasping for air between long, deep kisses.

He pulled his lips from hers and pressed her head against his heaving chest. She wrapped her arms around his torso, clutching his frame to hers. Nothing on earth had ever felt so good.

Sound rumbled in her ear as Jace cleared his throat and instructed, "Come in."

Penny hadn't heard the knock. The loving beat of Jace's heart was the only sound she cared to hear. Nor was she interested in knowing who was interrupting their time together. She refused to lift her head from the comfort it was enjoying.

"Oh, excuse me. I didn't know you were home, Mr. Owens!" Cody's young voice was laced with embarrassment and enjoyment.

Penny sighed as she pulled her face up to look at the boy. A satisfied smile remained on her lips.

"I just arrived," Jace paused to look down at her before he continued, "home. A few minutes ago."

"It's good to have you back," Cody admitted with delight. "I, uh-missed seeing you around." The boy attempted to make his voice sound more masculine as he walked across the room and offered his hand in greeting.

Jace took the boys hand in a firm shake. "It's good to be home. I missed seeing you, too. I missed everything about the Copper Cow," he confessed as he tightened the arm still holding her.

Cody handed Penny a large basket. "Merry Christmas, Ma'am. My Ma asked me to bring this over to you this morning. We really appreciate the job you've given me."

Penny took the basket filled with jars of foodstuffs and set it on the sofa beside her. "How nice of her. Thank you, Cody, and Merry Christmas to you." She glanced at her husband, "Mr. Owens and I sincerely appreciate the wonderful job you have been doing. We are very lucky to have you working for us."

His freckled cheeks turned red as he shuffled his feet, he cleared his throat, but didn't say anything, just continued to look around the room.

Jace must have sensed the boy's uneasiness and took sympathy on the young lad. He stood, bringing Penny with him and laid a hand on Cody's shoulder. "Have lunch with us Cody. There is someone I want you to meet." Jace led them to the door and instructed the lad. "Go wash up, we will meet you in the kitchen."

"Yes, sir!" Cody ran to do as told.

"Someone you want him to meet?" Penny asked as they paused in the doorway.

"You'll see," Jace nodded as he lowered his head. "You called me Mr. Owens."

"No, I referred," she started to protest. "Oh, yes, I guess I did, didn't I?" Penny readily agreed as she stepped up to meet his lips half way.

"Music to my ears," he whispered as their mouths met.

An hour later, Penny sat across from Susan Leigh as the woman explained the illness and death of her husband. The sad widow talked about the poison that had been fed to Bob and how it had destroyed his organs with agonizing slowness.

But Penny wasn't really listening. Instead, she examined how pretty Susan Leigh was. Her brunette hair was pulled back in a fashionable bun. Her skin still looked youthful and gave no signs of her age. Her form and behaviors were graceful and feminine in every way.

She felt the jealousy. It grew stronger as she thought of Jace and Susan Leigh's journey, all the way from Yankton. Traveling alone, together, during the shortened, chilly, winter days and the long, cold, winter nights.

Jace sent her a questioning look and then followed her gaze- no interpreted her gaze. A broad smile grew on his face as he read her mind. He reached over, took her hand fidgeting with her coffee cup and raised it to his lips.

The green-eyed monster ran away as she felt the soft caress. She leaned over, until their faces where inches apart. Her mind accepted the words his sent to her.

A warm glow entered her body. His unspoken reassurances were easy to understand. There wasn't a person on earth or in heaven who could ever threaten their life together. There was no bargain or circumstance that would ever cause uncertainty or misunderstanding about his or her love ever again.

"Penny? Jace?" Mary Alice interrupted, "Susan Leigh asked if you would like to ride over to the O'Brien's with her?"

"Of course," Jace said as a soft chuckles surrounded the table. "Cody, why don't you hitch up the sleigh and we will all go."

"Yes, Sir," the boy complied as he slid his chair away from the table.

****

Penny arranged the pile of gifts she had acquired for the O'Brien's into the soft hay that covered the floorboards of the sleigh. She bubbled with joy. The bright afternoon sun made every snowflake glisten and sparkle. The world around her dazzled with perfection. Hands reached around her waist and pulled her against a solid frame. She leaned into the welcoming embrace for a moment before the hands guided her climb into the sleigh. When everything was prepared for their trek across the wintry prairie, her husband climbed in beside her.

With pride, Cody sat in the driver's seat next to the watchful Sam. She, Jace, Susan Leigh, and Mary Alice settled into the back and wrapped thick quilts around their legs to ward off the cold gusts that would accompany them. Lighthearted conversation filled the air as the team of buckskins lifted their heavy hoofs and began to pull the deep skis of the carriage through thick drifts of snow.

Penny huddled closer to her husband, delighted in the convenience of the opportunity to snuggle, but also in the reason for their journey. Susan Leigh had returned one final time to Elm Creek, for two reasons. One, to see for herself the grave of the man who had killed her husband; his own son: and two, to rid herself of any connection to the Dakota Territory. She and her daughter Katie Jo would move to Europe after the first of the New Year. During this holiday journey, she wanted to present the deed for the James Ranch to the O'Brien's. A payment of sorts for the losses her stepson had caused them.

Jace had told Penny the story while they adorned

protective layers of clothing before they left the house. The widow had first offered the ranch to Jace in Yankton. He had declined, knowing Penny would want nothing to do with the property. Susan Leigh had then suggested giving it to Sam and Mary Alice, who in turn had also refused her offer. Jace had assured Penny he had assumed as much and had suggested she sell the property while they had been visiting in the restaurant near the train station. Susan Leigh had profoundly objected, adamant she would not accept payment of any kind for the land. She proclaimed too many people had already paid too much, too dearly.

He further explained letters from the mercantile owner's wife, Ann Marie Watson, had kept Susan Leigh abreast of all of the happenings in and around Elm Creek. He now agreed Ann Marie was the best source of knowledgeable, accurate news for miles around. This explained how the widow recognized his name when they met on the boardwalk.

Penny no longer cared who knew what, when, where, why, or how. She only cared that she was part of this exciting gesture of righteousness and that her husband was home, to stay. Her hand found its way between the buttoned flaps of his winter coat. The warmth of his chest and the steady, solid beat of his heart was pure bliss. His arm wrapped her tighter against his side and snuck into the hip pocket of her winter cloak. His fingers caressed her hip through the silk lining. The hidden petting continued as the sleigh glided across the winter wonderland.

****

Penny was happy the jaunt was successful. It had taken some convincing, but the O'Brien's were now planning for the move to their new home to happen the day after Christmas. She and her husband, as well as the rest of the travelers returned home to dine on a festive Christmas Eve meal before settling around massive pine tree in the back parlor.

Susan Leigh lifted her fingers from the piano and sighed as she looked around the room. "I can't thank you enough, all of you! For your aid and friendship. And for the invitation to join you for Christmas, it has been a wonderful day."

In silent agreement Penny nestled closer to her husband on the small sofa. Sam and Mary Alice sat in matching rockers beside the fireplace. They had just enjoyed a round of holiday melodies. Susan could play beautifully, but the evening had long since turned to night and Penny searched her mind for a way to suggest it was time to retire.

"Yes, it has been a perfect Christmas," Mary Alice agreed.

"Yup," Sam supplied, "one we will all remember. I'd say it's a perfect night to make lasting memories." He winked at Penny as he pulled his body out of the rocking chair and turned to his wife. "Are you ready to turn in, my dear?"

Mary Alice leaped to her feet, "Yes, Dear." She turned to their company. "I'll show you to your room, Susan Leigh."

Penny was just as quick to rise. Jace followed suit and stood beside her.

Sam prepared the room for departure, dowsed the small tree candles and stoked the night fire. Leaving a single lamp burning, he waited until the women said good night to Penny and Jace before he crossed the room and held his hand out. "Good to have you home, Son." Then he placed a soft kiss on Penny's cheek, "Have a good night, Princess. Merry Christmas."

"Merry Christmas, Sam," she replied as the older man slipped from the room. With grace, she melted into the open arms of her husband, rejoicing in their solitude. "Merry Christmas," she wished him.

"Merry Christmas, my love," Jace met her lips with his. A few moments later, he pulled his mouth from hers. "I have something for you." One hand dug into his hip pocket.

"Oh, what is it?" Penny asked as he handed her a small package.

"Open it," he suggested.

It was wrapped with red paper and tied with a bright green bow. She cherished it already, just because it was from him. With slow movements her fingers removed the ribbon and pulled off the paper. A small box appeared.

Her eyes glanced up at his. He smiled and looked back to the gift. His hand rose to remove the lid. A single band of gold lay in a bed of cotton.

Her heart beat in her throat as he lifted the ring from the box. The wrapping supplies slipped from her hands and fell to the floor. He knelt down, gathered the droppings and placed them on the table. His body continued to lower until he was kneeling on one knee. Looking up at her, he grasped her left hand with his.

"I love you, Penny. I love you with my heart and soul. And I will love you forever."

Penny explored the deep love shining in his eyes. Her thoughts came out of her mouth on their own accord. "I love you too, Jace. I have loved you since the minute you rescued me on the front porch of this house, the day you awoke. And I will love you forever."

"Penny Jordan, will you marry me?"

Penny's breath stilled, words she thought she would never hear floated through her mind and created the sweetest song. "Yes, oh, yes!" she answered and he slipped the gold band on her finger. She admired the gold as it glistened, the song still floated- *will you marry me- will you*...her mind stilled. Thoughts formed.

Pulling her eyes from the ring, she watched him stand. *Will you marry me?* Echoed in her ears. She raised her arms to circle his neck and started, "Jace, I'm not waiting any longer to become your wife. I have a marriage license that..."

Laughter floated in the air before he stopped her words with a deep, meaningful kiss. "That is completely valid and more than we will ever need," he finished her sentence before his lips met hers again.

After a long bout of playful petting she separated their bodies, convinced he wouldn't be making her wait much longer and asked, "Shall we go upstairs?"

Without a word, Jace extinguished the lamp and led her to the stairs. He caressed the ring on her finger during their climb. When they stepped onto the top landing he raised their hands, kissed the ring and said, "I thought you might want one of your own."

Penny clutched his hand and used it to lead him to the room she now considered theirs. With her other hand she pushed the door open wide. Twisting to face him, she assured, "Oh, I did. I do!" Both arms wrapped around his neck and she pulled his head down to meet hers. "But I think you know what I want even more, Mr. Owens."

Jace lifted her body into his arms as he deepened the kiss. Without breaking their embrace, he carried her into the room. As his foot kicked the door shut behind them, he whispered, "Get your pencil ready, my dear wife."

Epilogue

Philadelphia, Pennsylvania 1875

The screen door of the red, brick house fluttered shut. The sweet smells of honeysuckle filled the air. Penny strolled over to the wooden, porch swing. Rays from the warm, afternoon sun settled on her back as she sat down and sighed in contentment. With love her fingers caressed the round bubble that her abdomen had become.

The high-pitched squeal of excitement reached her ears. "Daddy! Daddy home!"

A little girl with long, red curls tumbling down her back and short, chubby legs ran across the yard to the rod iron fence. "Rebecca Jo, stay in the yard!"

"Don't fret, Penny, I'm right behind her!" Mary Alice said as she emerged from the side of the house, following the child.

"Wait here, Sweetie, that road is too busy for you," Mary Alice stopped the child before the youngster had a chance to push open the gate latch.

Jace felt his heart overflow. He waved to the two-year old girl waiting for him on the other side of the gate. She was as beautiful as her mother.

His step became quicker as he strutted down the roadway. When her eyes momentarily turned from his, he ducked down behind the leafy hedge that ran along the fence and crawled on his hands and knees the remaining few feet. Sticking his face up against the warm metal bars even with his daughter's height he exclaimed, "Boo!"

Her little body jumped with surprise. "Daddy!" Rebecca Jo giggled with delight. Her chubby fingers pressed down on her knees as she bent forward. Bright blue eyes stared back at him and she yelled, "Boooooo!"

His wife laughed aloud at witnessing the scene from the porch. Happiness jiggled her shoulders. He flashed her a look of love before he rose to his feet. Unlatching the gate, he whisked their daughter high into the sky then settled her onto his hip. Jace ambled up the brick walkway of the prominent, Philadelphia home, nuzzling his daughter's baby soft cheeks and tickling her round tummy along the way.

He gave the happy, little girl one final kiss and handed her to Mary Alice before he climbed the steps onto the wide veranda. "Hi," he knelt to place a soft kiss on his wife's lips. One hand went to massage her round belly at the same time.

"Hi," she returned and covered his hand with both of hers.

He settled onto the swing and placed his other arm around her shoulders. "How are you feeling today?"

"Fine, thank you. I have been through this before you know. I'm almost an old hand at it by now," Penny answered.

"Have I told you today how much I love you?" His heart hammered in his chest, as it did each time he thought of touching those wonderful, delightful lips with his own.

"Hmmm, I don't believe you have." She leaned forward with enthusiasm.

He made sure she was not disappointed. The world around them once again failed to exist as the kiss allowed them to become one.

"Will you two stop that constant petting?" Candice pleaded as she carried a tray of beverages out the door. Twin, three-year old boys popped out of the open door, one under each of her arms. "Jackson! Jefferson! You two slow down!" she exclaimed as they caused her tray to jostle.

Identical faces with bright blue eyes and bushy blond hair, looked up at their mother as if she had two heads. The boys then looked at each other and shrugged before they raced down the steps to join their cousin and Mary Alice on the thick green grass of the plush lawn.

"No," Jace stated.

"Excuse me?" Candice questioned as she handed him a tall glass of lemonade.

"No, I won't quit petting my wife-ever." His let his eyes dance across Penny's smiling face.

"Tell me something I don't know," Candice bantered. "Remember you only have her because of me-your favorite sister-in-law," she stated with show and handed Penny a glass.

Jace rolled his eyes. "You are my *only* sister-in-law, so by default you are my favorite, therefore you also are my least favorite." Winking at Penny he continued, "Which means you are also the ugliest, the most unpleasant, the most dangerous..."

"Shut up you beast!" Candice placed both hands on her hips in mock anger.

"Are those two going at it again?" Daniel asked as he made his way out the door to join the others.

"Yes," Candice answered as she turned to her husband.

"I was talking to Penny," Daniel informed his wife as he chucked her under the chin.

"Yes, unfortunately they still can't be in the same room together without bickering." Penny responded to the man who closely resembled her husband. Just not nearly as handsome-a fact she and Candice still didn't agree on. The one thing the two friends did agree on was that they were two of the luckiest women alive. She looked up at her husband with a bright smile.

Daniel took a seat at the small wicker table and pulled his wife down on his lap. Candice turned into his embrace, accepting the seat as well as his kiss.

"And she was reprehending us," Jace whispered in Penny's ear.

Penny patted his face, pretending to provide solace to an injured child.

"How did the meeting go?" Daniel asked Jace. The entire group grew into a more serious mood.

Penny held her breath, she wanted to hear, but had been afraid to ask after she saw Jace walk up the roadway alone.

"Very good, actually "terrific" might explain how Cody feels about it." Jace glanced at her and explained, "He stopped to send a wire to his parents."

She nodded expectantly.

"He passed the exam with flying colors. The Dakota Territory will soon have two veterinarians." Jace stuck his chest out with exaggerated pride.

Penny rolled her eyes, poking fun at him as she repeated an often-heard phrase, "Excuse me, don't you mean two farriers, Mr. Owens?"

His eyes flashed with pretend disgust. "You are such a slow leaner. For three years I've been punishing you for calling me that."

Penny accepted his kiss with her whole heart and murmured against his mouth as it started to withdraw, "Maybe your punishment isn't severe enough."

He smiled and patted her pregnant stomach. "You think not?"

Her face squished together and pretended to form a look of deep concentration before she shook her head. "Besides you, my dear husband, are the one who is a slow learner."

"Oh?"

"Yes. That was some pretty important information you —uh- *forgot* to tell me about. How many times have I told you I need to know everything?"

"What? What are you talking about?"

"That you and Daniel are twins."

"Oh, that again. I told you I assumed Candice had told you in one of her many letters. You two write about everything else." One hand rose to the locket hanging from her neck. "And you had pictures."

"I thought they were both of you," she whispered.

Looking deep into her eyes, his hand began to caress her stomach once again. "I thought you knew. I really am sorry."

She leaned in for one more kiss. "I forgive you."

Daniel interrupted the interlude, "What about your meeting with Charles? How did that go?"

With interest Penny listened to her husband's explanation. "About as well as can be expected, President Grant has abandoned any attempts to keep gold miners out of the Black Hills. His decision will ultimately mean the Army will have to reverse their position. Instead of protecting the Lakota from the infiltrators, they will now be commissioned to protect the miners and settlers from the Indians. It is going to be difficult for the Indians to understand the change. We knew the discovery of gold would cause trouble, but I'm afraid we may have a crisis on our hands before long." Jace patted her hand in response to her sad expression. "Charles will continue to work on it from this end. Our goal now is to prevent the Lakota from being forced to move onto reservations." He tightened his arm around her shoulders and invited her to press her cheek against his chest. "We will be leaving for home day after tomorrow."

"Jace, that's just not possible." Candice shook her head, "You have only been here for a week, that just hasn't been enough time."

Jace held his hand up. "I'm sorry Candice, but we must return home. Two Bears is anxiously waiting to hear what I was able to learn. My practice there is twice as busy as I ever was here. Our winter wheat crop is promising to be one of the best in the nation this year. And my wife can't miss the Cattlemen's Association meeting, especially since she is the newly elected president."

"Well then, we will have to discuss it right now." Candice turned to her husband and asked, "Don't you agree, Darling?"

Daniel nodded his head, "Yes, Dear."

"Talk about what?" Penny questioned, for some reason she had a tingling sensation running up her spine.

"Our plan of course," Candice informed them with a grin that stretched from ear to ear. "Daniel and I have been thinking and we believe we know of a way we can help the Lakota's with this whole gold issue."

"Stop right there!" Jace stood and issued his command with force. "Uh-huh! No. You two are not," he glanced toward Penny.

She shook her head, answering his silent question of her involvement.

"No, no! We are not going to let you try one of your hair-brained schemes out on Singing Dove's family." He was close to glaring at his brother. "Your schemes are dangerous. I almost died because of one of your ideas."

"Jace, please. When are you going to get over it? You didn't die and you wouldn't be sitting here today with a lovely wife, an adorable daughter, and possibly a fine son, or two, on the way if it wasn't for my wonderful-uh-arrangement," Candice reminded him of how well her plan had worked.

Penny watched as Jace looked at the other couple. Both Candice and Daniel had sincere smiles on their faces. Her husband rubbed his temples as if thwarting an ache. He turned to her and he held out a hand. Without question, she took it and rose to stand beside him.

An arm encircled her waist as he glanced to the front lawn, "Mary Alice, will you please keep Rebecca Jo with you?"

"Of course," Mary Alice agreed from where she was making crowns out of long dandelion stems for all of the children.

"My wife needs her rest. I can't allow her to become uh -upset in her condition. Please excuse us. We are retiring to our room, to take a nap before dinner is served," he informed the other couple on the porch.

"But, Jace, I really think you should listen to what Candice has to say," Daniel insisted.

"No, no, no, I really don't think I want to hear what she has to say."

"Fine, we will discuss it at dinner," Candice said as she brought her feet to the floor.

Jace shook his head, "What part of *no* don't you understand?"

Candice folded her arms across her chest with a loud, "humph" and looked at her husband for aid.

"Jace..." Daniel began.

Jace shook his head and led Penny through the screen door. It slipped shut behind them and he leaned down to whisper, "We can only hope Candice doesn't have General Custard's mailing address."

Penny shuddered at the thought. Fear flowed from her eyes as she glanced up at her husband. His blue eyes twinkled in humor. A chuckle rose in her chest. She placed both hands on his cheeks and leaned up to give a soft kiss. "I love you."

"Good, because I love you back."

"But, I'm really not tired." Penny let her hand run down his chest.

"Good, because I'm not tired either."

"Oh, Mr. Owens, whatever are we going to do until

dinner time?"

He raised both eyebrows as he lifted her into his arms and sauntered toward the stairs. "I have a plan," he whispered.

"Mmmm, so do I," she muttered against lips that descended to meet hers.

A word about the author...

As a young girl I remember spending warm summer days and long winter nights with Nancy Drew and Laura Ingalls-Wilder. As the years slipped by the books evolved into romance novels by Kathleen Woodiwiss, LaVyrle Spencer and a host of others. In 2000 when my husband said I should write one, I took the challenge, and have loved every moment of the journey. To create characters from once upon a time and lead them through a life that ends in happily ever after is such fun. Of course, you have to torture them a little bit along the way, and just like real-life children you often have to clean up after them. But, just like real children, they are worth it.

My husband of more than twenty-five years, and I live in Minnesota, have three grown sons and the most precious gift ever-a granddaughter, Isabelle. I work as the resource development manager for our local United Way program, am a life-long Elvis fan (yes, I've been to Graceland) and love spending Sunday afternoons watching NASCAR with family and friends. My previous published works include magazine articles, children's activities and a contemporary romance novel, A Message of Love with PublishAmerica in 2005.

Printed in the United States
127300LV00004B/1/A

9 781601 540621